THR
B

# THREE GO BACK

James Leslie Mitchell

(Lewis Grassic Gibbon)

Introduced by Ian Campbell

Polygon
Edinburgh

© This edition 1995
Polygon
22 George Square
Edinburgh
EH8 9LF

Printed and bound in Great Britain by
Short Run Press Ltd, Exeter

ISBN 0 7486 6203 0

A CIP record is available

The Publisher acknowledges subsidy from

THE SCOTTISH ARTS COUNCIL

towards the publication of this volume.

My dear Mégroz,

I wrote this novel as a holiday from more serious things and in dedicating it to such distinguished critic as yourself might be guilty of some temerity were it not for the fact that convention will forbid you reviewing me. But though this may be my loss I hope it will not be your gain!

You've impressed on me that a novel should need neither footnote nor forenote. I agree – and happily escape the reproach of either by embodying their contents in the dedication.

First, the continent where Clair and Sinclair and Sir John adventure: many respectworthy people in all ages have professed to find the ocean shores littered with proofs of its one-time existence.

The litter leaves me unconvinced.

Secondly, the character and characteristics here and elsewhere ascribed to the "grey beasts": There is not a scrap of proof that the "grey beasts" were ferocious and gorilla-like; for that matter, and to employ a very just Irishism, there is not a shred of evidence that the gorilla in his native haunts behaves in the least like a gorilla.

But though these two apparent fictions, continental and temperamental, are employed for dramatic effect, they have no direct bearing on the main theme and contention of the story, which seem to me quite unassailable.

And with these cautions I pass you the book in company with my gratitude and good wishes. May you like the reading of it as much as I enjoyed the writing!

Yours,

J. LESLIE MITCHELL

London, 1932

# INTRODUCTION

by

Ian Campbell

The outline of Lewis Grassic Gibbons's life is well-known;
born in Aberdeenshire, growing up in Arbuthnott, the
Kinraddie of *Sunset Song*, he drew on memory for the warmth
of a farming community and the memory of a Scottish
youth brutally destroyed by the First World War. Kinraddie
in fiction, like Arbuthnott in fact, yielded to a kind of
progress which destroyed traditional patterns of agriculture
and the small Scottish farm, killed many of the young men
and saw the steady drift to the cities which depopulated the
Mearns, and set the scene for the Depression years in which
Grassic Gibbon wrote. He himself had lived in Aberdeen (an
experience which produced the very recognisable *Grey Granite* descriptions), Glasgow (which fired the essay in *Scottish
Scene*), and after he enrolled in the armed services he had
endured squalor in England and the Middle East, laconically
but feelingly described in *Stained Radiance*. Marrying, he had
endured with his wife a search for cheap lodgings, political
involvement in the slums of London, witnessing the living
conditions of the poor and the desperate illness of his wife
which again all too clearly emerges from *Stained Radiance*.
James Storman, striding down to the Thames Embankment
at the start of the novel and eyeing the confusion and the
warehouses, the decay of Western capitalist society after the
Great War, echoes his creator: it cannot last.

> James Storman, the noted Communist who was an ex-captain of Artil-
> lery, came down to the River from Covent Garden and walked along the
> Embankment. The plane trees shook in a little wind. The muddy waters
> sparkled. A tramp slept on a bench. The Communist ex-captain walked with a
> swinging stride.

He was six feet in height, his complexion sallowly brown, his eyes a shade of brown, his hair brown. But his eyes denied the neutrality of their colour. They were the shining, humorous eyes of a man fundamentally unhumorous. He had a cleft chin and a small, closely-clipped moustache. Keen, calm, a mathematician, he was a mystic and religious, with Communism his religion. He looked at the world with the blind, clear eyes of faith.

Presently he ceased to talk, and leaning his arms on the stonework above the River, surveyed the dying capitalist system. Opposite him, in confusion and multitude, warehouses, wherries, and docks sprawled down to the water's edge. Their blue backgrounded signs jostled everywhere. They uplifted advertisements to Heaven. They flaunted an obscure, obscene, vulgar life. They did not look dead. Only ugly.

'It cannot last,' said Storman.[1]

The other Grassic Gibbon, something of a shock to those who know *A Scots Quair* or particularly only *Sunset Song*, is at work here both as writer and, sardonically, as autobiographer. Readers of *Three Go Back* will recognise in Keith Sinclair something of James Storman, something of the maturing Ewan Tavendale in *Grey Granite*, something no doubt that Keith Stratoun might have become in *The Speak of the Mearns* had Grassic Gibbon lived to complete what was so obviously autobiographical a piece of writing.[2] Gibbon was fond of playing self-distancing autobiographical games: in the essay "Glasgow" in *Scottish Scene* (which he co-authored with Hugh MacDiarmid in 1934) he refers to "my distant cousin, Mr Leslie Mitchell", and to Mitchell's description of Glasgow ". . . in one of his novels as 'the vomit of a cataleptic commercialism'." And, having given his *alter ego* a plug, he is happy to cap the point:

> But it is more than that. It may be a corpse, but the maggot-swarm upon it is very fiercely alive. One cannot watch and hear the long beat of traffic down Sauchiehall, or see its eddy and spume where St Vincent Street and Renfield Street cross, without realizing what excellent grounds the old-fashioned anthropologist appeared to have for believing that man was by nature a brutish savage, a herd-beast delighting in vocal discordance and orgiastic aural abandon.[3]

---

1 J. Leslie Mitchell (Lewis Grassic Gibbon), *Stained Radiance* (London, 1930: Polygon, 1993 reprint), p. 5

2 (Edinburgh, 1982; Polygon, 1994).

3 'Glasgow', in *Scottish Scene* published under the names of Lewis Grassic Gibbon and Hugh MacDiarmid (London, 1934); essay reprinted in *The Speak of the Mearns*, p.119. See also 'Gibbon and MacDiarmid at Play: The Evolution of *Scottish Scene*', *The Bibliotheck* 13/2 (1986), 44-52.

The same hypersensitivity and gusto fasten on to his rather
more affectionate reminiscences of Union Street, Aberdeen:

> If you escape the trams and the drays and the inferno where Market
> Street debouches on Union Street, and hold west up Union Street, you will
> have the feeling of one caught in a corridor of the hills. To right and left
> tower the cliffs, scrubbed, immaculate and unforgiving. Where Union Terrace
> breaks in upon Union Street there is an attempt at a public Garden. But the
> flowers come up and take one glance at the lour of the solicitors' offices
> which man Union Terrace, and scramble back into the earth again, seeking
> the Anitpodes.[1]

Here too, the author looks for "the high cheek-bones
in the brachycephalic heads of the males, that singularly
disharmonic head that is so singularly Aberdonian".[2] In
Glasgow, the human types are degenerate but also degener-
ated by the system they endure in the slums. And Aberdeen's
slums paled beside what Gibbon was to see in Glasgow, and
the inhabitants who "live on food of the quality of offal, ill-
cooked, ill-eaten with speedily-diseased teeth for the tending
of which they can afford no fees", who endure mind-
numbing work in shipyard or factory as an alternative to
even more mind-destroying unemployment, "frittering away
the tissues of their bodies and the spirit-stuff of their souls"
in the ghastly years of the Depression.[3]

Enough, then, to establish Lewis Grassic Gibbon as the
well-known face of James Leslie Mitchell, socialist, anarchist,
hater and despiser of a system which had produced the cities
of the 1930s, and poverty and hopelessness which degraded
his environment and threatened to degrade his life.

The thought was to recur in Grassic Gibbon's work. Each
successive part of *A Scots Quair* ends with it, the destruction
with Kinraddie of "the last of the Peasants, the last of the Old
Scots Folk", the destruction of the world Robert Colquhoun
stood for in *Cloud Howe*, the struggle for a newer and a juster
Britain to replace the decay of Depression Scotland in *Grey*

---

1 'Aberdeen', in Scottish Scene: reprinted from *The Speak of the Mearns*,
pp. 142-3.
2 *The Speak of the Mearns*, p.147.
3 *The Speak of the Mearns*, pp. 119-20.

*Granite.* The deeply-felt essays in *Scottish Scene* on the antique
scene, Glasgow, literary lights, Aberdeen, the land, religion
– they share the sense of a scene in its last stages, something
coming to replace it, not yet clear, but change inevitable.

\*\*\*\*\*\*\*\*\*\*\*\*\*\*\*\*\*\*\*\*\*\*

*Three Go Back* fits completely with this definition of Grassic
Gibbon's work – for in his hectic writing career he accomplished much in a variety of styles and genres, and science
fiction was only one of his accomplished modes. James
Storman surveys a city rioting with a kind of life – but one
which cannot last. *Gay Hunter* (1934)[1] projected Storman's
vision to the future, visiting a world where London and its
society had not lasted, had simply been left behind, rusted,
crumbled, fallen apart. *Three Go Back* (1932) takes the opposite tack: it goes to the far past, surveys a world where
the machine that London had become in 1932 did not yet
exist, looks at the people who lived in an unspoiled Atlantis
not yet sunk beneath the ocean, not yet trapped in Grassic
Gibbon's today.

Of course there is a distinguished tradition of writing out
societies which could be described both as utopia and as
dystopia, and more recently still a tradition of filming them:
Storman could be looking at the set of *Blade Runner,* and Gay
Hunter and her friends are close to several post-holocaust
visions of the far future. *Final Count-Down,* by contrast, finely
envisions in the cinema an American aircraft-carrier and
crew from the present day transported back through time,
as Clair Stranlay and Keith Sinclair are, to the past. With
one difference: in the film, captain and crew are fully armed
with modern nuclear weaponry and find themselves just in
time to stop, if they wish, the Japanese invasion of Pearl
Harbor and change the course of history. Clair and Keith
have no such clear-cut choice at their disposal: the airship
*Magellan's Cloud* is completely destroyed when it crashes, and
they escape to their island as defenceless and impoverished

1 (Polygon, 1990).

as Wells's time traveller or Defoe's Robinson Crusoe – and rather less resourceful than Robinson in adapting to their new environment.

The three who go back – Clair, Keith and Sir John Mullaghan, who does not long survive the crash and effectively makes the book about two time-travellers – land on Atlantis, the fabulous island long held by cultural historians to have existed to the West of Gibraltar (or perhaps, as recent theory suggests, in Turkey) and by many held to have been one of the cradles of modern civilisation. Gibbon was himself a cultural historian of some distinction: his own views are best described as "diffusionist"[1]. Diffusionists, briefly, believe in civilisation as the conclusion of a long process of corruption of a once-free human race; after the replacement of nomadic freedom by settlement (in the Nile valley and the growth of layered, hierarchical civilisation spreading from Egypt to Greece to Rome) comes European "civilisation", renaissance, reformation – industrialisation, world war – finally the Depression. All the ghastliness James Storman sees in London at the outset of *Three Go Back* is the last stage of commercial civilisation – unemployment, corruption, pollution, greed – corruption of the mind as well as the body.

The same corruption which debases the human beings, and the social organism of Kinraddie in *Sunset Song* – sexual dysfunction, gossip, greed, hypocrisy – is what the travellers in *Three Go Back* leave behind. In Atlantis, the diffusionist writer imagines a world before the whole sorry process begins. The human beings are naked and not ashamed of their nakedness, sexually instinctive without shame, free of property and its responsibilities and social guilt. They welcome the time travellers with frank curiosity and equally frank appraisal: they invite them into the group without social reserve and all join together in the business of hunting and survival. To Gibbon, to the convinced reader, it is the

---

1 For discussions see Douglas Young, *Beyond the Sunset* (Aberdeen, 1973), William K. Malcolm, *A Blasphemer and Reformer* (Aberdeen 1984), and Jeremy Idle, unpublished PhD thesis (Edinburgh, 1994). See also Use Zagratski, *Libertäre and Utopische Tendenzen in Erzählwerk James Leslie Mitchells/Lewis Grassic Gibbons* (Frankfurt, 1992).

most natural thing in the world – their world, the world Gibbon hopes the reader accepts as "normality" after a few chapters of description. Clair, after all, finds little difficulty in reconciling her twentieth-century ideas to the past: as her defences fall, so do the readers'.

> Here there was no hate, no compulsion in love. These people played no game of sacrifice, because sacrifice was a stupidity beyond their understanding . . . It was the mentality of the slave, the bond-woman of all the weary years of civilization that had allowed those caresses while Sinclair went away.
> All their thousands of grey, suppressed years! And, hating and resenting all that tradition of sacrifice and servitude, she was herself submitting to it. Why? (225).

At the same time, Gibbon shows the change of relationship between people of "today" when the normality of "today" is subject to the stress of time travel. Although the idea is a commonplace of science fiction, Gibbon handles it with skill and with the removal of Sir John the plot can be simplified down to one of human – comprehensible – relationships to divert attention from the shakier fictional ground of inadvertent time travel. For Gibbon is asking quite a lot of his readers with dialogue like this:

> "Then they can make fires – they *are* men", she said.

> "They are men, but not Man. They are the sub-human species that are almost men, and are to be in occupation of most of Europe when our Cro-Magnards wander there thousands of years hence. If they do so wander" (212)

Chapter III of the last section of *Three Go Back* plays between Neanderthalers – "the sullen, individualist beast whose ferocity is perhaps maladjustment of body", and the Cro-Magnards, "decently, kindly animals of anthropoid blood". The originality of Gibbon's plot lies mainly in this last section, the battle between the two prototypes of humankind, the sudden jolting back of Clair and Keith to their own time at the moment they are killed in the far past – the moment of realisation, the slow process of readjustment to the present.

Above all, Gibbon's plot reaches its effective end by the device which makes Claire the Lizair of her own time, Keith

the Aerte. The past has not been altered by their time travel;
it has been prolonged into their present, and memory (unlike
clothes and artefacts) has travelled with them. "They'll live
as long as we do. They're things undying. They live though
human nature go into an underground pit for a million
years" (254). Clair had taken to the past "that dim twentieth
century of three weeks ago the memory of her boy-lover who
had screamed away a night of agony beyond the parapets of
Mametz; and he – he had brought memories kin enough to
hers, dying soldiers and starving miners, the Morlocks of the
pits" (224). Back in their own world, they bring memories
of the golden hunters before civilisation, the earthquakes
presaging the end of Atlantis, Winter, "a foretaste of that
winter that was gradually creeping down on all the northern hemisphere, presently to crystallize into the spreading
glaciers and the long silences of the Fourth Ice Age" (227).
They bring no clear memory of coming back, no pat explanations which would make the book too neat and too easily
explained: only conjecture that "Perhaps the Neanderthalers
never pursued them after our end. Somehow they went east
and south and found a place safe from the winter. And then
they went east again, into the beginnings of history". (248)

   *Three Go Back* owes a debt here to William Morris's *News
from Nowhere*, with its splendid concluding moment where
the time traveller, having lived in a perfected future, finds
himself suddenly and inexplicably back in his own time, its
mean architecture and above all its squalid working class
which had been simply missing in Morris' socialist future.
*Three Go Back* uses different reference points for the present
– the train whistling on the distant slope, the incongruity of
clothes, "the ghastly, ghastly smell of the place",

> "My God, did you see that crucifix? And servants – diseased animals
> sweating to tend diseased animals! Why do they? Why the devil do they?
> Pack a room like this? All this nonsense of furniture. Pottering in that damned
> garden. . . Flowers: they grow much better wild; any fool knows it . . ." (251)

Here is Swift's contempt for mankind, in Gulliver's voice
as he returns to London at the end of the fourth book of his
travels from the land of the horses, but without Gulliver's in-
cipient insanity. Clair and Keith are their author's creatures,
and their mission at the end of the book will be to alert people

to the mess civilisation has reduced them, unwittingly, to. The world of airships and leisure living is replaced by real, unembarrassed love – and by a crusade to help the rest of mankind.

*Three Go Back* is at its strongest in visioning the moment of going-back, the shock of recognition of each part of Atlantis and its life, the moment of returning to the present. Its weaker points are its preaching, its Shavian set-piece speeches, the shallow characterisation of the main actors as vehicles for those speeches, the frequent over-writing. But over-writing is balanced by fine moments of character imagining, the relationship between Clair, Aerte and Keith, the slow penetration of an innocent state of mind by people from an unimaginably different world, the realisation that the old world is not necessarily worse, the very human sense that even if the society of the past is better, the comforts of the present would be welcome. Keith's notion (174) of teaching the Atlanteans technology before their time – "we can leap twenty thousand years and take these people with us" – would have made for impossible complexity, very unwilling suspension of disbelief.

The sudden, unexplained return to to-day requires no rationalisation, rather the balancing of memory with reality, and the commitment of the two central characters to a union begun twenty thousand years before. Clair had noticed (135) "these people without religion are the most spiritual the world will ever see!", and her shuddering at the crucifix, back in her own time, is the natural response. In the past she had learned unashamed sexual pleasure: back in her own time, she and Keith will share the pleasure and the commitment.

So yes, *Three Go Back* ends with a "message" as well as with an ingenious end to a science-fiction plot and as Edwin Morgan has described it Gibbon had

> "a desire to map out origins and futures . . . taking him back into an ill-recorded or unrecorded past. . . . [which] could not but shade off into more imaginative constructs where belief rather than fact encouraged him to describe places and races, rituals and adventures, with a sort of didactic semi-fictionality, as in *The Conquest of the Maya* (1934), or in the full-blown fiction of his scientific romances".[1]

---

1 Introduction to Gay Hunter (Edinburgh, Polygon, 1989), p. ii. Morgan notes sardonically (p.viii) the novel's success in that it "manages — just — to conquer its own bathos" in the concluding section where Gay returns to her own time.[9]

*Three Go Back* uses the form of scientific romance to illustrate its writer's conviction that there is an alternative to James Storman's London, and one within reach. Like Ewan at the end of *Grey Granite*, the characters have to feel enough commitment to devote their lives to persuading their contemporaries to fight for it. Perhaps more convincingly than *Grey Granite, Three Go Back* gives the fighting central characters not only a mission, but a real human existence which has survived time travel, and is ready to live with joy in their present.

*Three Go Back* takes its place in the work of Grassic Gibbon now being republished and given long-overdue critical attention – and reading. Small wonder that Wells acknowledged Gibbon's short stories: here is an uneven but memorable imagining of two great set pieces (the arrival in the past, the return to the present) and a slow, methodical exploration of what it would be like to go back before civilisation, to create healthy societies and healthy relationships, taking the cold and the danger with the freedom and the love. Living himself in 1930s London, Grassic Gibbon had to imagine most of it, but the commitment he felt to a better society is the mainspring of his writing which makes *Three Go Back* one of his most consistently readable essays in visioning a better world.

*Ian Campbell*

*November, 1995*

## Some further reading

Works by Lewis Grassic Gibbon in print include:

*A Scots Quair* (1932-34) in three parts and in one volume from
Canongate Press in Edinburgh and from Penguin;
*Gay Hunter* (1934) from Polygon (1989);
*Stained Radiance* (1930) from Polygon (1993);
*The Speak of the Mearns* (1934) from Polygon (1994);
*Three Go Back* (1932) from Polygon (1995).

Malcolm, W K, *A Blasphemer and Reformer* (1984)
Young, Douglas, Beyond the Sunset (1973)
Zagratski, U, *Libertäre and Utopische Tendenzen in
Erzählwerk James Leslie Mitchells/Lewis Grassic Gibbons (1992)*

There are bibliographies of Grassic Gibbon and Grassic
Gibbon studies in *The Bibliotheck,* and an important unpublished PhD thesis by Jeremy Idle (Edinburgh, 1994). The
main collection of manuscripts is in the National Library
of Scotland in Edinburgh. The Grassic Gibbon Centre in
Arbuthnott contains important archives, publishes annually,
and has a bookshop where a wide variety of publications
is available including a recent (1994) biographical study by
Peter Whitfield. Details are available from the Grassic Gibbon
Centre, Arbuthnott Parish Hall, Arbuthnott, Laurencekirk
AB30 1YB telephone 01561-361668.

# CONTENTS

# BOOK I

## WHERE?   WHEN?

*"And if you conquer the air, and if you
compass the earth,
It will not sweeten your death, and it will
not better your birth,
And though you out-distance the swallow,
with a song of pride in your mouth,
What if you barter your soul for speed –
and forget the way to the South?"*

– OLAF BAKER

# THREE GO BACK

CHAPTER I:   THE WRECK OF *MAGELLAN'S CLOUD*

*Subchapter i*

A skyey monster, cobalt and azure-blue, it sailed out of the heat-haze that all morning had been drifting westwards from the Bay of Biscay. It startled the crew of the Rio tramp and there was a momentary scurry of grimy off-watches reaching the deck, and a great upward gape of astounded eyes and mouths. Then the second engineer, a knowledgeable man and discreet in friendship with the wireless operator, voiced explanations.

"It'll be the airship *Magellan's Cloud* on her return voyage."

The Third spat, not disparagingly, but because the fumes of the engine-room were still in his throat. "Where to?"

"Man, you're unco ignorant. Noo York. She's been lying off for weather at Paris nearly a week, Sparks says. Twenty o' a crew and twenty passengers – they'll be payin' through the nose, I'll warrant. . . . There's Sparks gabblin' at her."

A subdued buzz and crackle. A tapping that presently ceased. High up against a cloudless sky, the airship quivered remoter in the Atlantic sunshine. The Third spat again, forgetfully.

"Pretty thing," he said.

The Rio tramp chugged north-eastwards. One or two of the crew still stood on deck, watching the aerial voyageur blend with the August sunhaze and the bubble walls of seascape till it disappeared.

And that was the last their world ever saw of the airship *Magellan's Cloud*.

*Subchapter ii*

Clair Stranlay could not forget her lover who had died on the wire outside Mametz. A series of chance encounters and casual conversations overheard had filled out in tenebrous vignettes each letter of the cryptic notice, Killed in Action. He had died very slowly and reluctantly, being a boy and anxious to live, and unaware that civilization has its prices. . . . And at intervals, up into the coming of the morning, they had heard him calling in delirium: "Clair! *Oh, Clair!*"

Fourteen years ago. And still a look, a book, a word could set in motion the little discs of memory in her mind, and his voice, in its own timbre and depth and accent, would come ringing to her across the years in that cry of agony. . . . She thought, stirring from the verge of sleep in her chair of the *Magellan*'s deserted passenger lounge: 'What on earth made me think of that now?'

". . . no, madam, quite definitely I've nothing to say about my deportation from Germany."

"Oh, please, Dr. Sinclair, *do* give your side of the case. Just a par. I'm Miss Kemp of the C. U. P., you know, and it would be rather a scoop for me. Shame to miss it."

"I've nothing to say. And I'll be obliged if you'll stop pestering me."

"Oh, *very* well."

An angry staccato of heel-taps broke out and approached. Clair, deep in her basket-chair, saw the doorway to the swinging gallery blind for a moment its glimpse of ultramarine skyscape. Miss Kemp, short, sandy, stocky, stood with flushed face, biting her lips inelegantly. Then, catching sight of Clair, she came across the cabin in her religiously-acquired svelte-glide. Clair thought, with an inward groan: 'Oh, my good God, now *I* am in for it.'

She closed her eyes, as if dozing. Unavailingly. The near basket-chair creaked under the ample, svelte-moulded padding of Miss Kemp.

"Hear me try the beast? You're not asleep, are you? I saw your eyes open.... Hear me tackle him? Hope I'm not disturbing you. . . . Beast. Hear his answers? But I'll give him a write-up that'll make him and his precious league squirm, though. Dirty deportee."

"Dirty what?" Clair opened reluctant eyes.

"Deportee. Haven't you heard of him?"

"Quite likely. Who is he?"

"Why, Keith Sinclair, the agitator who's been travelling about Europe organizing the League of Militant Pacifists. Says that another war's inevitable with the present drift of things and that it's up to the common people to organize and shoot down or assassinate their militarists and politicians at the first hint of it."

"Sounds logical." Clair thought: 'And I hope I sound bored enough. . . . No result? Oh, well.' Aloud: "And what happened?"

"Haven't you heard? He was kicked out of Italy a month ago and deported from Germany last week."

"What fun. And where's he going now?"

"Beast. To gaol, I hope. Returning to America in a hurry to attend some demonstration in Boston." Miss Kemp's chair creaked its relief as she rose. "Hear that Sir John Mullaghan's on board?"

"I'm awfully weak on the auricular verb. . . . Never heard of him at all."

"Oh, you *must* have. Awfully important. Conservative M. P. Head of the armaments people. I'm off to get his opinion of the trip. Rather amusing, you know; he and Sinclair have met before."

"Have they?"

"Didn't you hear? Awful shindy. Sir John was making a speech at some place in Berlin. Said there would always be wars and that honest men prepared for them. Sinclair stood up in the audience and interrupted and started a speech on his own. Told them things he'd seen on the Western Front when he served there as a doctor with the Canadians. Sickening things; he's a beast. Women began screaming and some were carried out fainting. . . . Ended up by saying that the obvious duty of the British public was to cut Sir John Mullaghan's throat, and the Germans to hamstring Frau Krupp. . . . Police had to interfere, and that led to his deportation. Sinclair's, I mean. Wonder if Sir John knows he's on board the *Magellan*?"

"I haven't heard."

"*Will* be a scoop if they say anything when they meet. Did you hear – oh, there's Sir John crossing to the steering cabin. I'll get him now."

Clair cautiously raised the eyelids below her pencilled brows. Like talking to the bound files of the *News-Chronicle*.

The lounge was empty, the passengers in their cabins or on the galleries. Miss Kemp's high-heeled footfalls receded. . . . Blessed relief. Please God, why did you make Miss Kemps?

Clair closed her eyes again, and remembered with a drowsy twinge of amusement various gossip paragraphs in the less sanitary weeklies. Inspired by Miss Kemp. No doubt as to the inspirer. . . . What had they been?

> WE'D LOVE TO KNOW –
> If it's true a certain lady novelist acquires a new "lover for life" with every fresh novel she writes?
> If she's made this *clair* to the seventh successor in the rôle?
> And if London isn't rather tired of both her literary and personal promiscuities?

Poor Miss Kemp! That had been the case of Gilbert Trolden she'd heard of and exploited at half-a-crown a par. And poor Gilbert with his desperately respectable sins – how the pars had shocked him! Almost burst his bootlaces. Didn't realize Miss Kemp must live, or that he himself suffered from quite as many pitiful spites and repressions as the journalist. . . . That article in *Literary Portraits* had been sheer claw, however.

> BEST- SELLER FROM THE SLUMS
> Miss Clair Stranlay, whose real name is Elsie Moggs . . . born in a tenement house in Battersea . . . best-seller in England and America . . . Mr. Justice Belhuish, delivering judgment in the case of her banned novel, "Night on Sihor", said: "It is obscene and unclean . . ."

Most of it true enough, of course. Except for the Elsie Moggs bit. A bad mix-up that on Miss Kemp's part when searching out antecedents in Thrush Road. She'd missed the story of how fond Stranlay *mère* had been of novelettes – even to the extent of christening her daughter out of one of them . . .

Romance! Romance that had beckoned so far away beyond the kindly poverty of Thrush Road!

'My dear girl, you came this voyage for rest, not reminiscence. Now's your time.'

But not even the *Magellan's* soothing motion could recapture that drowsiness from which the sound of Miss Kemp's attempted interviewing has evicted her. She thought, with a laggard curiosity: 'Wonder, if the Sinclair man is the one with the beard and false front who ate so hard at lunch? Throat-cutting is probably hungry work. Let's look.'

And, as idly as that, she was afterwards to reflect, she stood up and strolled out of the *Magellan's* lounge and out of the twentieth century.

*Subchapter iii*

Below her, trellis-work of wood and aluminium, and, in the interstices, the spaces of the sun-flooded ocean. The beat of the engines astern sounded remote and muffled. There was not a cloud.

Then, raising her eyes, she saw Keith Sinclair for the first time. He turned with blown hair at the moment, glanced at her uninterestedly, looked away, looked back again. He scowled at her with the sun in his eyes.

He saw a woman who might have been anything from twenty-five to thirty years of age, and who, as a matter of data, was thirty-three. She was taller than most men liked, with that short-cut, straight brown hair which has strands and islets of red in it. And, indeed, that red spread to her eyelashes, which were very long, though Sinclair did not discover this until afterwards, and to her eyes, which had once been blue before the gold-red came into them. Nose and chin, said Sinclair's mind methodically, very good, both of them. She can breathe, which is something. Half the women alive suffer from tonsilitis. But that mouth . . . And he definitely disapproved of the pursed, long-lipped mouth in the lovely face – the mouth stained scarlet with cochineal.

"Weather keeping up," said Clair, helpfully.

He said: "Yes." She thought: 'My dear man, I don't want

to interview you. Only to collect you as a comic character. Sorry you haven't that beard.'

Nearly six feet three inches in height, too long in the leg and too short in the body. All his life, indeed, there had been something of the impatient colt in his appearance. He had a square head and grey eyes set very squarely in it; high cheekbones, black hair, and the bleached white hands of his craft. Those hands lay on the gallery railing now.

"Wish I could go and smoke somewhere," said Clair.

"So do I."

"A little ambiguous." He stared rudely. Clair, said, suddenly: "Goodness!"

Startled, they both raised their heads.

The metal stays below their feet had swung upwards and downwards, with a soggy swish of imprisoned lubricant. The whole airship had shuddered and for a moment had seemed to pause, so to speak, in its stride. Sinclair leant over the gallery railing.

"Hell, look at the sea."

Clair looked. The Atlantic was boiling. Innumerable maelstroms were rising from the depths, turning even in that distance below them from blue-green to white, creamed white, and then, in widening ripples, to dark chocolate . . . Clair felt a kindly prick of interest in the performance.

"What's causing it?"

The American was silent for a moment, regarding the Atlantic with a scowl of surprise. He said: "Impossible."

"What is?"

"I said impossible." He brushed past her towards the doorway of the lounge. Paused. "See the dark chocolate?"

Clair nodded, regarding him with a faint amusement.

"Well, don't you see it must have come from the bottom?"

"So it must." She peered down again. "And it's deep here, isn't it?"

"Perhaps a couple of miles." He disappeared.

News of the submarine earthquake spread quickly enough. Passengers crowded the galleries, Miss Kemp coming to the side of Clair in some excitement. Another passenger, the inescapable portrait-hound, appeared with a camera of unbelievable price and intricacy, and snapshotted the Atlantic closely and severely. From the flashing of lens in the gallery of the engine-house it was obvious that a member of the crew was similarly engaged.

"The chocolate's dying away," said Clair Stranlay.

So it was. The Atlantic had reassumed its natural hue. The maelstroms had vanished, or the airship had passed beyond the locality where they still uprose. For, after that first shudder, the *Magellan's Cloud* had held on her way unfalteringly.

The snapshotter beside Clair wrinkled a puzzled brow.

"Very strange. I could have sworn there was a ship down there to the south only a minute or so ago. It's disappeared. . . . Quick going."

The airship beat forward into the waiting evening. Sky and sea were as before. But presently there gathered in the west such polychrome splendour of sunset as the *Magellan's* commander, who had crossed the Atlantic many times by ship, had never before observed.

And suddenly, inexplicably, it grew amazingly cold.

*Subchapter iv*

The airship's wireless operator fumed over dials and board, abandoned the instrument, went out into the miniature crow's nest that overhung his cabin, glanced about him, and beat his hands together in the waft of icy air that chilled them.

"Damn funny," he commented.

He went back to his cabin and rang up the *Magellan's* commander. The latter had donned the only overcoat he had brought on board and was discussing the weather with the navigator when the wireless operator's voice spoke in his ear.

"Is that you, sir?"

"Yes."

"I'm sorry, but it seems impossible to send that message."

"Eh?"

"I thought there was some fault in the set. I've been sitting here for the last two and a half hours trying to tap in on France or a ship. There's no message come through. I've sent out yours, but there's been no reply."

The commander was puzzled. "That's strange, Gray. Sure your instrument is functioning all right?"

"Certain, sir. I've broadcast to the receiving apparatus in the passengers' lounge and they heard perfectly."

"Damn funny. Get it right as soon as you can, will you?"

"But . . . right, sir."

The commander put down the telephone and turned to give the news to the navigator. They were in the steering cage and it was just after eight o'clock. But the navigator, instead of standing by with his usual stolid expressionlessness, was at the far end of the cage, staring upwards fascinatedly.

"Gray says the infernal wireless has gone out of order. Bright look-out if we go into fog over the banks. . . . Hello, anything wrong?"

"Come here, Commodore."

The commander crossed to the navigator's side. The latter pointed up to a darkling sky which, ever since the sudden fall of temperature, had been adrift with a multitude of cloudlets like the debris of a feather-bed. The commander peered upwards ineffectually.

"Well, what is it?"

"Look. Up there."

"Only the moon. Well?"

"Well, it's only the 22nd of the month. The new moon, in its first quarter, isn't due till the 27th. And that one's gibbous."

"Good Christopher!"

They both stared at the sky through the lattice of airship wire, amazed, half-convinced that some trick was being played upon them. From behind the clouds the moon was indeed emerging, round and wind-blushed and full. It sailed the sky serenely, five days ahead of time, taking stock of this other occupant of its firmament. The *Magellan's* commander brought his glasses to bear on it. It appeared to be the same moon.

"But it's impossible. The calendar must be wrong."

"The only thing possibly wrong is the date. And it's not – as of course we know. Look, here's to-day's *Matin*."

He showed it. It was dated the 22nd.

The airship *Magellan's Cloud* beat forward into the growing radiance of moonlight which had mysteriously obliterated the last traces of the day.

*Subchapter v*

Looking out from his cabin window as he prepared to undress and go to bed, the American, Keith Sinclair, was startled. He was aware that it had grown intensely cold, as indeed was every soul on board the *Magellan's Cloud*, whether on duty or in bed. But now his gaze revealed to him the fact that the airship's hull was silvered with frost in the moonlight. Frost at this altitude in August?

For a moment he accepted the moonlight. And then, standing in the soft hush-hush of the flexible airship walls, realization of the impossibility of that moon came on him, as it had done on the navigator.

'Now how the devil did you come to be there?'

The moon, sailing a sky that was now quite clear, cloudless and starless, made no answer. The notorious deportee whistled a little, remembering a Basque story heard from his mother – of how the sun one morning had risen in the semblance of the moon. . . . But that didn't help. It wasn't nearly morning yet. And it was an indubitable moon.

Still whistling, he felt his pulse, and, as an afterthought, took his temperature. Both were normal. Meanwhile, the cold increased. Sinclair pulled open his cabin door.

'Look up the navigator again. He had precious little explanation of that submarine earthquake, but the moon's beyond ignoring.'

But, crossing the lounge, glimpse of the dark seascape beyond the open door drew him out on the passengers' gallery. There it was even colder, though there was no gale. The ship was travelling at a low altitude. Below, smooth, vast, and unhurrying the rollers of the Atlantic passed out of the near sheen of moonlight into the dimness astern. . . . Abruptly Sinclair became aware that the gallery had another occupant.

Clair Stranlay; in pyjamas, slippers, and wrap. Intent on the night and the sea. But, imagining for a moment that she had air-sickness, the American groped along the handrail towards her.

"Feel ill?"

She started. "What? Dr. Sinclair, isn't it? I'm quite well."

"You'll be down with pneumonia if you stay here."

She thought: 'You must be a blood relation of the Irish policeman — "You'll have to be moving on if you're going to be standing here." But I'd better not say so. Thrush Road imperence, Miss Kemp would diagnose it.' Aloud: "Don't think so. I do winter bathing and icy baths. What's happened?"

"The cold?"

"Yes."

"Early bergs down from the north, I suppose."

"But it's not nearly the season yet."

He had seen something in the moonlight below them. He caught her arm. Clair brushed the short, red-tipped hair from her face with one hand, clung to the handrail with the other, and looked down.

Out of the deserted Atlantic was emerging what appeared to be an immense berg – a sailing of cragged, shapeless greyness upon the water. The moonlight struck wavering bands of radiance from it, and for a moment, in some trick of refraction, it glowed a pearled blue as though lighted from within. It passed underfoot, and as it passed a beam of light shot down from the navigating cabin, played upon it, passed, returned, hesitated, hovered, was abruptly extinguished.

But not so quickly that the two occupants of the passengers' gallery failed to see an accretion such as no iceberg ever bore. For beyond the berg had showed up a long, sandy beach, and beyond that the vague suggestion, a mere lining in the moon-dusk, of a flat and comber-washed island.

Sinclair swore, unimpassioned. "I'm going to find out about this. Are we making for the Pole?"

Clair, to her own amusement, found herself shaking with excitement. "But what could it have been? There are no islands on the France-New York track."

"We've just seen one. I'm going to find out what the navigating cabin knows about it. Unless we're Pole-bound – and that's nonsense – the submarine earthquake may have thrown it up."

"It must have done other things as well, then." Clair began to stamp her feet for warmth. The rest of her felt only the glow of well-being that falling temperatures nowadays gifted her unfailingly as guerdon for much braving of wintry dips. "Haven't you noticed something entirely missing from the sea – even though this is the crowded season?"

"What?" he sounded impatient.

"Ship-lights. Not one has shown up since sunset."

"Who said so?"

"One of the riggers I spoke to just now."

She saw, dimly, his puzzled scowl, and thought, with the unfailing Cockney imp for prompter: 'Disapproving of the Atlantic again!' He said:

"The submarine 'quake we saw couldn't have affected shipping. It was quite localized. If it had caused great damage the wireless bulletins they post in the lounge would have told us."

"Don't they?"

The same thought occurred to them simultaneously. Clinging to the handrail, she followed Sinclair into the cabin. The case with wireless transcriptions was hung against the further wall. They crossed to it, looked at it, and then looked at each other. Clair's face close to his, a flushed and lovely and easily-controlled face, he found for a moment irritatingly disconcerting.

No notices had been posted since five o'clock in the afternoon.

"Look here, Miss —"

"Stranlay."

"Stranlay, I'm going to find out about things. Something extraordinary seems to have happened. But if any of the other passengers come out, don't alarm them."

Clair shook her head, regarding him with upraised brows. "Much too."

"Eh?"

"Dictatorial. . . . And I alarm people only in my books."

"Oh. Do you write?"

"Novels."

"Oh. I'd go to bed if I were you. I'll tap on your cabin door and let you know what I hear."

Fortunate she hadn't seen anything peculiar in the moonlight itself . . .

Passing through the hull, he stopped at a window and himself noted another happening.

The moonlight was pouring lengthwise into the long hull

of *Magellan's Cloud*, not striking due in front, as a moment before.

The airship had turned southwards.

*Subchapter vi*

Clair Stranlay arrived in her cabin meditating the deportee from Germany. And, looking out at the far, moon-misted horizon of the Atlantic, she thought:

'He'd never heard of me! Publicity, where are thy charms? ... Any more than I of him. But how desperately important folk we are to ourselves!' She yawned. 'Must insert that reflection in my next serial. It can't have been used in more than a million novels already.'

And, because that Cockney insouciance of Battersea days seldom deserted her, and she had long ceased to feel even mildly vexed that there lived a world which devoured not best-sellers, she forgot the matter. She slipped out of wrap and pyjamas, rubbed her white and comely self until she felt warm and pringling and the possessor of an altogether enjoyable body. A spear-beam of moonlight splashed on her shoulder and she raised her head, with the red lights in her hair, and looked at it. She put up her hand.

'The blessed thing feels almost cold.'

Something quite extraordinary had happened to the *Magellan's Cloud*. But what? Delay it much reaching New York?

'Oh, my good God!' sighed Clair, getting into bed.

For, escaping England and boredom to go and lecture in America, the awfulness of the ennui, hitherto concealed, that lay awaiting her appalled her. The shore. Miles and miles of ferro-concrete, macadam, pelting rush and automobilist slither. Packing of clothes – scanty though they were. Mooring mast. Elevator. Customs shed. Forms. Beefy officials. Forms. "Are you an atheist or anarchist?" Solemn no, instead of writing, as the spirit always moved her, "Yes, both, and then some." Auto. Becky Meadow's house. Literary gathering. Stylists. (Accent on the sty.) Prudent pornographers. Platform. Brisk skittishness with tiredness commingled – correct best-seller attitude. Husky American voices stilling.

"The New Schools in England." Woof, woof, woof. Woolf, Huxley. Blah, blah, blah. And rows and rows of eyes set in faces more like those of paralytic codfish than human beings – faces of women combed and powdered and bathed to excess, living hungrily on the mean grubbing and sweating of mean and shrivelled hes. Shes! Oh, my good God, the shes of the world!

And, thinking of them, Clair's mind-mask of insouciance, brittle and bright, quivered and almost showered her soul with its flakes. Sometimes, indeed, it cracked and fell about her entirely, and she'd hear that boy on the wire outside Mametz, and her desperate distaste for her work, her lovers, her life and her century crescendo'ed in her heart into the cry of a prisoned, tortured thing. . . .

'Oh, forget it. The mess of our lives! Civilization! Ragged automata or lopsided slitherers. Our filthy concealments and our filthy cacklings when the drapings slip aside! Our hates, our loves – oh, my good God, your own loves, my dear! Better to have kept to the memory of the boy always, perhaps – and turned to a shrivelled virginal spite like the Kemp. Your lovers. . . . Poor simulacra! Remember them? Sneak and strategy. Devotion. Starryeyedness. Thrill and masculinity. . . . Instead of —

'What else? What else is there? Physical love or life – could there ever be anything very much better? For we're not human beings, of course. There was never such a thing as a human being. We're only apes repressing our blood-lusts and sex-lusts and God alone knows what unhygienic lusts – in the interests of feeding better! And the repressions'll grow and grow as we eliminate the beast entirely. Exit Tarzan. . . . And when that's happened there won't be a codfish in a N'York audience but'll be an intelligent codfish, discussing hormones with its intimate hes. Utopia. . . . See old Moore —'

But here Clair Stranlay found the blessedness of sleep now close upon her. Her body had lost its surface cold. She curled up her toes a little under the quilt – they were even, uncramped, and shapely toes – and sighed a little, and wished she could smoke a cigarette, and fell fast asleep – and was shot out of sleep five minutes later by a knock at the door of her cabin.

*Subchapter vii*

"Yes, come in," she called, good-tempered even then; good temper had dogged her through life. Was it morning already and had they sighted New York?

But there was no daylight, only moonlight, entering the cabin window. She reached up to the switch and in the pallor of electric light looked at the American. Keith Sinclair, shutting the door, thought: 'Pretty thing' – a thought in the circumstances that was a considerable feat of detachment.

"About what's happened, Miss Stranlay – Can I sit down?"

"Can you?" said Clair, blinking her eyes and looking round the small cabin. Then, entirely awake, she solved the difficulty by drawing herself into the smallest space possible. "Yes, do, here on the side of the bed. If anyone comes in you can be taking my temperature." She put her hands behind her head and leant back comfortably.

The American grunted. "It'll probably want taking when I've told you the news." He brooded, his high-cheek-boned face dourly thoughtful. "We're in this together, in a fashion, I suppose, seeing we were the first to see the submarine 'quake. Well – the commander refuses to talk sense. Scared I alarm the others, I suppose. But he has to admit that no wireless messages have been received since the time of the submarine disturbance, though the apparatus of the *Magellan* appears to be perfectly in order. Also, he's turned the airship south."

"South?" Clair's hands dropped from her neck at that. "Then we're not making New York?"

"We're not" – grimly. "We'll be lucky if we fetch up in Brazil at this rate."

"Thank God," said Clair.

"Eh?"

"Nothing. Not particularly anxious to reach New York. The codfish can wait. . . . Sorry, I'm still half-asleep. Nice of you to come and tell me the news. Why has the *Magellan* turned south, then, and what does the captain say about that island with the berg we saw from the gallery?"

"Turned south because he's scared about the effect of the continued cold on the airship's envelope. I don't wonder, either. I met your garrulous rigger just now and he says we're carrying tons of ice. As for the island – the navigator says we're mistaken."

"Astigmatism or booze?"

He grinned – a softening relaxation. ('Possibility that some day he'll laugh,' recorded Clair's imp.) He said: "Neither in his case and both in ours, he seems to think. Truth of the matter is that the crew is as puzzled as we are, but they think if the passengers knew they'd blame them for all these extraordinary phenomena." He considered his pyjama-jacketed listener for a moment. "There's another thing, Miss Stranlay, which you didn't notice. The most serious of the lot, though the commander refuses to have anything said about it. It's the moon."

"What has it done?"

"Arrived five days ahead of time. There shouldn't be a full moon for another fortnight; there shouldn't be a moon at all just now."

Even Clair felt startled at that. "But – that *is* the moon."

He looked through the cabin window at it. "It is." he rubbed his chin impatiently. "And it isn't. . . . Eh?"

"I said: Clear as mud."

"Oh. It's a thing not easy to explain." He stood up. "But I've a telescope with me – probably the most powerful magnifier on the *Magellan* – and I've had a peek at the moon through it. Just a minute."

He was back in less. He opened the cabin window and poised the telescope on the ledge. Clair sat forward and looked through it.

"Keep both eyes open," advised the American.

So she did, and for a moment was blinded in consequence. The moon was sinking. Stars were appearing, pallidly. Clair gazed across space. Then:

"Nothing very different, is it? I've looked at it through the big glass at Mount Wilson. Why – the nose!"

The Man in the Moon lacked a nose. Clair turned her face to Sinclair's moon-illumined one. He nodded.

"Exactly. That mountain-range on the moon is missing. Something is happening up there."

She thought for a moment, caught a glimpse of a possible explanation. "Then – the tides are caused by the moon.

Mayn't that submarine earthquake have been caused by the change in the moon?"

"Perhaps. I'm not an astronomer. But something abnormal *has* happened to the moon – both to her surface and her rate of revolution. The submarine earthquake we witnessed may have been the result. Probably it's had other effects in the far north – God knows what. Bringing down bergs and so forth."

"And the wireless interruptions due to the same cause?" Clair lowered the telescope from her cabin-window in the *Magellan*. "Most interesting thing I've seen for years. Pity we've explained it all so nicely."

But, as they were later to learn, they were very far indeed from having explained it.


*Subchapter viii*

And presently, while Clair slept again and Sinclair tried to sleep (for his mind was vexing itself with notes for his Boston speech to the League of Militant Pacifists), and the commander sat peering at an almanac, and the navigator peered into the west – a pale shimmer of daylight arose in the east, lightening the surface of that strange Atlantic, flowing liquid almost as the Atlantic itself till it touched the southwards-hasting, high-slung cars of the *Magellan's Cloud*. A moment it lingered (as if puzzled) on that floating monster of the wastes, and then, abruptly, like a candle lighted for a hasty glimpse of the world by some uncertain archangel, was snuffed out. . . . And the navigator from his gallery was shouting urgent directions into the engine-room telephone.

It is doubtful if they ever reached the engineers. For at that moment the nose of the *Magellan*, driving south at the rate of eighty miles an hour, rustled and crumpled up with a thin crack of metallic sheathing. The whole airship sang in every strut and girder, and, quivering like a stunned bird, still hung poised against the mountain-range that had arisen out of the darkness. The drumming roar roused to frantic life everyone on board, asleep or awake. Most of the passengers probably succeeded in leaving their beds, if not their cabins. On the lurching floors of these they may have glanced upwards and caught horrified glimpses of the next moment's happening.

The airship's hull spurted into bright flames, green-glowing, long-streaming in the darkness that had succeeded the false twilight. Then the whole structure broke apart, yet held together by the tendrils of the galleries and cabins, and, an agonized, mutilated thing, drew back from the mountainside and fell and flamed and fell again, unendingly, in two long circles, the while the morning came again, hasting across the sea, and the noise of that sea rose up and up and reached the ears of some on the *Magellan* . . .

And then suddenly the Atlantic yawned and hissed, while the dawn passed overhead and lighted the mountains and hastened into the west.

CHAPTER II:   THE SURVIVORS

*Subchapter i*

NOW, what happened to Clair Stranlay in that dawn-wrecking of the *Magellan's Cloud* was this:

The preliminary shock, when the nose of the airship drove into the mountain which had mysteriously arisen out of the spaces of the Atlantic, did not awaken her, though she twitched in dreams, and, indeed, may in dream have had a momentary startlement. She stirred uneasily, though still asleep, freeing her pretty arms from the quilt during the period that the *Magellan* hung, death-quivering, against her murderer. Then, abruptly, sight, hearing, and a variety of other sensations, were vouchsafed to her fortissimo, crescendo.

She heard the first explosion which shattered the hull of the airship, and leapt up in bed to see through the cabin window, phantasmagoric against a grey morning sky, the flare and belch of the flames. She sat stunned, uncomprehending, the while the floor of her cabin tilted and tilted and the metal-work creaked and warped. Then the cabin-door, a groaning, flare-illumined panel, was torn open, a figure shot in, crossed to Clair's bed and caught her with rough hands. It was the American deportee, Sinclair.

'Oh, my good God, he's been reading one of my novels,' thought Clair, as his hands touched her. It was the kind of thing the overwrought hero always did when he couldn't abide the fact of the heroine sleeping alone any longer. . . . She struggled, thinking: 'Shall I blacken his eye?' then ceased from that as, fully awake, she heard him shout:

"Come on, damn you! The ship's a flaming wreck. . . . Clothes – some clothes!"

He swept a pile into his arms from the locker. Clair jumped from bed, plucked something – she could not see what it was – from the floor, and groped across the cabin after

Sinclair. He tugged at the door. It had jammed. Now, out of the corridor, above the babel of sounds, one sound sharp-edged and clear came to them; a moan like that of trapped cattle. For a moment it rang in Clair's ears in all its horror, and then – the floor of the cabin vanished from beneath the feet of Sinclair and herself.

Below, the Atlantic.

And Clair thought 'Oh, God,' and fell and fell, with a flaming comet in wavering pursuit. Till something that seemed like a red-hot dagger was thrust to the hilt into her body.

*Subchapter ii*

Breakers, and breakers again – the cry of them and the splash of them, and their salt taste stale in her mouth. In and in, and out with a slobbering surge. Water in pounding hill-slopes, green and white-crested. Pounding tons of water whelming over into those breakers. . . . Clair Stranlay cried out and awoke.

"Better? I thought you'd gone. . . . My God, look at the *Magellan*!"

Her body seemed wrapped in a sheet of fire that was a sheet of ice. She could not open her eyes. She tried again. They seemed fast-gummed. Then, abruptly, they opened. She moaned at the prick of the salt-grime.

She and Keith Sinclair were lying in a wide sweep of mountain-surrounded bay, on a beach of pebbles. Beyond and below them the sea was thundering. And out in the bay, a splendour like a fallen star, the *Magellan's Cloud* was flaming against a dark-grey, rainy sky momentarily growing lighter, as if the *Magellan* were serving as tinder to its conflagration.

This was not what Clair saw immediately. It was what she realized as she looked around her. Sinclair lay at right-angles to her, propped on his arm, vomiting sea-water in horrid recurring spasms of sickness.

Clair stared at him, sought for her voice, found it after an interval, manipulated it with stiff and painful lips.

"How did we get here?"

"Swam." The American swayed to his knees. His high cheek-boned face looked as though the blood had been drained from it through a pipette. "We hit the water before the *Magellan* did, and sank together. Came up clear of the wreck and I pulled you ashore. . . . Oh, *damn* it!"

He was very sick indeed. There was an inshore-blowing wind, bitterly cold. With a shock Clair discovered she was dressed in her pyjamas only. Through those garments the rain-laden wind drove piercingly. It was laden now with other things than rain – adrift with red-glowing fragments of fluff, portions of the *Magellan's* fabric. The *Magellan*?

In that moment the airship blew up. A second Clair saw its great girders, like the skeleton of a great cow, then they vanished.

The eastwards sky was blinded to darkness in the flash, Clair and Sinclair momentarily stunned with the noise of the explosion. Then a great wave poured shoreward out of the stirred water of the bay, leapt up the beach, snarled, spat, soaked and splashed them anew, tore at them, retreated. Gasping, Clair saw Sinclair's hand extended towards her. She caught it. Unspeaking, now crawling, now gaining their feet and proceeding at a shambling run, they attained the upper beach. Fifty yards away, across the shingle, there towered in the dimness of the morning great cliffs of black basalt. Against their black walls Sinclair thought he discerned a fault and overhang. He pointed towards it and they stumbled together across sharp stones that lacerated their feet. Anything to get out of the wind and spray. Clair almost fell inside the crack in the rock face. Sinclair crumpled to the ground beside her. Clair heard someone sobbing and realized it was herself.

"What's wrong?"

She looked up at him, her teeth chattering, thinking: 'I suppose we'll both be dead in a minute.' She said: "I'm all right."

Prone, he began to laugh crackedly at that. Clair stuffed her fingers in her ears and looked out to sea.

It was deserted. The *Magellan's Cloud* had disappeared without leaving other trace than themselves. Green, tremendous, with tresses upraised and flying through the malachite comb of the wind, the Atlantic surged over the spot where the wreck had flamed. An urgent fear came upon Clair. She shook the American's shoulder.

"Where are the others?"

"Dead."

He had stopped laughing. He lay face downwards, unmoving. Clair shook him again.

"You mustn't! You must keep awake . . ."

But she knew it was useless. Her own head nodded in exhaustion. She laid her face in the curve of her arm and presently was as silent as he was.

*Subchapter iii*

The morning wind died away and with its passing the sky began to clear. One after another, like great trailing curtains drawn aside from an auditorium, sheets of rain passed over the sea. But they passed north-eastwards, not touching the little bay. Lying exhausted and asleep in their inadequate shelter under the lee of the cliffs the two survivors of the airship's wreck stirred at the coming of the sunlight. Sinclair awoke, sat up, looked round, remembered. He whistled with cracked lips.

"Great Spartacus!"

Wrecked. The *Magellan's Cloud* blown up. And cold – the infernal cold . . .

He was in pyjamas – green-striped silk poplin. The suit clung to his skin in damp and shuddersome patches. He stood up. His feet were cut and bruised, black with congealed blood. The salt bit into them as he moved. Alternate waves of warmth and coldness flowed up and down his body. He pulled off the pyjama-jacket, stripped himself of the trousers, and spread the soggy things to dry in front of the shelter. Setting his teeth against giving way to the pull of the urgent pain in his feet, he began to knead and pound his throat and chest and abdomen and thighs, then took to massaging them, plucking out and releasing muscles like a violin-maker testing the strings of a bow. Suddenly something screamed at him, menacingly.

He glanced up, startled. It was a solitary gull. He thought: 'And a peculiar one, too.' It swooped and hovered, its bright eyes on the occupants of the shelter. Man and bird looked at each other unfriendlily. Then the gull, with slow beating wings, flapped out of sight. Sinclair resumed operations on his now tingling body.

Behind him, Clair Stranlay began to moan.

He had thought her dead. He wheeled round. Lying with her face and throat in the sun, she was moaning, again unable to open her eyes. Her hair was a damp mop. The American frowned at her, lightedly, considered a moment, reached out for his pyjamas, found them almost dry, donned them.

Then he knelt down by his fellow-survivor, straightened out the crumplement in which she lay, loosened at waist and throat her ornate sleeping suit of blue and gold, and began with great vigour to massage her body into such warmth as he had induced in his own. The muscles of her stomach, usually a very flat and comely stomach, were bunched in cold. He smoothed that out, gently enough. She quivered under his hands. Her eyes opened at last.

She sat up, remembering at once, as he himself had done. "Any of the others turned up?"

He shook his head, searching her body the while with skilful, nervous fingers. She became aware of that, surprisedly.

"Thanks. What about yourself?"

"I attended to myself before tackling you. The sunlight woke me."

"I'm horribly thirsty."

"So am I. I'll go and look for water in a minute."

"Where do you think we are?"

"Somewhere in the Bay of Biscay. Coast of Portugal, perhaps."

Clair's undrowned imp raised a damp head. "Hope it's the sherry district. People inland must have seen the wreck of the *Magellan*. They're bound to come down to the shore, aren't they?"

"Bound to, I should think. Feel certain enough to rise now?"

She stood up with his arm supporting her. Instantly, in the full sunlight, she began to shiver. He nodded.

"Strip and do exercises. Know how? Right. I'll go and look for water and see if any people are coming down the cliffs. Don't overdo things. Shout for me if you feel faintness coming on."

He went, limping bloody-heeled. Clair stared after him till his black poll vanished round a projection of rock, and then emerged slowly from her dejected sleeping-suit. She thought, hazily: '"Exercises. . . ." Honest to God Amurrican ones. This can't be happening to me. It's a scene out of a novel.'

Her feet, like Sinclair, she discovered bloody, though not so badly cut. Excepting its craving for water, her body in the next few strenuous minutes acquired comfort and familiarity again. The pyjamas steamed in the sunlight; ceased to steam. In ten minutes they were dry. She was putting them on when Sinclair returned.

"There's water round to the left – a cascade over the rocks. Can you walk?"

She essayed the adventure, gingerly. "Easily."

Out in the full sunlight she stopped to look round the bay. Desolate. The navigator, the commander, Miss Kemp – a fit of shuddering came on again. She covered her face with her hands.

But the horror lingered for a moment only, and then was gone. She turned to the American, a pace behind her, waiting for her, a grotesque figure in his shrunken pyjamas, his blue-black hair untidily matted. He stood arms akimbo, scowling at the sea. A gull – there seemed but one gull in the bay – swooped over their heads. Clair thought, after that one swift under-glance: 'We must look like a bridal couple in a Coward play. But I'd better not say so.'

She became aware that the silence around them was illusory. It was a thing girdled by unending sound, as the earth is girdled with ether. The tide was no longer in full flow, but the serene thunder of the breakers was unceasing. Clair's voice sounded queer to herself as she spoke, as though voices were scarce and alien things in this land.

"Funny no Portuguese have come down to look for the wreck."

"Damn funny." The scowl went from his face. He looked at her expressionlessly. He glanced up at the surrounding walls of basalt. "They'll come. You'd better have some water."

The pebbles underfoot were slimily warm. From the sea a breath of fog was rising, like a thin cigarette-smoke. Not a ship or a boat was in sight, nothing upon or above the spaces of the Atlantic but a solitary cirrus low down in

the north-eastern sky. Clair's heels smarted. The American
limped. They turned a corner in the winding wall of cliff
and were in sight of the waterfall. In distance it seemed to
hang bright, lucent, unmoving, a silver pillar in a dark phallic
temple. Clair loved it for its beauty; she had the power in any
circumstances to love beauty unexpected and unwarranted.
She bent and scooped from it a double handful of water. She
gasped.

It was icily cold. Some drops splashed through her jacket.
They stung like leaden pellets. She shivered and, squatting,
rinsed her mouth and laved her face. Sinclair looked down
at her; knelt down beside her. They scoured their faces in
solemn unison. Standing up, Sinclair looked round about
him, involuntarily, for a towel. Clair wiped her face with
the jacket of her pyjamas. Sinclair followed suit. Wiping, he
suddenly stayed operations.

"Here's someone at last."

He pointed towards the leftward tip of the bay. A black-
clad figure was descending the inky, sun-laced escarpment,
apparently less steep at that spot than elsewhere. It was
descending in haste. It had descended. It stood hesitant,
glancing upwards, not towards them. Clair put her fingers
to her mouth and startled the bay, Sinclair and the stranger
with a piercing, moaning whistle which the rocks caught and
echoed and re-echoed.

"Stop that!" said Sinclair, angrily.

He was to see often enough in succeeding days that
look of innocent, amused surprise on the lovely face turned
towards him. The black-garmented figure had started violently, seen them, stood doubtful a moment, but now, with
gesticulating arm, was coming towards them.

"I can't speak a word of Portuguese," said Clair. "Can
you?"

There was a pause. Then:

"It won't be necessary. I don't suppose he knows
Portuguese himself."

"No?" Puzzled, Clair examined the nearing stranger. He
was finding the going punishing. He stumbled. His features
changed from a blur to discernible outline. "Who is he?"

"A fellow-passenger on the *Magellan*. Sir John
Mullaghan."

*Subchapter iv*

"I was washed ashore at the far peak of the bay when the *Magellan's Cloud* struck the water. I imagined I was the only survivor."

The grey-haired man with the gentle, sensitive face was addressing Clair. She held out her hand to him.

"I'm Clair Stranlay. Dr. Sinclair rescued me." She glanced from one to the other, thinking: 'Don't bite. . . .' "You know each other?"

The American smiled thinly, but otherwise took no notice of the question. Sir John Mullaghan began to unbutton. Clair said, wide-eyed: "What's wrong?"

"You must wear my coat, Miss Stranlay."

"No thanks. I'm quite comfy. However do you come to be wearing your clothes?"

"I found it too cold to go to bed, and was sitting up studying some documents when the wreck occurred." His small, neat form was clad in the shrunken caricature of a dress suit. Collar and tie were missing, the breast of the shirt very limp and muddied. Sinclair glanced sideways at his feet and scowled again. Shod in thin pumps that were at least some slight protection. . . . Clair said: "Let's sit down. What did you see at the top of the cliff?"

They sat down, Clair and Sir John. Sinclair remained standing. Clair folded one shapely knee over the other, and twisted a little on the boulder, thinking: 'Oh, my good God, how I *would* like some coffee and a soft chair to sit in!' She repeated her question to the new arrival.

"–and what made you come down so quickly?"

The armaments manufacturer was sitting with his grey head in his hands. He looked up.

"A lion, Miss Stranlay."

"A – what?"

"A lion. One of the largest brutes I have ever seen. It stalked me close to the cliff-head." He trembled involuntarily.

Clair glanced at Sinclair, glanced back at Sir John, looked up at the cliffs. The Atlantic said: "Shoom. Surf. Shoom." The cirrus cloud trailed its laces across the face of the sun, and for a little the faces of the three derelicts on the beach were in patterned shadow. "A *lion*? But I thought we were in Portugal?"

"I don't know where we are. But this is not the coast of Portugal. At the top of the cliff there is a further terrace-wall to be climbed. It is fringed with bushes and trees. I expected to get some view of the country from there and went up about half an hour ago."

"What happened?"

"I pushed through the fringe of bushes until I came to a fairly open space. I was certain that I would see some village near at hand, or at least houses and some marks of cultivation." He paused. The Atlantic listened. "There are no houses and the country is quite wild. It is natural open park-land, dotted with clumps of trees, stretching as far away as one can see. And on the horizon, about five or six miles distant from here, are two volcanoes."

"Volcanoes?" The American was startled into speech. "You must have been mistaken."

"I have quite good eyesight, Miss Stranlay."

The American bit his lip. Clair said: "Where do you think we are, then?"

"Somewhere on the coast of Africa."

"But it's much too cold. And I never heard of volcanoes on the coast of Africa."

"There *are* no volcanoes on the coast of Africa. Most likely the lion was some beast escaped from a menagerie."

This was Sinclair. Sir John Mullaghan flushed. Clair, wondering bemusedly if there were ever an armaments manufacturer who looked less the part, wondered also if the beast of which he spoke had had any existence outside the reaches of a disaster-strained imagination. She looked again at the cliff-top, shining in the cool sunlight. "We'll have to go up there and look for food, anyhow. I'm horribly hungry."

All three of them were. It was nearing noon. They licked hungry lips. Both men, if for different reasons, had been too preoccupied to realize the emptiness within them. Sinclair, peering up at the cliffs in the breaker-hung silence, thought: 'Hungry? As hell. But if this patriot warrior didn't dream, there's a lion up there. Still – without food we'll never last another night.'

Clair thought: 'Now, if this were a good novel of wrecked mariners, we'd toss up for it to see which was to eat t'other.' And she began to giggle, being very hungry and somewhat dizzy.

"Miss Stranlay!"

She regarded the American placidly. "It's all right. I was thinking of a funny story."

"Oh."

"Yes." She stood up, suddenly decided. "Wrecked people sometimes eat each other if they can't get other food – at least, they always do in my profession. *De rigueur*. Let's climb the cliff and see if the lion's gone."

"Come on, then," said Sinclair, shortly, striding over the shingle. They followed him, Sir John Mullaghan dubiously, Clair satisfiedly, and once surreptitiously trying to rub some feeling into her oddly-numbed stomach. Sinclair was making for the point ascended and descended by the armaments manufacturer. His survey of the cliffs had told him that no other spot was climbable.

They went on along the deserted beach. The tide was going out. Sinclair glanced back, casually, halted in his stride, stared, abandoned the other two, strode past them.

"Wait."

They looked after him. Ten yards away he bent over something at the wet verge of shingle. He picked it up. It glittered, wetly. He shook it vigorously. Clair called: "What is it?"

"An eiderdown quilt."

So it was. Brought nearer in Sinclair's arms, Clair recognized it.

"It's off my cabin-bed in the *Magellan*! I'd know those whorls anywhere. . . . That was the thing I must have picked up when you came to get me."

"Lucky that you did."

"Why?" She regarded it without enthusiasm. "It's very wet, isn't it?"

"It'll dry. And the nights are likely to be cold."

"But —" Clair looked out to sea, looked round the deserted bay again. The possibility that this was not, after all, a few hours' lark struck upon her. "We'll be rescued before then."

Neither of the men spoke. Sir John passed a grey hand over his grey hair. Sinclair's comment was the usual impatient frown. . . . They resumed their progress cliffwards, the barefooted refugees slipping on the moist pebbles, Sir John in slightly better case. The thin, sun-flecked wind bit casually through pyjama-fabric. At the foot of the cliff-ascent, hearing a swish of wings, Clair looked back.

The bay's solitary seagull was following them. Clair held out her hand to it. At that, as if frightened by the gesture, it turned in the air in a wide loop, and planed away steeply down towards the retreating tide. The American was speaking to Sir John.

"You've got shoes. Will you lead?"

The armaments manufacturer hesitated only a moment, nodded curtly, and began the ascent. The silence but for his scrapings over the rock was more intense than ever.

Sinclair and Clair followed, the American in a little beginning to swear violently underbreath because of his cut feet. Clair said: "Say something for me as well."

He glanced at her – almost a puzzled glance – from below his fair, unhappy brows. Then he went on. Clair, panting, poised to rest. She was more than a little frightened, though she refused to think of the fact. . . . Where were they? And what on earth was going to happen? And how long would her pyjamas last?

Sinclair's toiling back, quilt-laden, reproached her sloth. Sir John Mullaghan had almost disappeared.

From the shore the circling gull saw the three strange animals – it had never seen such animals, nor had any gull on the shore of that strange Atlantic ever seen their like – dwindle to spider-splayed shadows against the face of the cliffs, dwindle yet further to hesitant, fore-shortened dots on the cliff-brow, and then vanish for ever from its ken.

CHAPTER III:   IN AN UNKNOWN LAND

*Subchapter i*

THREE days later, and the coming of nightfall.
Almost it came in countable strides. All the afternoon
the line of volcanoes beyond the leftward swamps had
smoked like hazy beacons, like the whin-burnings on a
summer day in Scotland. They had drowsed in the clear,
sharp sunshine that picked out so pitilessly the hilly, wooded
contours of the deserted land. Swamp and plain and rolling
grassland, straggling rightwards forest fringe, swamp and
plain and hill again. Unendingly. But with the westering
of the sun these things had softened in outline, blurred in
distance, and now, on the hesitating edge of darkness, the
great chain of volcanoes lighted and lighted till they were
a beckoning candelabrum, casting long shadows and gleams
of light over leagues of the bleak savannah. The coming
nightfall hesitated a little on the stilled tree-tops of the great
western forest, and then, with uncertain feet, walked westwards, delicately, like Agag, to meet the challenge of those
night-beacons kindled far down in the earth's interior. So,
walking, it paused a little, as if astounded, by a spot in the tree
sprayed foothills that led to the volcanoes' range.

For here, in all that chilled and hushed and waiting
expectancy, were three things that did not wait, that bore
human heads and bodies and cast them anxious glances at
the astounded and brooding nightfall. For three sunsets now
the nightfall had come on those three hasting figures. Each
time they were further south, each time they greeted the
astounded diurnal traveller with the uplift of thin, ridiculous
pipings in that waste land overshadowed by the volcanoes.
They did so, now.

"'Fraid it'll beat us," said the middle figure, a short
bunched shapelessness.

The leading figure, tall and hasting, grunted. The last

29

figure, breathing heavily, said: "I also think it's useless. We had much better try the forest."

"What do you think, Dr. Sinclair?" asked the midway shapelessness. The leader grunted again. "Damn nonsense. We'll climb towards the volcanoes, where we've a chance of getting warm. Another night in the open may finish us. And the forest's not safe."

Underfoot, the heavy-fibred grass rustled harsh and wet to the touch of naked feet. Overhead, the dark traveller still hesitated. The heavy-breathing rearward figure said:

"There is probably no danger in the forest. You saw things while you were half-awake. In daylight we've seen no animal larger than a small deer."

The leading figure swore, turned a shadowed face, halted and confronted the rearguard, and disregarded a restraining motion made by the shapelessness. "Damn you and your impertinences. Did you imagine that lion you originally saw, then? I tell you I saw a brute twice as big as any lion hovering round the tree-clump we slept in this morning. And you make me out a liar, you – you damned straying patriot freak!"

And the middle shapelessness which, under the endrapement of the eiderdown quilt salvaged from the wreck of *Magellan's Cloud*, contained Clair Stranlay, thought: 'Goodness, they're both nearly all in. And I don't wonder. What on earth am I to do if they start scrapping now?'

That question had vexed her almost continually for some seventy hours. The American and Sir John Mullaghan had seemed to her designed from the beginning of the world to detest each other. For seventy hours they had lived on edge. And now —

Clair thought: 'Oh, my good God, I could knock your silly heads together. And I'm cold and miserable and hungry. And if ever we get out of this awful country I'll write an account and lampoon you both —"

*Subchapter ii*

There would be plenty of copy for that account.

. . . The wreck. The rescue. Sir John Mullaghan arriving on the scene, complete with tale of discourteous lion.

Climbing the cliffs. No lion. Wide view of the sea. No ships. No food. And before them an unrecognizable landscape about which Sinclair and Sir John had at once begun to disagree. Labrador or North Canada, said Sinclair – abruptly deserting Portugal. There were supposed to be lost volcanoes in the wilds of Canada. Sir John had asked if there were also lions, and how the *Magellan*, turning south just prior to being wrecked, could have reached Canada? No reply to that. Scowls. All three growing hungry. Finally, exploration in search of food.

It had led them further and further inland, that exploration. No animals. Not a solitary bird. Strange land without the sound of birds, without the chirp of grasshoppers in those silent forest clumps! Clair had shivered at that voicelessness, though, far off beyond the cliffs, they could still hear the moan of the lost Atlantic. They had strayed remoter and remoter from that moan, out into thinner aspects of the parkland, till the landscape they saw was this: Distant against the eastern horizon a long mountain sierra, ivory-toothed with snow, cold and pale and gleaming in the cool sunshine, except at points lighted with the lazy smoking of volcanoes. To the right a jumble of hills that must lead back to the Atlantic eventually, and those hills matted and clogged with forest. But not jungle. Pines and conifers and firs.

"Likely-looking country for lion," the American deportee had remarked acidly, and then hushed them both with a sharp gesture. Something stirred in a clump of bushes only a yard or so away. They'd stared at it, making out at last the head and shoulders and attentive antlers of a small deer. Sinclair had acted admirably then, Clair had thought – albeit a little ridiculously. He'd motioned them to silence, unwound the damp eiderdown from about his shoulders, crept forward, suddenly leapt, landed on top of the deer and proceeded to smother the little animal in the quilt's gaudy folds. Squeals and scuffling. Deer on top, deer underfoot. Sinclair in all directions but hanging on grimly and cursing so that Clair, running to his aid, had thought regretfully how she'd no notebook with her on this jaunt. . . . She had halted and gasped.

For at her forward rush all the bushes round about, probably held paralysed by fear until then, had suddenly vomited deer; a good two score of deer. A hoofs-clicking like the rattle of an insane orchestra of castanets, the bushes were deserted, and the deer in headlong flight. Clair had stared after them, fascinated, been cursed for her pains, then had knelt down and, rather white-faced, assisted Sinclair to strangle his captive . . .

Sir John Mullaghan, who had tripped and fallen in *his* forward rush, had arrived then.

They had kindled a fire and fed on that deer. The making of the fire had been a problem until it was discovered that the armaments manufacturer had a petrol-lighter in his pocket. Ornate, gold-mounted thing. No petrol. But the flint had still functioned and there had been lots of dry grass available. Fire in a minute. How to cook the deer? No knives. Sinclair had said: "Miss Stranlay, go away for a minute. You, Mullaghan, I want your help." Clair had turned away, reluctantly, had heard an unfriendly confabulation, had heard the sound of scuffling, smelt the reek of blood and manure, had wheeled round with a cry. . . . The men had torn a leg and haunch from the body of the deer. Clair had been quietly sick.

The meal had been good, though singey and tough. Sinclair had burned his fingers in tearing off a half-cooked portion and handing it to her. Sir John, his dress suit spattered with drops of blood, had helped at the cooking efficiently enough. But there had been no co-operation be-tween him and Sinclair. They had sat, replete, and disagreed with each other, never once addressing each other, but talking through the medium of Clair. It had then been late afternoon.

"It's obvious we must hold inland and southward," said Sinclair. "There's no sign of human beings or habitations hereabouts. And if this, as I suspect, is Northern Canada in a warm spell, it is only southward we are ever likely to meet with anyone."

"I doubt if there's anything in that, Miss Stranlay." The grey head had been shaken at her; the gentle eyes held determination. "Probably you, like myself, wish to get back to civilization as soon as possible? Then, I think, it's obvious we ought to return to the cliff-head before sunset and light a fire there and wait through the night. Some ship is bound to see the signal, for there are plenty of ships on the African coast."

Clair had wiped her greasy, slim fingers on the coarse grass, and thought about it, sitting cross-legged and massaging her sweetly pedicured toes. "I don't know. Canada? I don't think we can be there, Dr. Sinclair. It's too far away from the eastern Atlantic, as Sir John Mullaghan says. But this is not a bit like Africa." She had glanced round the unhappy landscape. "Not a bit like anything I ever heard of." She had thought of adding: 'Like hell it isn't!' because that would have been funny, and was always appreciated in her novels. But she had restrained herself, being judicious, and looked at the three-quarters of deer left to them, the while the two men looked at her, Sinclair with apparent indifference, Sir John with courteous attention. On the other hand, there doesn't seem to be any food in this place. All those little deer ran away south. They may have been strays from the south. I think we ought to follow them. After all, we're bound to meet people some time."

The American had stood up at that, handed Clair the quilt, seized the deer, gutted it – a sickening task – with his hands, and then slung it across the shoulder of his pyjama-jacket. "You've the casting vote. Come on, then."

And they had gone on. They'd camped that night a few miles inland, under the lee of a ragged and woebegone pine on the edge of the great, silent forest itself. They had made another fire with the aid of Sir John Mullaghan's lighter, and broiled more deer and eaten it, all three of them by then weary and footsore from the few miles they'd covered, but Clair in no worse plight than the others, except that she wasn't of their sex. When she strolled into the bushes Sir John had called out warnings about the lion. Clair had called back: "No lion would be so unlionly," and then wished she hadn't, and thought: 'Oh, Battersea!' and sighed, being tired.

When she came back they had apparently settled down for the night. Sir John lay to the left of her entrance. He had taken off his pumps and wrapped his feet with grass. He had also removed his coat and draped it round his thin shoulders. He lay close enough to the fire. It had grown cold, though there was no wind. Neither was there a star in the sky. Sinclair lay near the fire also, but more directly under the lee of the pine. He was swathed about by bundles of grass, and Clair had thought, appalled: 'Oh, my good

God, I'll have to do some hay-making.' But that had proved
unnecessary. Between the spaces occupied by the two men,
and directly opposite the bole of the pine, the quilt had
been outspread to dry and had dried. This, Clair understood,
was her sleeping position. She had sunk into the eiderdown
gratefully.

"Good night, you two," she had called, muffling the soft
folds round about her. Sinclair had merely grunted. Sir John
had said, uncovering his face: "Good night, Miss Stranlay.
Call me if you want anything."

"Tea in the morning, please."

He had laughed, with pleasant courtesy, and there had
been silence.

Such silence! All her life she would remember it, though
the second night had made it commonplace. The night was
a stark and naked woman, asleep. But sometimes you could
hear her breathe. Terrible. And against the lightless sky,
unlighted though it was, you saw her hair rise floating now
and then. The pine-foliage . . .

Miles and miles of it, this cold, queer country. Where was
it? What would happen to them?

Clair had stirred in the light of the fire, and turned on her
left side, staring at the dead wood and hearing the soft hiss of
burning cones. She lay half-in, half-out, the spraying circle
of radiance. Beyond that: the darkness. Fantastic position to
be in! She had thought, 'To-night? I should have been in
N'York. Betsy would have been coddling me. Bedtime cock-
tail. Slippers and – oh, my good God, a clean pair of pyjamas.
Lighted bedroom. Bed. Blankets. Sheets. A *soft* bed. . . .' She
had drowsed then and wakened to find the fire dying down
and her shoulder cold where the eiderdown had slipped
aside. Also, her hip-bone had been aching unbearably. She
had turned over and lain on her back, thinking: 'Is it
really me?'

Three or four yards to her right she had seen the outline
of the sleeping form of Sir John Mullaghan. He was snoring.
Catarrh. That was what had awakened her. She lay and
stared at him, thinking: 'I do wish he'd realize he's a lost
and desperate refugee and wouldn't saw at his backbone like
that.' But Sir John had sawed on. She had turned her eyes
towards Sinclair's place.

No more than herself was he asleep – or sleeping only fitfully. His grass wrappings had fallen off, and she saw the gleam of the dying firelight on his skin where the pyjama-jacket had failed of its purpose. At that sight she had called to him, softly, but he had made no answer. Reluctantly, she had disencased herself from the eiderdown and stood up, finding the night a pringling coldness and underfoot something that rustled like salt. Hoar-frost. She'd danced to the fire, seized the ready collected pile of cones and branches, and fed the heap of red cinders till it kindled to a glow, eating hungrily into the resinous cones, more slowly engaging in mastication of the branches. She'd stood and shivered until it was well under way, and then bent over the American.

"Are you sleeping, Dr. Sinclair?"

"No. Why?"

"Come under the eiderdown with me."

"Nonsense. Go back to it. You'll freeze there."

"And you'll freeze here with nothing but pyjamas. Do come."

"No thanks. Ask Sir John Mullaghan."

She'd felt herself flush a little at that, in spite of the cold. She'd turned round and gone back to her place, picked up the quilt, wheeled round and returned to Sinclair's side.

"I'm not asking you to become my lover," she had explained. "Only not to be a silly ass."

He'd stared up at her, the firelight in his eyes. He had looked rather ashamed. He'd stood up. "All right, Miss Stranlay. Sorry. Stand back and I'll arrange the grass. We'll lie on it. . . . Now."

Even so, he had been diffident. Clair had said: "Please just forget it. We're both very sleepy. . . . So. Comfortable?"

He'd said "Yes." And added, as an afterthought: "Thank you."

He'd been asleep before she was, and she'd lain listening to his quiet breathing and thinking: 'This is a fine scene for a novel. But there ought to have been all kinds of drama. Instead of which the hero's so tired he'd have bitten the Queen of Sheba if she'd suggested being naughty. . . . Has a nice, strong chest. Hope to goodness he doesn't snore. . . .'

And then, though she didn't know it, she had snored a little herself, gently, adding her soft pipe to the deep bass notes that smote the night from the nose of Sir John Mullaghan.

Next day they had held south again, with little conversation except that Sir John, some sternness in his gentle eyes, had drawn Clair aside after breakfast and asked her if the American – last night —

"Oh, no, I went and forced myself into his bed," Clair had said, looking at him wide-eyed.

He'd coloured a little, looking at her undecidedly. "Remember, Miss Stranlay, I can always protect you."

"From lions, you mean?"

Catty, that, she had thought remorsefully as he turned away. He'd addressed few remarks to her from that time onwards until the evening. Neither had the American. Willy-nilly, he had taken the lead. There was no compulsory obedience, but the other two had followed. Water in ponds and in streamlets was plentiful enough, but the character of the country did not change. As one volcano receded to the right, another took its place. Clump on clump of forest, dark-green, erupted from the face of the tundra. The great forest itself marched on their left, watching them. Again and again Clair had the feeling that they were being watched from that half-mile distant forest. She had told the two men of the feeling. Sinclair had shrugged his shoulders.

"We may be. But it doesn't look like it." He waved his hand around. "Look, it's completely desolate."

There was no sign of other living thing than themselves until late afternoon, when they again startled a small herd of the small deer. Perhaps it was the same herd. It disappeared from view within two minutes of their rousing it. Sinclair had sworn. "We could have done with more venison."

There had been only a quarter of the deer left by then. Camping at sunset, this time in the midst of a cluster of bushes, itself in the midst of a tree-clump out in the tundra, Clair had taken stock of herself and her companions. First, herself: her pyjama-trousers were ripped and scratched from the knee downwards; otherwise intact. The jacket was still serviceable, though one of the loops had been torn away. Her feet ached, as indeed did all her body, especially knee and thigh joints. But otherwise she was quite well.

Sinclair – it did not do to look very directly at Sinclair.

In matters sartorial he had suffered the worst of the three, though he did not seem very conscious of the fact. . . . All right if he didn't feel cold.

'And anyhow,' Clair had consoled herself the while she gathered brushwood for the fire, 'we've still got a dress suit in the expedition. Even though the pumps have given way.'

They had, abruptly abandoning their allegiance to the armaments manufacturer in a swampy place. Prior to that they had abandoned their soles. Now Sir John tramped barefooted, like his companions, displaying small, handsome and well-cared-for feet. 'Fortunate he hasn't got bunions,' Clair had meditated, and had gone on to think that it was fortunate indeed that all three of them were comparatively healthy people. Her own penchant for winter bathing had inured her to almost any extreme of temperature that almost any climate could provide. Sinclair, she had discovered, was a trained athlete, combining with militant pacifism some gospel of the unpadded life which had taken him on tramping expeditions through half the Western States. Sir John was the least well equipped, yet compared with the average passenger on the *Magellan*! What would Miss Kemp have done? *Miss Kemp*!

Sinclair had divided up the last leg and haunch for the evening meal. "We don't know when we'll get any other food." The others had assented, Clair silently regretful, for she found herself very hungry in those hours of marching through the clear, cold sunshine. Suddenly she had thought, and said aloud with a rush of longing: "Oh, my good God, I do wish I had a cigarette!"

Sir John Mullaghan had come to her aid unexpectedly. "I have two," he had said, and had drawn a small silver case from his pocket the while Clair stared at him unbelievingly. Opened, the case disclosed two veritable Egyptians. Clair had reached for one, starvingly, lighted it from a twig, drawn the acrid, sweet smoke down into grateful lungs. Sir John, similarly employed, had sat at the other side of the fire. Sinclair, looking tired, looked into the fire. She had suddenly disliked Mullaghan with great intensity.

"Share with me, Dr. Sinclair?"

"No, thanks. I don't smoke."

"Now, isn't that a blessed relief?" Clair had said, but

she had not said it aloud. Instead, she had leant back on the long, coarse grass and smoked slowly, carefully, lingeringly, finishing long after Sir John, and indeed, had she known it, finishing the last cigarette ever smoked in that unknown land.

Nightfall. Bed with Sinclair under the eiderdown quilt, Sir John, grey-headed, watching them across the fire. The American, settling down, had resented the stare.

"What the devil are you glowering about?"

"To see you take no advantage of Miss Stranlay's kindness."

Clair had felt Sinclair's arm muscles tauten beside her. She had interposed, sleepily. "It's quite all right, Sir John. We sleep together for warmth, not love." Then she had laid her head against Sinclair's unyielding shoulder and gone to sleep again. So presently had Sir John. But Sinclair had slept in fits and starts, turning uneasily and twice awakening Clair. Finally she had whispered: "Whatever ails the man?"

He had answered in a whisper. "There's something prowling round the fire."

Clair had sat up beside him, peering forward. Nothing. Nothing but the crackle of a consuming twig. Not even a breath of wind. Nothing to see, except far off, remote across the tundra, the nearest volcano, crowned with quiet flame, burning watchfully. Perhaps five miles away. Utter darkness and silence. Sir John Mullaghan, dim-seen, sleeping quietly now. Or was he also awake? Not a sound. Or was there?

It was a deep, steady, full-lunged breathing a little distance away from them. "There's some beast there," whispered Sinclair, unnecessarily, staring across the fire. He had slipped out of the eiderdown. Clair had caught his wrist. "Stir up the fire."

"I'm going to."

He had, and then, suddenly snatching up a branch which was crackling into flame, had emitted a blood-curdling yell and rushed round to the other side of the fire, waving his torch. He had crashed through the bushes, spark-spreading, and to Clair, thinking unalarmedly: 'Goodness, his poor pyjamas!' it had seemed he was preceded by an even more distant crash. Sir John awoke, startledly.

"What is it? Miss Stranlay – are you all right?"

"Quite. Dr. Sinclair thought he heard a wild animal prowling round and went after it with a torch. Here he comes."

Sinclair returned, piled the fire with all the wood they had collected, and sank down by Clair. Crouching on his elbow, the armaments manufacturer had looked across at them.

"What was it?" Clair had asked.

"Sorry I'm so damn chill. . . . Eh? Some kind of bear, I think."

"A big one?"

"Brute like a cart-horse."

"Did it run away?"

"Near the equator by now, I should think."

Clair had gurgled drowsily and laid her shapely head on the grass pillow. It was the first spark of humour she had heard struck from the American's angry, flinty personality. Soon she and Sinclair slept. But until dawn Sir John had watched the moving shadows of the bushes beyond the radiance of the camp-fire.

Next morning – the third morning – they had eaten the last of the deer and tramped southwards again, across country still unchanged and unchanging in promise. But this morning had greeted them with rain, so that they had been forced to shelter under a great fir, watching the sheets of water warping westwards over the long llanos. It looked almost like grey English countryside, grossly exaggerated in every feature. Clair had early felt very tired, and standing under the fir had become aware of the cause. Of course, the damn thing *would* happen now. She had questioned Sinclair, who had looked curiously into her white face.

"Do you know what the date is?"

"It should be the 25th."

"The 25th? But it can't be. Why —" She had stopped, calculating, very puzzled as well as otherwise distressed. Sinclair she had discovered to have singularly gentle eyes. Sir John Mullaghan was a little apart.

"Why can't it be?"

She had remembered his profession, with relief, and had explained. He had stood thoughtful, draped in his ragged pyjama-suit, pulling at his rather long upper lip. Then:

"If it's only twenty days since the last occurrence, Miss

Stranlay, you can put it down to shock, I suppose. Hardship. Different life. Though I never heard of such a case."

"The moon!"

"Eh?"

"Don't you remember?" she said. "The moon we saw from the *Magellan*. You said it was five or six days too early."

He had stared away from her. "So I did. And it was. Been too cloudy since we landed to see the moon again. . . . But the connection's a myth —"

Clair had smiled at him ruefully, lovely even then. "It's a fact."

He had nodded, impersonally. "Right. Now —"

When Sir John Mullaghan turned to them again, with the clearing of the rain, he had stared in some surprise at Sinclair's legs. He was clad now in knee-length shorts. Clair, considerably more comfortable, moved forward by his side.

But the day had held little of comfort in it, what with the rain. Somewhere in the early afternoon Sinclair had stopped near a stream which meandered out of the forest and filed away into the beginnings of a tract of long-grassed, mush-eared swamp. "I'm going to hunt around and see if there's any food to be had, Miss Stranlay."

"I think I'll also look round, Miss Stranlay."

"There's a fire required," the American had flung over his shoulder. "And Miss Stranlay's tired."

Sir John Mullaghan had searched around for dry grass and twigs, scarce enough commodities, both of them, the while Clair lay under a thing that looked like a whortleberry bush, but wasn't, and wished she was dead. The quilt was damp, and presently kindled to a slimy warmth from the heat of her body. She had fallen asleep in a self-induced Turkish bath, with the slow patter of the rain on the leaves overhead and a view of Sir John Mullaghan, in a considerably battered dress suit, squatting on bruised and dirty heels, doing futile things with his petrol lighter against a dour loom of treey, desolate landscape. Sinclair had not yet returned.

They had no method of measuring time, with the sun's face draped in trailing rain-curtains, but it must have been at least another two hours before he did come back, coming from the direction of the forest, and walking wearily, a soaked and tattered figure.

"You'll catch pneumonia," Clair had called, and tried to stir the fire to warmth-giving. But both she and Sir John had looked at the doctor with sinking hearts. Clair had said, casually: "Any luck?"

Sinclair had opened his right hand. "These."

They were half a dozen half-ripened beech nuts, picked up below a high, solitary and unclimbable tree. Sinclair told, shortly, that he had wandered for miles without sighting any animal or bird, or fruit-bearing tree. "And we'd best be getting on again."

"Why?" Clair had queried, eating her two nuts.

"Because you can't stay unsheltered on a night such as this promises to be. We'll try nearer the mountains for some ledge or rock shelter."

So once again they had set out southwards, with the rain presently clearing merely to display a sun hovering on the verge of setting.

*Subchapter iii*

And now, in the last of the daylight, lost, desperate, and foolish, they stood on the brink of a disastrous quarrel, Sinclair with every appearance of being about to assault the armaments manufacturer, Sir John with his gentle face ablaze. Clair looked from one to other of them, wanly, but still with that gay irony that was her salvation, and, after a little calculation, did the thing that she thought would be best under the circumstances.

She burst into tears.

The two men paused. The American, she observed through her fingers, went more white and haggard than ever. Sir John laid his hand on her arm.

"Miss Stranlay, you must keep up. We can't be far now from some town or village or a trapper's hut."

"It – it's not that." Clair thought, swiftly 'Am I overdoing it? Oh, God, I hope it doesn't take long, because I really am sick and tired and ill, and all this crying isn't in jest.' She resumed: "It's you and Dr. Sinclair. You're spoiling all our chances because you won't act together."

There was a silence. Sinclair looked at the volcanoes,

looked at Clair. "That's true, Miss Stranlay. . . . I'm sorry, Mullaghan."

"And I, Dr. Sinclair. If you'll lead on —"

The American turned again and led. Clair thought: 'Triumph of the civilized habit. Or is it? According to all the books they should have flown at each other's throats in this primitive milieu, and the winner grabbed me as prize. . . . Goodness, a damp and dejected prize I'd have been!'

Suddenly they found themselves in the lee of one of the foothills, under the mouths of two great caves.

CHAPTER IV: THE LAIR

*Subchapter i*

"WE don't know what may be in them," said Sir John Mullaghan.

They stood and looked at the cave-mouths. They stood almost in darkness, in a thin line of light, a space-time illusion of luminosity, for the sun had quite vanished. Hesitating, they peered at each other in the false twilight. A little stream of water, hardly seen, ran coldly over Clair's toes. She felt iller than ever.

"What can there be? There are no animals in this country. Do let's get out of the rain – it's coming on again."

"Can't you smell?" said Sinclair.

Clair elevated her small, rain-beaded nose and smelt. A faint yet acrid odour impinged on the rainy evening. Ammoniac. "Like the Zoo lion-house," said Sinclair, very low, staring at the near cave-mouth.

The armaments manufacturer showed his latent quality. He bent down, groped at his feet, and straightened with a large stone in his hand. He motioned them aside. Clair stood still. Sinclair seized her roughly by the shoulder and pulled her to one side of the near cave-mouth.

"Come out!"

The stone crashed remotely in the bowels of the cave, ricochetted in darkness, stirred a multitude of echoes. Nothing else. The twilight vanished. They stood in the soft sweep of the rain, listening.

"I'll step into the mouth and try the lighter on a bit of my underclothes," said Sir John, practically.

"All right." The American's voice, imperturbable.

Clair could see neither of them now. But Sinclair's shoulder touched hers. She heard cautious, bare-foot treadings in the dark. Sir John had left them. Clair thought: 'Oh, God, why doesn't he hurry?' Her thoughts blurred. She leant against Sinclair. "I'm going to be sick."

He put his arm round her and the quilt. "Not now. Don't be a fool."

She bit her lips, holding herself erect, dizzily. "You've shocking bedside manners."

"Sh!"

The forward darkness spat sparks, intermittently. The lighter. Spat. Spat. Something dirty white. A catch. Vigorous blowing. A glow. The mouth of the cave. Porous-looking rock. Sir John Mullaghan's face. His voice.

"It winds inward. I'll go and see if there's anything."

"All right."

Clair said: "No, you don't. Dr. Sinclair thinks he's protecting me. I don't need it." She prodded her protector. "Go with him."

His support was withdrawn. "Keep where you are."

A faint glow, over-gloomed by a titanic shadow, illumined the cave-mouth. Betwixt her and that glow passed another tenebrous titan. The glow failed, lighted up again, receded. Alone. Soft swish of rain. Clair began to count, found herself swaying, shook herself out of counting. 'Makes you sleepy.' A long wait and then suddenly Sinclair's voice close at hand: "Miss Stranlay!"

"Hello?"

"Give me your hand." She found herself drawn forward. "Careful."

"Nothing inside?"

"Not a thing except a queer kind of nest."

She stumbled in blackness. "Has the light gone out?"

"The cave twists."

The ground underfoot had a porous feeling; it was as though one walked over the surface of a frozen sponge. A few more steps and Sinclair, by the aid of disjointed gropings with his disengaged hand, guided Clair round a corner of the ante-cave. She saw then a roof nine or ten feet high over-arching a cave-chamber something of the size and appearance of her own small drawing-room in Kensington. It glittered greyly. On the uneven floor, tending a small fire that seemed to be fed with his undergarments and a pile of ancient hay, squatted Sir John Mullaghan, naked to the waist. In the far leftwards corner was a hummock. The "nest".

"All right, Miss Stranlay?"

"As rain, Sir John." Clair stumbled again. Sinclair pushed her past the fire. She sank down on the nest. Its straw crackled dustily under her weight. The fire, Sir John and Sinclair, began to pace a hasting gavotte. Clair closed her eyes.

"I'm going to faint."

She did.


*Subchapter ii*

She passed from the faint into a sleep, and awoke several hours later, Sinclair's hand shaking her.

"Miss Stranlay! . . . I'm afraid it's going to spring —"

She sat up with a twinging body, brushing back the hair from her face. The American crouched beside her, a red-ochred shadow in the light of the fire, his head turned towards the fire. The fire itself burned and sputtered sulkily under a strange, brittle heaping of fuel. And beyond its light, in the darkness, glowed another light.

Two of them. Unwinking. Clair felt an acid saliva collect in her mouth. Suddenly the two lights changed position; they had sunk lower towards the floor of the cave. Clair understood. It was crouching.

"Don't scream."

Sinclair's words were in a whisper. But the Thing in the darkness beyond the fire must have heard them. Its eyes reared up again. Clair shut her own; opened them again. The eyes were again sinking. Spring this time?

And then the fire took a hand. It spiralled upwards a long trail of smoke, red-glowing gas which burst into crackling flame. There came a violent sneeze, a snarl, the thump of a heavy body crashing against the side of the cave in a backwards leap. And then the three survivors of the *Magellan's Cloud* saw – saw for a moment a bunched, barred, gigantic body, a coughing, snarling, malignant face. Then a rushing patter filled the cave. The fire died down. Beyond its light no eyes now glowed in the darkness.

Clair sank on her elbow, dry-mouthed. "What was it?"

Someone beyond Sinclair drew a long breath. "A tiger."

Sinclair spoke very quietly. "Like one, but it wasn't."

"What was it, then?" Clair saw Sir John Mullaghan also crouching, a keyed-up shadow.

The American, answering, still stared across the fire. "*Machaerodus.*"

"What?"

"*Machaerodus* – a sabre-toothed tiger."

There fell a moment's silence – of stupefaction on the part of all three. Clair, ill, closed her eyes and opened them again. She must be dreaming. "But – it can't be. They're extinct."

"Didn't you see the tusks?"

She had. So had Sir John. The latter got to his feet. He spoke and moved doubtfully.

"It may come back."

The fire purred and crackled again. He had fed it from a pile of fuel not in the cave when they first entered it. The American got up and helped him. Clair's head, sleep-weighted, sank again on the nest. She thought: 'I'm dreaming. Don't care though it's a mammoth next time.' The smell of the fuel was nauseating. She voiced a sleepy question, and, voicing it, was asleep, and never heard Sinclair's answer.

"What are you burning?"

"Bones."

*Subchapter iii*

When next she awoke, she was in complete darkness. No fire burned near at hand. She had a sense of having slept for many hours. She stretched, cautiously, remembering everything, and found that someone had tended to her while she slept. Her rain-dampened pyjamas had disappeared. She was lying not merely covered by the quilt, but wrapped in it. A keen, cool current of air blew steadily in her face.

If that three-days' Odyssey across the deserted savannah was a dream? ... She was at home in Kensington. ... Wrapped in a quilt, lying in fusty hay? She called, cautiously: "Dr. Sinclair!"

No answer. She released her left arm, and sought in the place where he had crouched while they looked at the eyes beyond the fire. Her fingers touched bare rock. She sat up, a little frightened, desperately hungry.

"*Dr. Sinclair!*"

A far-off voice called: "Coming, Miss Stranlay."

Footsteps, and the darkness receding from the light of a smoky torch, held in Sinclair's hand. In his other he carried a shapeless bundle.

She said: "Goodness, nice to see you. Where's the fire? Have I slept long?"

Sinclair's mind said, absorbedly, and for a second or third time in looking at her: 'Pretty thing!' Tousled red-tipped hair, comely sleep-flushed face, clear, friendly, questioning eyes. Miraculous to wake from sleep like that. . . . Aloud:

"The fire's in the outer half of the cave. It's about noon. I've brought you your things."

He dropped them in her hands. They were her pyjamas, dry and warm.

"You *are* a dear – though you try so desperately not to be." The dear grunted. Clair's eyes twinkled at him. "Is that a smell of something cooking?"

"We've found some food. I'll leave you the torch to dress by."

He set it against the rock-wall, turned about, and went. Clair stood up and shook off the eiderdown quilt, and felt her body with disgust. Grimy, gritty and granulous. But her sickness of the night before had passed. She thought: 'Wonder if it's safe to bathe yet? Nice things, warm pyjamas. Wonder —'

She had remembered the beast which had stalked them in the dark hours. Had there been any beast? She snatched up the torch and walked past the ashes of the fire. On the damp floor were multitudes of impressions, and superimposed on these great pug-marks of a cat.

"A sabre-toothed tiger!"

She picked up the eiderdown quilt and groped her way through to the front part of the cave, and so came on the sight of it suddenly, the entrance flooded with sunlight, and against that sunlight a hazy drift of smoke, as from the lips of a contemplative smoker, engendered by the fire. Either side of this fire sat Sinclair and Sir John – Sinclair in his ragged pyjamas, Sir John with his slight form even slighter than of yore. Minus underclothes. Neither of them heard her coming and she stood for a moment and looked at them with some little modification of that gay, ironic, contemplative scrutiny she usually turned upon the world. Their lives had interwoven in hers with a dream-like abruptness and intimacy —

'Sinclair – no more a gentleman than you're a lady. No more an American than you're an Englishwoman. Why? Fifty years ago we might have been both – the tricks are easy enough to learn. . . . Sir John – no doubt about *him*. A lost aristo who's mislaid his guillotine and ruffles —'

Sinclair – he had begun to fray badly, poor boy. Soon be a catastrophe with that sleeping-suit of his. The faces of both men were lined with stubble, an unchancy harvest, Sir John's a red wiriness of vegetal promise, with hints of grey, Sinclair's a blue-black down. Their hair stood up in tufts and feathers. But both of them seemed to have washed, and Clair noted the fact with an interest that put an end to her survey.

"'Morning, Sir John. I've already met you, doctor. . . . Oh, not in the wilds." She motioned them to sit, but flushed a little with a touch of reminiscent wonder. The cosmopolitan had been at least as quick as the aristo. . . . "Where did you get the food?"

Sir John was toasting on a sliver of wood a strange-looking, yellowish piece of meat. Sinclair bent his dark poll over a roundish, smooth-polished object. Sir John seemed to hesitate a second in his reply.

"Dr. Sinclair found it, Miss Stranlay. We've already eaten some, but you slept too soundly to be awakened. Better now?"

Something funny about this meat. "Yes, much." She stared at Sir John's preparations. "*Found* it?"

The American glanced up, impatiently. "Nothing mysterious. It won't poison you – I saw to that. It's horse-flesh. There was a partly-eaten carcase about a hundred yards from the mouth of the cave here."

"Oh. So I didn't dream last night. There *was* a beast like a tiger prowling on the other side of the fire?"

The armaments manufacturer held up the skewer of yellowish meat, looking the most incongruous of cooks as he did so. "Yes. Some kind of tiger. It probably killed the pony after it ceased to stalk us."

Clair regarded her breakfast uncertainly.

"I think I'll bath first. Both of you have. Where?"

"Just outside the cave, to the left."

Clair went out. Sinclair looked after her, looked at Sir John, said something. The armaments manufacturer rose up and followed Clair. She glanced round from bending over the streamlet that had gurgled over her feet the night before.

"I'm sorry, Miss Stranlay, but one of us had better be near. That beast may come back, though it's not very likely."

"I see." Clair felt and sounded ungracious – and, as usual, regretted it. She looked away, across the tundra flowering into swamp, at the sun-hazed surface of the mile-distant forest, and then southward, where swamp and forest crept down to the foothills, and their long journey through the llanos-land seemed to end. What was beyond that cul-de-sac? . . . She became aware of Sir John waiting. "Sorry. Shan't keep you a minute. Do wish I had some soap."

"There's red earth on the bank here. I used it." He felt his unshaven face, wryly. "It seemed fairly effective."

He thought she looked like an absurd boy in her thin, stained garments. Not at all as he had pictured her. For he had heard of Clair Stranlay before that meeting on the beach, had once, on a train journey, read one of her books. Crude, calamitous, vicious thing. Very vivid, too. . . . How had he pictured her? A dark and beetle-like best-seller, perhaps, or one of those blowsily mammalian women you meet in French magazines. Instead: this charming, impertinent boy . . .

He sighed and turned away from that thought. He turned his head away from her also, looking round the deserted countryside. The sun seemed warmer. A little breeze stirred the long grass. The stream glimmered and its gurgling passage was the only sound to be heard. And the same thought came to him as to Clair: What lay south? What country was this, with wild ponies and tigers? Tigers? A sabre-tooth? But that was absurd. Probably some freak animal.

He became aware of Clair standing beside him, dabbing at

her face and hands with a bunch of grass. "That was good . . .
Sir John."

He looked gently into her grave eyes.

"*What* country is this? It can't be Canada. And it can't be
Africa."

He shook his head. "I'm afraid I haven't an opinion worth
knowing, Miss Stranlay. Tigers, I think, are found in the East
Indies. But to suppose the *Magellan's Cloud* drifted across the
Atlantic, America and the Pacific in those few hours four
nights ago is absurd. And I cannot imagine this stretch of
uninhabited country in the East Indies."

Clair finished dabbing, re-tied the fraying neckloop of
her jacket. "No. But we *must* be getting near some inhabited
place."

"I hope so."

He wouldn't say more than that, though her eyes still
questioned him. They went back to the cave. A smudge of
smoke, fainter now, for the fire was dying down, rose from
it against the limestone hillside. Sinclair was standing in the
sunlight at the mouth of the second cave, looking intently
southward, as both of them had done. He came and joined
them. Clair was surprised at the look on his usually dour face.
It was alive with some strayed excitement.

"Feel hungry?" he asked her.

"Shockingly." But indeed her appetite felt oddly reserved.
She sat down beside the fire, but still in the sunlight. She
picked up the piece of charred horse-flesh and began to eat
it. Sir John stayed outside, leaning against the cave entrance,
his greying head down-bent. "How did you manage to
cut it up?"

"With this." Sinclair was back at the other side of the fire.
He held up an object. Clair peered at it. He passed it to her.
She turned it over, wonderingly.

It was a fragment of stone, she thought, though it was
flint. Even to her unaccustomed eyes it seemed to have a
certain artificiality. She held it away from her with her left
hand, the while she fed her small, stained mouth with the
right. She saw the shape of the thing better then. It was in
the form of a smooth-butted axe-blade – an incredibly crude
stone axe-blade.

"Why – it's *made*."

The American nodded. "It's *made*."

"Where did you find it?"

"In the next cave. Among a pile of bones."

She remembered something. She questioned him with her eyes. He nodded.

"Human bones. Though I didn't know that in the darkness last night when I was searching for fuel. Fortunately I didn't burn them all."

She looked at the thing at his feet, and somehow didn't want any more of the horse-flesh. It was a skull he had been examining. She stood up and went to the entrance. Sir John glanced at her. Something like a smile of sympathy flickered over his face. The American said, abruptly: "You people."

They both turned. Sinclair had the skull in his hands. He came towards them. The stone axe-blade slipped out of Clair's forgetful hand as she backed away from the skull. Sinclair sprang forward and caught it, bruising his fingers. He swore. Sir John turned his head, Clair tried hard to repress herself, failed; giggled. Sir John's laughter joined with hers.

"I'm so sorry." Genuinely contrite.

"All right. I want to talk to you both about these finds." He addressed Sir John, still with something of an effort. "Know anything about crania?"

Sir John shook his head. "Nothing at all." He took the skull in his hand, however, and examined it. It was complete to jawbone and teeth. He held it out to Clair. She waved it away.

"No thanks. Ghastly thing. It's got a permanent frown, too."

Sinclair: "Exactly. That's the point. It's not an ordinary skull."

The other two regarded it, back in Sinclair's hands. "A savage's?" said Clair, helpfully.

"Of course it's a savage's. Otherwise he wouldn't have had a flint hand-axe in his possession when he was carried back in there and devoured by the sabre-tooth."

Clair shivered. "Was that what happened?" She looked over the undulating waste of grass to the dark boles of the sun-crowned forest. "Ugh."

Sir John glanced at her, and interposed, gently. "And what is peculiar about the skull?"

"It's as Miss Stranlay says. It has a permanent frown – look, this ridge above the eyes. And practically no forehead." He loosened the clenched jaw. "Look at the teeth."

They looked. "Funny," said Clair, at once repulsed and fascinated. Sinclair closed the jaw again, set the skull at his feet, stared at it, fascinated also.

"Not a human skull at all, you know, as we understand the term human. By rights it belongs to a race that died off twenty thousand years ago."

Clair was startled into dim memories of casual reading in pre-history. "What race?"

"The Neanderthal. It's a Neanderthal skull."

*Subchapter iv*

By early afternoon they had left the caves some four or five miles behind, and, tramping along the edge of the foothills, were nearing the spot where hills and forest converged. Sinclair, as usual, walked in advance. He was burdened with the remains of the horse-flesh, a great haunch, and the cord of his pyjama-shorts sagged under the weight of the flint axe-head. The strange skull he had abandoned with reluctance.

Clair and Sir John walked side by side, half a dozen yards behind him. Sir John said: "I'm afraid we're rather a drag on our leader. By the way, have you noticed how much alike your names are? – Clair and Sinclair."

She looked after the long-striding figure of the American, and unconsciously increased her own pace. "He's the saint and I'm the Clair. . . . *Is* energetic. I'm sure that's why they used to martyr saints." (But it wouldn't do to discuss one with the other.) "What do you think of the skull?"

"I don't know what to think. Though I should imagine that the chances are Dr. Sinclair has made a mistake."

"Neanderthal man. . . . They all died off in the last Glacial Age – I think. Or was it just after it? Perhaps it was a fossil skull."

The armaments manufacturer, striding bare-footed, bowed-shouldered beside her, shook his head. "No, it wasn't that. I'm afraid I know little or nothing of such matters, but it was comparatively fresh bone."

"Funny if there are any more of them about."

Sir John also thought that, but did not say so. Funny? The coarse grass was warm and dry under their feet. The last of the volcanoes had disappeared on the northwards horizon. Sinclair slowed down till they caught up with him. He pointed.

They were at a slight elevation by then. The forest did not close completely on the hills, but left a narrow corridor, a waste, bush-strewn space. Across this space they looked, and it was as if they were at no slight elevation, but on a mountain-side. For beyond the passage-way the land failed completely, as it seemed. Yet, remote and far away, downwards, southwards, something like a lake shimmered, forest-fringed; and blue and golden, there shone under the sunlight a suggestion of immense tracts of waste country. All three of the travellers stared, Clair with sinking heart. It must be miles to that lake. And no sign anywhere of a native village or trading station.

"We're on a high level – a plateau with mountains," said Sinclair, unemotionally. "We've been travelling across it for days. That's why we've seen so few animals, probably. There's nothing here but strays from down there."

Sir John said: "And we're going down?"

"Yes."

Clair smiled at the American, casually, friendlily. "There's no 'yes' about it. Not until we've all made up our minds."

Sinclair's ears tinted themselves a slow red. "*I* am going down."

"Do."

Sir John interposed. "Really, Miss Stranlay, I don't think there is anything else to be done now. ... Though possibly Dr. Sinclair might word his invitations a little more courteously in future."

Sinclair scowled at him, angrily. "Courtesy! Do you realize we're absolutely lost somewhere in absolutely unknown and unexplored country? That there are *machaerodi* and possibly other wild beasts in it – to say nothing of Neanderthalers?"

"That seems to be the case," said Clair. "But it doesn't alter the fact that your manners are badly in need of improvement."

He glanced from one to the other of them, as though he were looking at idiots. He shrugged. "All right. Bad though they may be, I think it would be ruinous if we split into two parties." He bowed, a ludicrous, angry figure. "Would you mind coming down into the low country, Miss Stranlay?"

Clair had a ridiculous impulse and a lovable singing voice – a deep, untrained contralto. They stared at her startled as she held out her arms and smiled at the wild lands below them:

> "Oh, ye'll take the high road,
> And I'll take the low road,
> And I'll be in Scotland afore ye;
> But me and my true love
> We'll never meet again
> On the bonny, bonny banks of Loch Lomond!"

She felt her eyes grown moist, involuntarily. Sir John said, gently: "Thank you, Miss Stranlay."

"Silly," Clair confessed.

"Not silly at all, Miss Stranlay." It was Sinclair, unexpectedly. "Thank you also. I was a lout."

"You're a dear," said Clair, soberly, and for the second time that day.


*Subchapter v*

It was a steeply-shelving descent of nearly a mile, over the usual coarse grass. At the foot Sinclair waited – as usual. He avoided Clair's eyes. He had avoided them since that remark. "We have about an hour until sunset."

Sir John, panting, sat down. "And what are we going to do until then?"

The American pacifist seemed for once at a loss. "Find a place to camp, I suppose."

"Looks different somehow," said Clair.

It did. The forest was more widely spread or the tundra more enforested, according to one's fancy. Some oaks – young-looking oaks – grew near at hand. Smooth, hog-backed hills rose here and there in the tree-set waste, but there were no mountains, no volcanoes. Also, near sunset though it was, this low country was much warmer than the plateau they had just deserted. Nor was it so silent. A long-necked grey bird flitted among the oaks; they could hear the swish of its wings through the leaves. Remote among the low, smooth-humped hills a vast, long-drawn moan rose and fell; they had not noticed it at first, because it was part of the landscape. Now, as it ceased, they peered in the direction from which it had come.

"A cow," said Clair.

It did indeed sound like the lowing of a cow – a gigantic cow. Presently it ceased with some decision, and was not resumed. Sinclair stood with his fingers on his hand-axe. "Bison, perhaps."

"What *is* this place, Dr. Sinclair?"

The question worried all three of them continually. Clair put it into words most frequently. Sir John glanced up at her, then at the ragged bearer of the horse-haunch. The latter started.

"Eh? . . . God knows."

"I doubt it," said Clair.

The American began to move across the grass towards the trees. Clair held out her hand to Sir John, but he stood up without assistance, albeit with a grimace. Presently they were threading a new belt of trees, very green and lush with undergrowth, and with their shadows pointing long, dark fingers into the east. The grey bird was silent. So was all else of the hidden life of the tree-spaces – if there were life. Clair heard herself call in a whisper:

"Where are we going?"

Sinclair's voice also was low. "Some place where there's water."

They emerged from the trees then, into another clearing. Doing so, Clair seemed to hear a sound of low rumblings, like the borborygm in a large and placid stomach. She thought, rather ruefully: 'Not mine'. And went on, following the sunset-reddened back of Sinclair. Neither he nor Sir John had heard anything.

But suddenly they did. Fallen boughs crunched and snapped, and something with heavy tread came after them from the twilight darkness of the trees.

They all halted, looking back. For a moment they could distinguish nothing, though the heavy tread paced towards them. And then they saw it against the dun light of an open patch – its swaying bulk, its matted shagginess. Its trunk was lowered, sniffing the track they had taken.

They stared appalled. They had all seen its like before – in this or that museum or illustration. There could be no mistaking those curved immensities of tusk.

It was a mammoth.

## Chapter V:   AND I'LL TAKE THE LOW ROAD

*Subchapter i*

THEY camped a quarter of an hour or so later, by the mere of the lake that had glittered its invitation from the northern plateau. Tall reeds grew far out into the water, and, remotely over that water, unknown birds croaked and dipped amid long grasses that Sinclair certified were – of all things – wild wheat. The American knelt under the moss-shaggy boughs of a great oak, coaxing Sir John's lighter to imbed a spark in a tuft of withered grass. Sunset was again close – the lingering sunset of a temperate country. It might have been eight o'clock in the evening.

Clair padded to and fro, bough-collecting, with even her bare feet a little chilled by the evening dew. Sir John, outside the obscuring bulk of the oak, was looking back to the dimness of the plateau – that high land where they had adventured through three long days.

And the mammoth continued to watch them.

It was halted at a distance of ten yards or so, not facing them, but in profile. Its great ears flapped meditatively and every now and then its trunk would stray upwards into the foliage of a bush, or down into the unappetizing grass. The sunset glimmered on its watching eye . . .

It had trailed them like a great retriever, halting when they halted, coming on again as they moved hesitatingly away. While they crossed a clear space it would stop and watch them, pawing a little, rubbing a gigantic, hair-fringed shoulder against a tree. Then it would pace swingingly after them. Once, apparently imagining them lost, it had frolicked wildly amid the bushes, hunting the scent of them with uplifted trunk.

"It must be harmless," Clair had whispered, walking between the two men.

"Trying to summon up courage to charge," hazarded Sinclair.

"Hope it comes of a timid family."

"I'm afraid we can't do anything to prevent it charging, anyhow," said Sir John, glancing over his shoulder and starting a little. " . . . I thought it was coming that time."

But it had not, and, the lake opening out before them, there had been no other course obvious than to camp. It was eerie doing so with that watching monster pretending not to watch them. Clair knelt by Sinclair with a handful of twigs, seeing he had caught a spark and was cherishing the grass into the parturition of a flame.

He glanced at her. "The fire may scare it off or may madden it into making an attack. Scoot round the back of the tree if it comes." He spoke in a whisper, "Frightened?"

Clair fed the flame with a twig, resolutely keeping her eyes from the watcher. "Not now. Rather a thrill. . . . What's it doing now?"

Sir John came to their side. "I think it's going to charge."

The mammoth had knelt on its knees, embedding its immense tusks in a great clump of grass. There came a crackling, tearing sound. The mammoth stood up. Its tusks were laden with grass, like the rake of a hay-maker. Elevating its trunk to the fodder, it proceeded to test and devour great wisps.

"Bless it," said Clair, "it's having its supper."

The armaments manufacturer ruffled his grey hair. "One certainly didn't expect such mildness. A *mammoth*!"

There the brute stood, real enough, feeding and watching them, with the brown night closing down behind him. The flame came now in little spurts and glows and the twigs caught and cautiously, Sinclair administered first small branches, then larger ones. The firelight went out across the gloaming shadows, splashing gently on the red-brown coat and bare, creased skull of the mammoth. It paused for a little in its eating, turning its trunk towards them. Then resumed. Clair sat down and held her head between her hands.

"A mammoth in the twentieth century! It's – oh, it's ridiculous."

Sir John, standing and looking at the watcher, patted her shoulder. Sinclair hacked at the dried horsemeat with the Neanderthal axe. The meat had a faint smell of decay. He said: "I've been thinking about where we are. I know now it can't be Canada."

"And it's certainly not Africa, as I thought at first," murmured Sir John.

"No. I think we're in Patagonia."

Clair drew back warmed toes from the fire. Abruptly the last of the daylight went. The lake misted from a pale sheen to a dark, rippling mystery. The sound of the mammoth feeding was oddly homely. . . . Patagonia?

"But I understand practically all of it has been explored," said Sir John.

Sinclair toasted yellow meat for a moment. "I don't think so. Delusion we North Americans and English have about every country which is shown plainly on a map, with the main mountains and rivers and a political colouring. We can't get it into our heads that these places are much larger than a home country. And of course —" He stopped and frowned at the piece of meat. He addressed Clair. He still avoided, as far as possible, speaking directly to Sir John Mullaghan. "Did you notice from the plateau brow the mere tips of a mountain-range – they must be more than fifty miles away – down there in the south, Miss Stranlay?"

Clair nodded.

"I think they must be the Andes. We're somewhere in the western Argentine or the foothills of Chili – the country where Pritchard went to hunt the great sloth. We may be traversing a mountain kink or fold that up to this time has escaped notice completely."

Clair thought. Then: "A kink with sabre-tooth tigers and fresh Neanderthal skulls in it – and mammoths?"

"All possible." But his voice sounded less certain.

Sir John said: "But not very probable. We landed on a sea-coast, somewhere, went inland, and turned south. That sea-coast, if this is South American, must have been the Atlantic. And Patagonia, if my memory serves me, is remote from the Atlantic. Also, it has grown warmer the further south we have come. If we are south of the equator it ought to grow colder."

Sinclair detached the piece of meat from its wooden skewer and handed it to Clair. He nodded acknowledgment of Sir John's arguments and was silent. All three of them sat and ate the tough meat. Then, stumbling among the reeds, they went down to the lake in search of water. At a spot that glimmered faintly Sinclair lay down full length and drank. Sir John followed suit. Clair squatted and cupped the water in her hands and drank that way. As they came back to the fire they noted the mammoth still in guardianship. Overhead there was a faint pearliness in the darkness of the sky.

Sir John raked about in the shadows outside the fire, collecting damp grass and arranging it for drying to act as pillows and mattresses. Clair sat a yard or so from Sinclair, looking into the fire, drowsy and still a little hungry after her meagre ration of horse-flesh. Sinclair had procured a long bough from amid the tree-litter and was whittling at it doggedly with the flint-axe.

"Stone Age idyll," murmured Clair.

"Eh?"

She repeated the words, and, as she did so, remote away beyond the lake, strange and eerie, that lowing they had heard in the early afternoon broke out again. It rose and belled and fell, the calling of some stray of a Titan herd. Unexpectedly, for he had been quiet enough until then, the mammoth answered, lifting his trunk to the remote washings of the firelight and trumpeting screamingly. Clair thought her ear-drums would burst. She covered them and heard the noise die down. The ensuing quietness held no hint of the distant lowing.

But to Clair, with it dead, there came an almost passionate wish that it would break out again. She looked at the two men, at the darkness around them, at the bulk of the strange beast that guarded them so queerly. That lowing and wild trumpeting seemed to have torn down a barrier inside her heart – that calling across wild spaces heard in the shelter of the camp-fire. . . . She had heard it before, somewhere, at some time, in an era that knew not print and publishers. Often. And of all sounds it had lived with her through changes innumerable. She had heard it before in lives not her own —

Fantastic dream!

"Miss Stranlay!" Sir John's hand on her shoulder. "You'd best lie down if you're so sleepy. You nearly fell into the fire."

## Subchapter ii

"Did I?"

She shook herself and looked at them. Sinclair, hafting his axe-head on the bough and binding it with sinews he had saved from the tiger-killed pony, had half-risen to catch her just as Sir John forestalled him. He sank down again. The armaments manufacturer, padding about bare-footed, arranged the grass beds. He looked over at Clair, hearing her low laugh.

"Nothing much, Sir John. But I'd just said to Dr. Sinclair, before that trumpeting started, that this was a Stone Age idyll. And just now I caught sight of your clothes."

The firelight twinkled on a grey head and the smile on a gentle, cultured face. "And they don't fit the part?"

"Not very well."

The American laughed shortly. "The warrior was the armaments manufacturer of the Stone Age, Miss Stranlay, and no doubt wore appropriate habiliments."

Clair felt a little pang of shame for him. The fire simmered cheerfully. Sir John straightened and looked across at the deportee.

"Yes, the warrior was probably the equivalent of the armaments manufacturer," he said quietly. "He brought order and a livable relationship into primitive anarchy. And his task isn't yet finished."

Clair said: "Perhaps it hasn't begun in this country yet. . . . Funniest nightmare of a country we've landed in! I'd give anything for clothes and a bathroom and electric light and – oh, for a cigarette!" She paused and tried to put into unfacile words that strange aching that had been in her heart hearing the lowing in the distant hills. She looked at Sinclair's and Mullaghan's listening faces. "But there's something in it that's not terrifying at all. Lovely, rather. The silence and starkness. . . . Those primitives of the Old Stone Age – they

had some elemental contacts with beauty that we've lost
for ever."

Sir John Mullaghan sat clasping his knees, rubbing his
chilled, bare feet. He shook his head. "They had this kind of
country, perhaps, but it was not the country you see with
your civilized, romantic eyes, Miss Stranlay. It was a waste
of ghouls for them. The night was a horror to the squatting-
places – the time when the dead Old Men of the tribes
returned as stalking carnivorae, the time of shuddering fear.
It was a life livable only for the strongest and most brutal.
For thousands and thousands of years life was that only.
And here and there rose the soldier and the inventor, the
men who subjected the squalid and lowly, who built the first
classes and sowed the first seeds. And the long climb from the
filth and futility of the night-time camps began."

"Poor ancestors!" Clair said it soberly, her eyes on
the night.

Sinclair finished bonding his axe, and laid it on his knees
and looked into the fire.

"That was the life of the Stone Age savage, Miss Stranlay.
And the strong men and wise men, the warriors and the
witch-doctors, bound him in chains of taboo – the first laws –
and made him less of a beast. For twenty thousand years
they've fashioned new chains for him, till civilized man has
taken the place of the savage. But it's been no simple case
of design. The old, meaningless taboos and loyalties – once
necessary and just – are things that threaten to strangle
us nowadays. The age of the witch-doctor and the warrior
is over. But they won't believe it. They still preach their
obscene gods and raise and equip armies that now threaten
to smash to atoms the foundations of civilization. It is they
who are the ghouls who haunt the contemporary world."

Sir John said, steadily: "They are the ghouls, if you like,
that guard civilization. The strong man keeps his house and
the wise country an army on the *qui vive*. The soldier is civilization's safeguard, and still, thank God, defends it against
anarchic sentimentalities. . . . Do you people know *nothing* of
the beast that is in human nature unless there is force and
discipline to keep it down? I had a daughter once. Twelve
years of age. Bright and clean and very glad to be alive. Like
Miss Stranlay in some ways. . . . She was missing one night.

She was found under some bushes a mile or so away from home next day. She had been raped and murdered by a tramp."

Clair made an inarticulate sound of sympathy. Sinclair's knuckles whitened round his axe-haft. "I also have seen human beings mutilated and murdered – in thousands. And through no chance accident of lust or madness. Sentimentalist? My God, you old men! Sentimentalists we are then, and our fight is for human sanity. Don't think we shirk facts. And we've learned from experience. We know that man's a fighting animal by nature, that cruelty's his birthright; and we also know that what keep us in the pit as animals are the armies and the armaments. We're out to smash both, we who have had some personal experience of both. And we'll do it. There's a league of men coming into being that'll send a bullet into the brain of every clown who preaches war in future, Sir John – and a bomb into the office of every armaments manufacturer who trades in blood and human agony. . . . It is you and your kind who will not let the ape and tiger die. And they're prepared to your challenge."

Clair's voice startled them. "I had a lover in 1917. A boy. He'd have hated to hurt the hatefullest human on earth. He went to France because I taunted him. He died on the barb wire at Mametz. All night. He screamed my name all night. . . . And at heart he was just a savage filled with lust and cruelty?"

They said nothing, uncomfortably. Clair thought, suddenly weary: 'Idiotic to speak about that. Oh, my dear, my dear, who died there at Mametz, that's a time long ago, and I can't do anything for you now . . .'

She leant back with her hands under her head. They had all three forgotten the mammoth. Now they heard its steady munching. Clair thought, with a reckless change to gaiety: 'It'll have tummy-ache if it's not careful.' She said: "There come the stars. We're hopelessly lost, but they're still the same as ever."

Unchanged, indeed, and remote and cold as ever. As though a lampman walked the dark spaces of the night they kindled in groups and constellations. The night was very still and cloudless. It was not yet moonrise. The evening star burned palely beyond the stance of the drowsily-shuffling mammoth. And over the darkness of the untrodden lands to the south Jupiter hung like a twinkling ball of fire.

*Subchapter iii*

In the morning the mammoth had gone. There was no trace of it but the trampled stretch of grass and a great heap of dung. Wakening the first of the three, Clair thought she heard remote trumpetings. But whether these were memories from night-time dreams, or the farewell callings of their mysterious guardian, there was nothing now in the quietude of the morning to tell her.

The fire was a grey fluff. They had slept beyond the first chill of the dawn, and the sunshine, like early spring sunshine in the greys and greens of England, sprayed through the lattice-patterns of the oak boughs. The reeds that hid the lake stood in long battalions, peering into the sunrise, with the urge behind them of a little wind from the places of the earth that the morning had not yet touched. Sinclair slept beside Clair with his arms outflung and begrimed, his bearded face hid in his shoulder. Clair touched that shoulder with the tips of her fingers, found it cold, pulled the eiderdown quilt over it, and herself stood up.

Sir John Mullaghan slept huddled in his stained coat, his grey-streaked hair ruffled every now and then by a stray waft of wind from the places of the sunset.

Clair wondered if she should make a fire. But either Sinclair or Sir John had the lighter. She moved about under the oak, and further into the bushes, collecting twigs. She found a stretch of gorse-bushes, very yellow and scented, still wet with night-mist. It was as she stood among them that the lark began to sing.

It was at first no more than a remote piping up in the grey pearlment of the sky. But it came nearer, and the sound hovered, and, shading her eyes, it seemed to Clair that she saw the fluttering singer for a moment. She stood and listened and found herself weeping. She dropped the bundle of firewood and, weeping, stood in that morning listening to the amazing sound. Shrill and strange and sweet, the piping of youth unforgotten! . . . And they took that youth and smeared it with the filth of the years, murdered it on barb-wire entanglements, gave it to torture and horrific agonies in the hands of lust-crazed lunatics . . .

Clair thought: 'But, even so, we've heard it. It's worth having heard it though the memory torture us all our lives.'

It died away. Clair picked up the firewood and went back to the camping-place. The men still slept. For a little she considered them and then went down through the dark, seeping peat-edges to the mere of the lake. A bird flew out of the reeds as she approached. A kingfisher. From her feet the cold of the ground spread up through her body. Accustomed though she was, she shivered in the sunlight. She bent and touched the water and found it – 'wet, of course. And cold enough. Doesn't matter. I'm too filthy for description.'

She undressed, a simple matter, and waded out, into a clamouring pain of coldness. Her hair fell over her face and she switched her mind to that matter as the water rose higher, over her knees, creeping upwards. . . .'Getting long, and where will you find a barber's shop? Unless Sinclair operates with his flint-axe. . . . Now? Deep enough? She halted, half-knelt, and flung herself forward.

Deep enough.

She swam into the sunrise through a long lane in the reeds. Beyond that lane cramp caught her right arm for a moment and she struggled with it, a little frightened, until it passed. The lake swept to the horizon almost, she saw, though from its surface there was no sign of Sinclair's Andes. . . . Alligators?

But there seemed nothing living in the region of the lake, apart from the skimming kingfishers. She turned round at last and swam towards the remote, solitary oak. As she did so she suffered from the curious illusion that it waved to and fro, violently, as in a high wind. A thin, pencil-point of smoke was rising. It did the same.

'Curious. Something wrong with my heart?'

Soberly, she reached the shore and dressed, and went through the reeds, hearing the anxious calling of Sinclair and Sir John, whom an earthquake of considerable intensity had disturbed in the preparation of breakfast.

*Subchapter iv*

Clair thought: 'We are in the Hollow Land.'

There were high hills both to right and left now as they still pressed south. For four or five miles they kept the bank of the lake, but that was soon left behind, a radiance that presently betook itself from the earth to the sky. The leftwards hills were the further away, and betwixt them rose and fell in long undulations a crazy scarping of nullahs. Underfoot was the long grass, but of finer texture here than on the northwards plateau, growing in places lush and emerald, especially where some stream hesitated and crept and slept and woke and shook itself and meandered uncertainly amid the llano.

It was a land of streams. They forded three – one at a trampled place, where were the imprints of both tiny hoofs and great paws.

"Why are we still going south?" Clair asked once.

"Because we might as well," the American returned, broodingly.

Sir John suffered from agonies of stomach-ache throughout that day. He walked beside Clair with distorted face and frequently distorted body. Several times he sat down while the other two stood and waited. Sinclair could do nothing for him – or at least offered to do nothing. Neither he nor Clair had as yet been affected by the saltless diet of horse-flesh. But the surviving piece quite definitely began to smell undaintily. It was fortunate that the country seemed almost entirely devoid of insects.

Sinclair carried his axe-blade hafted now on a five-foot pole. He stalked a sound in the bushes with it once, only to disturb a long, tawny shape which snarled at him sleepily. Then it turned and slunk unhurriedly into deeper cover. Sinclair, rather pale, rejoined the other two.

"What was it?" Clair asked.

He glanced at Sir John. "A lion."

They went on. Once, far towards the leftward hills, and beyond the nullahs, they heard that lowing break out again. Plangent and plaintive. Several times herds of small deer such as they had twice seen on the plateau were observable at a distance, feeding with some daintiness and apparent enjoyment. Clair looked at them carnivorously. But the wind went steadily south and at the first whiff of the travellers, and long before Sinclair could near them, the deer had gone.

"How many more meals?" Clair asked the American, looking without appetite at the shrinking haunch of horse-flesh. Sinclair had dropped back from his old position in the van and walked beside the other two now.

"Two, I think."

Sir John, padding along in pain, grimaced. "You may count it three. I – I don't think I'll be hungry for some time."

"Oh, the doctor may be able to stalk something fresh," said Clair.

Instead, it was something fresh which presently stalked them, though they never caught sight of it. The noise of its padding pursuit and appraisal began to the right of a long corridor of bushes. The three went on for a little while, and then halted, listening. The stalker had halted also. In the sunshine silence they heard the noise of its heavy breathing. And a sound of a swish-swish among the leaves. ('Its tail,' thought Clair.) Sinclair changed from the left hand side of the march to the right. They waited. No movement of approach. They went forward again. The paddings and cracklings came after them, till beyond the bushes they were in open grassland again and the stalker gave them up.

At noon they made a fire near the usual stream, and Sinclair toasted the meat. Sir John lay full-length on the ground, his face hidden, saying nothing. Clair, who had been looking about her as they trekked, walked a quarter of a mile or so away across the llano, into a patch of gorse-like bushes. Presently she emerged from these, coming back with her hands held like a cup. As she came near the fire she called: "Sir John!"

He looked up at her, and smiled wryly, his face drawn with pain. She knelt beside him. Her hands were filled with blueberries.

"Now you can lunch."

"You are a very sweet lady."

His eyes were grave and Clair looked at him as gravely. "Thank you," she said, and emptied the berries into his hands. Sinclair said, evenly: "You shouldn't eat too many of them, else it'll be as bad for you as the meat. Some horse, Miss Stranlay?"

They went on again, after Clair had fallen asleep and slept a dream-filled hour in the sun. The southwards nullah-jumble drew nearer with its background of hills. And on the upper ranges of those hills was a glittering yellow colourlessness.

In mid-afternoon they came upon the giant deer.

It stood with head lowered, drinking at a pool, with dark-brown back pelt and white dappled belly. It was quite close to them when they came through a belt of trees on it, and it was a moment before Clair realized its hugeness. Then she saw Sinclair's six feet two in outline against the thing: it had the bulk of a small elephant.

From its head uprose a twelve-foot spread of antlers, velvet-rimed. Clair thought: 'They must weigh half a ton.' The brute slowly lifted its head and regarded them with vague, indifferent eyes. Then it inhaled deeply, coughed, and trotted away, unhurryingly, westwards. They stared after it, seeing it clear the dip of a nullah in one magnificent bound, and then disappear through a pass in the hills.

And presently over those hills came the hunters.

*Subchapter v*

They came like figures on a Grecian frieze upflung against the colours of the sunset.

First, there was the afternoon quietness but for the scuffle of the grass underfoot. The sun overhung the hills, the country lay deserted since the great deer had vanished. Clair had bent to pick a thorn from her foot and her companions also had halted, Sir John lifting his face, smelling at some unusual odour he imagined upon the wind. Then —

The first intimation was a far, wild neighing and stamping. Clair straightened and looked at the other two. Their eyes were on the grass-covered hill-top perhaps a quarter of a mile away. Its rim was set with hasting dots – dots that changed, enlarged, were heads, shoulders, flying manes. It was a herd of wild ponies in panic flight. The drumming of their hoofs came down to the watchers. Up over the hill into full view they thundered, with flowing manes and tails, thundering against the sunset. And behind, company on company, racing into view, came the hunters.

They ran in silence, tall and naked, the sunshine glistening on golden bodies, their hair flying like the horses' manes. Golden and wonderful against the hill-crest they ran, and the staring Sinclair drew a long breath.

"Good God, they are running as fast as the horses!"

It was unbelievable. It was true. And while Sinclair and Sir John stared at now one hunter, now another, overtake his prey and spear it with whirling weapon, Clair Stranlay put her hands to her lips and whistled up through the evening that piercing blast learned long before in the streets of Battersea.

## Chapter VI:  THE HUNTERS

*Subchapter i*

THOSE ensuing moments! Looking back on them, Clair was to wonder, with a strange tautness of her heart-strings, if they were indeed as her memory pictured them. If the fervour of the sunset behind the hunters had indeed been so intense, their approach to the three survivors of the *Magellan* so rapid. They had come fleeting down the hill, a wash of gold, with the speed of converging clouds in a rainstorm. Abandoning the carcases of the ponies they had swooped downwards in a bright torrent, and in Clair's memory she had fast-closed her eyes at sight of their spears. She had thought:

'They will throw those spears.'

But they had not. She had opened her eyes again, to find that Sinclair, upright and with scowling face, had moved a little in front of her, as though to shield her from the approaching savages. Close now. Gold and naked, with flying hair.

And then indeed in her heart had leapt that strange quiver of unreality upon which her memory insisted – or was that a later-learnt thing from Sinclair's theories? For in that moment of mind-tremor it was a torrent of men from her own land – pale and pinched and padded – who bore down upon her. . . . Then that passed. She stood shaking, but seeing clearly again.

Two score or more of them, naked and tall and golden-brown, not one of them under six feet in height. Some of them mere boys; no old men. And their faces! They were the faces of no savages of whom she had ever heard or read: broad, comely, high-cheekboned, some with black eyes and some with blue, and one she noted with eyes that were vividly grey eyes in his golden face. . . . Sinclair barking out: "Damn you! Keep off!"

They took no notice whatever. Sir John Mullaghan put his arm round Clair, Sinclair fell back to her other side. The hunters at that manoeuvre halted, queried each other with surprised looks, and then burst into a loud peal of laughter.

Sinclair swung up his axe. "Keep off!"

For answer one of the hunters, armed with a piece of wood shaped like a boomerang, laughed in the American's face and came casually forward under the threat of the axe – so close did he come that he stood not three feet away. Clair stared up at him, saw him young, with white teeth uncovered in an enjoying grin ('and that completes his costume', added the imp in her mind) – then found her attention distracted. Sir John's arm shot past her, gripping Sinclair's just as it was about to descend.

"Keep steady, Dr. Sinclair. We can't do anything. . . . Ah, it's too late."

For the young hunter had wheeled round at a call from his companions. Most of them had halted in attitudes of casual surprise or cheerful indifference, but three of them, older men, were poising their spears, warningly. They called something again, and the young man, the mirth falling from his face, drew back. Unexpectedly, Sinclair dropped his axe and stood staring stupidly.

Next moment, apparently galvanized into action by nothing more than a co-operative impulse, the hunters swept in and surrounded them.

"They're friendly," said Sir John. "Keep cool, Miss Stranlay."

"I'm going to —"

A hand tugged gently at the eiderdown quilt draped round her shoulders. She wheeled round, clutching the thing. An impudent golden face smiled down at her. Behind came another tug, and she turned on that. The quilt was in the hands of the young hunter who had smiled under the threat of the Neanderthal axe. He dropped it, and stretched out his hands again, his eyes lighted with amused curiosity. Clair's heart contracted.

"No – *no!*"

The laughter of the savages echoed up the evening of the hills. The three survivors of the *Magellan's Cloud* found themselves patted and pinched and questioned in pantomime.

The young hunter, smiling, put his arms round Clair, and in a sudden panic she sank her teeth into a warm, muscular, golden arm.

The savage drew back with a cry of pain. Sinclair struggled free from the group surrounding him. He glanced round and caught sight of Clair.

"Miss Stranlay? What is it?"

"Nothing." She was already repentant. "I was a fool."

She bent to reclaim the eiderdown. One of the hunters, like a mischievous boy, kicked it beyond her reach. Thereat Sinclair flung him nearly as far. The laughter died down. The levitated hunter picked himself up, his face black with anger. He dropped his spear, came running into the circle again, pushed his face close to Sinclair's, and shouted excitedly.

"Don't touch him again, Sinclair!" Clair discovered Sir John Mullaghan, panting, standing by her side. The hunters had fallen silent, with eager, expectant faces. Sir John said: "God bless me!"

Sinclair, his head thrust forward as had been the angry hunter's, seemed to be replying to the savage in his own language – a torrent of consonants. At that the angry one suddenly smacked the American in the face, and then leapt back lightly out of range. Doing so, the anger vanished from his face. He laughed. Thereon all the others shouted with laughter as well, Clair's assailant being so overcome that he had to hold his sides. . . .

The *Magellan's* survivors stared astounded.

"Must be a colony of escaped lunatics," said Sir John. "I'll try and get you that quilt, Miss Stranlay. . . . What now?"

"*Utso! Utso!*"

The hunters, yelling, turned and ran, all but three of them. One of these seized Sinclair's wrist, another Sir John's, gesticulating the while towards the hill where the pony-battue had taken place. Clair found her right hand in the grasp of a savage whose face was vaguely familiar. It was he of the vivid grey eyes.

He waved towards the hill, urgently. Clair, with a last, desperate glance backwards, pointed to the quilt. He shook his head. Next moment, in the trail of Sir John and his captor, Clair Stranlay found herself running through the evening shadows of the unknown land by the side of a golden body and a golden head which stirred a misty clamour of memories in her mind.

*Subchapter ii*

There were half a dozen ponies on the hill-brow. They were no larger than Shetlands. One of them was not quite dead. As Clair and the grey-eyed hunter arrived, a savage bent over the beast and, poising a flint-axe in his hand, neatly split its skull. Half the hunters faced outwards, their flint-tipped spears held ready. Strange, grey-black things, with high shoulders and dragging hindquarters, came out of the gloaming dimness, glared at the groupings of dead ponies and quick men, snarled disappointedly, and wobbled backwards. A hunter made a feint with his spear at one of these unaccountable beasts. Thereat, scrambling away like a calf, it guffawed hideously. Clair felt she was going mad, standing in the gloaming chill among these laughing savages and laughing beasts. She found Sinclair beside her, and clung to him for a moment, thinking: 'That scowl of yours is the only sane thing in this country.' She shook him.

"Who are they? What are they going to do?"

"Wish I knew – the giggling swine! Especially that clown who slapped my face —"

"Oh, never mind your face."

"I'm sorry." Stiffly.

They looked at each other. Clair began to giggle. The American still scowled with twitching face. Clair realized he was almost as hysterical as she was. Realization was somehow sobering. A hunter near them, bending over the carcase of a pony, pushed his bearded face towards them, grinning inquisitively himself, as though desirous of sharing a joke. Sir John Mullaghan struggled to their side, though indeed no one made any effort to detain him.

"Sinclair, since you know their language —"

"Oh, yes, and what language is it?" Clair also had remembered.

"I don't know." He stared at them puzzledly in the twilight. "I've no memory of hearing it before. But when that circus clown came jabbering I found myself – answering him."

"But you *must* know what you answered."

"I don't. . . . Good God, are we to stand here while I'm put through an examination in linguistics? Stop that damned giggling, Miss Stranlay. . . . I'll ask them where they're going to take us —"

"No need," said the armaments manufacturer.

Nor was there. The hunters, half of them laden with portions of pony carcase, began to move down the southward brow of the hill. They seemed to have no leader. The move was made in a drift of mutual convenience. A large, elderly man, over-burdened, stopped beside Sinclair and motioned unmistakably. He wanted assistance.

"I'm damned if I do," said the American.

The man showed his teeth in a grin, lingered, moved on. It was almost dark. A hunter with his spear slung on his arm by a thong caught Sir John and Sinclair by the arms and urged them down the hillside. Looking after them it struck Clair, absurdly, that he was doing the thing in sheer friendliness. . . . Next moment she found herself alone on the hill-brow with the beasts, now a dark mass like a moving carpet, snuffling up the hill towards her. She would have run but that a hand came over her shoulder, and she almost screamed at that. It was the grey-eyed hunter. He was evidently the rearguard. He smiled and motioned southward. He smiled less frequently than the others. His body smelt of red earth. Clair thought, sickly: 'Some caveman stuff, now, of course.' And so thinking she was suddenly very sick.

The savage left her side. Being ill, she heard the sound of a furious scuffle, the impact of blows. The hunter returned, breathing heavily, glancing over his shoulder. He caught her arm anxiously. They began to run downhill together. Thereat a wurr of protest behind them changed into a scamper of many paws and a blood-freezing bay of laughter.

Sinclair, Sir John and the others had disappeared. Clair ran blindly in the darkness over grass and things that were probably bush-roots, for she stumbled on them. Behind, the pattering sound gained volume. Clair understood. The man beside her could run as fast as the beasts by whom they were being pursued. She was delaying him. She shook her arm free.

"Go on, you idiot, then! I can't."

For answer, still holding her hand, he swung to the right. Clair heard the scratch and scrape of the wheeling pack behind them. The hunter's hand shot up and gripped her wrist.

Next moment they trod vacancy.

Clair heard a feeble little ghost of a scream come from her own lips. She curved her body automatically and next moment struck water – water she could not see. It closed over her body like an envelope of red-hot steel. Down and down, with burning eyeballs. Something tearing at her, something holding her. . . . She found herself on the surface – the surface of a river it must be, for the current was strong – trying to swim and hampered in the effort by the grip of the naked hunter.

She tried to wrench her arm free, and then immediately stopped, realizing that he evidently knew in which direction to swim. Which she as certainly did not. A short distance away a snuffling clamour and bestial laughter grew fainter. Clair's knee struck soggy yielding ground. They crawled through a stretch of swamp; scrambled up an incline. Clair fell on the ground, panting. It was black as pitch. The savage was the vaguest shadow. He pulled at her shoulder impatiently, saying incomprehensible things. She raised her head.

Quite near at hand was the glow of five great fires.

*Subchapter iii*

So it seemed to Clair then, looking at that bright segmenting of the eastern night. But she was mistaken. There were five great openings into the cave, and the segmented glow had birth and being in a multitude of fires. The light grew brighter as she and the grey-eyed hunter climbed from the river. Far in ages past that river had driven through a higher channel in the limestone bowels of the hillside; once, indeed, it must have flowed eastwards an underground river. Then, in some catastrophic spate, it had burst those stygian bonds, broken free in an acre-wide vomit of great limestone boulders, and then sunk and sunk, sweeping eastwards and downwards, till it flowed, in rough parallel, a good hundred yards from the gaping cavern mouths that marked the riven bank of the original channel. The catastrophe had left a great cave, at some points narrow, at others wide and sweeping into a glow-softened darkness; fires burned in remote sub-caves far into the rock. . . . Clair stood in the wash of light, looking at a scene as remote from the life and times of her country as it was remote from all pictures she had ever built in imagination of the life of the savage.

There were perhaps two hundred or less human beings in that immense abandoned channel of the underground river. More than half were women and children. Some were grouped round the innumerable small fires, some lay flat and apparently asleep on skins by those fires, some stood in groups – surely in gossip! Ten yards from Clair an old man squatted, his greying hair falling over his eyes, and, in the unchancy light of the fires, smote with a mallet at a nodule of bright flint. The staccato blows rose at regular intervals, high above the hum of the cavern.

Men, women and children were entirely naked, and for a little they saw neither Clair, panting and dripping, nor her companion, dripping as well, but panting not at all. Then a voice called something from the group round the nearest fire, and Clair's hunter touched her arm and she found herself walking across the hard uneven floor of the cave into the concentrated, astounded stare of four hundred eyes. Then (so it seemed to her) the whole cave rose en masse and precipitated itself upon her.

She said, frightenedly, so frightened that she merely said it, not screamed it, "Sinclair."

A man touched her hair, found it unbelievable, ruffled it wildly, laughed. Two women stroked her breasts. Someone pinched her. A boy who might have been five years old slipped through the forest of legs and clasped Clair's knees, so that she almost fell. She clenched her fists and struck one of the women on the mouth. At that the touching hands left her. The babble hushed. The laughing, curious eyes darkened. And from somewhere Sir John Mullaghan's voice called abruptly:

"Don't do that, Miss Stranlay! They don't mean any harm."

So Clair had realized. It was impossible, but it was a fact.

The golden-skinned nudes were as friendly as they were unreticent. Clair did something then that was an inspiration – leant forward to the woman she had hit, and who had drawn back a pace, and kissed her on her bruised mouth.

"I–I'm sorry."

Thus haltingly (and appropriately, she was afterwards to think) her greeting to that world from her own. For answer the brown-haired woman put up her arms, held her head in a curious way, and kissed her in return!

('And, oh, my good God, she's a *savage*!')

Clair found her hand seized by the woman. She found herself being led away towards a fire burning solitary in a sub-cave of the great rock chamber. She found herself sitting on a badly-cured skin, with beside her the woman whom she had hit and kissed, bending over the fire, toasting a long, grey fish in much the same fashion as Sinclair had toasted the horsemeat. ('Like a figure from the Greek vases – a lovely figure,' said her mind.) She recovered her breath and looked about her.

The American and Sir John were hasting towards her, threading the dottings of fires. Behind them followed the grey-eyed savage.

"Where did you get to, Miss Stranlay?"

Sinclair was unreasonably angry. Also, it seemed to her he was still hysterical. He kept glancing from right to left, towards the cave-mouths, the cavern-ceiling, the groups of the golden-skinned. He waited for no answer, but, gripping his head with his hands, half-turned away. Clair thought, disturbedly: 'Good gracious, what's the fuss – now we've fallen among these nice natives? They'll guide us to a town or a trading-post in a day or so.' She smiled up at the two of them.

"Having a walk with a gentleman friend. There he is behind you."

The hunter came up, unsmiling. He looked from Clair to Sinclair, from Sinclair to Sir John. Then his grey eyes came back to Clair, questioningly. He made a motion from her to Sinclair.

She said to Sinclair: "What?"

The American stared at her and the hunter abstractedly. He was certainly on the verge of a breakdown. He said, "Eh?"

and then, to the savage, a bark of unintelligibility. The savage found it intelligible. He answered. Sinclair's hands went again to his head.

"He wants to know if you are my woman."

Clair sat up with some abruptness. "What have you told him?"

Sir John Mullaghan said, very evenly: "I think Sinclair had better say 'Yes', Miss Stranlay."

Clair found the three of them watching her – Sinclair with a strange, dazed look on his face. ('Not thinking of me at all.') The woman toasting the fish looked up with wondering, friendly eyes. Clair thought: 'Silly ass – go on, agree!' and so thinking found herself for some reason shaking her head at the grey-eyed hunter.

He smiled, gravely; nodded, and walked away. Clair, with a little catch of breath, watched him go.

To what had she committed herself?


*Subchapter iv*

That question was to return with frightening intensity a few hours later.

The fires had died down considerably. Heaped with damp grass and heavy boughs they smouldered with the smell of garden rubbish burned in an English garden. The smoke drifted out of the circle-radiance of each fire, coiled to the roof, and then, in an army of ragged banners, went north into the unexplored darkness of the ancient river-bed. Outside, a wind had risen that soughed eerily among the stars. On either side of the fires the naked hunters and their women slept, sometimes as many as eight or ten to a fire, sometimes only two. Clair had witnessed, and in the sleepy stirrings of the dark continued to witness, scenes of a kindly simplicity unbelievable. Naked savages in a naked cave in an unknown land! Sir John Mullaghan had emerged once from the bizarre cavern background and the neighbourhood of the distant fire where he had been adopted.

"Comfortable, Miss Stranlay? If you want Sinclair or myself during the night, just shout. One of us will keep awake."

"Oh, don't. I'm sure we're safe enough. Who on earth *are* these people, Sir John?"

The grey-haired armaments manufacturer – surely the most grotesque figure ever seen in these surroundings ! – put his hand to his head, bewilderedly, much as Sinclair had done.

"I've no idea – unless I'm to accept Sinclair's new theory. Perfectly mad." He stared down at her with something like horror on his gentle face. "At least, I hope to God he's mad. . . . Don't talk about it, Miss Stranlay. We'll discuss the matter to-morrow. Have you noticed the paintings on the roof?"

"Paintings?"

"Look. Amazing things, aren't they?" He muttered to himself, distractedly. "And the final proof for Sinclair's sanity. . . . Oh, they can't be." He shook himself. "Good night, Miss Stranlay."

"Good night, Sir John."

She had stared after him, troubled and puzzled. Sinclair? . . . And then her eyes had turned to the wild beauty and vigour of the painted beasts that stood and charged and fled in panic flight amid the coiling of the fires' smoke. Here was their sabre-tooth, in black and grey; yonder, a red mammoth; centre the great arch of the cave chamber a nightmare monster bunched in polychrome, gigantically, for an attack. . . . Savages – and these paintings! Where were they? What country was this?

She turned now, the heavy pelt of an unknown animal beneath her, and lay on her right shoulder. She pulled another skin, long-haired and warm, up to her neck, and lay sleepless, looking down the stretch of the caves. Savages. Awful people. Only – they were neither savage nor awful.

No other words than negatives in which to state the facts.

A yard away the woman she had hit slept by the side of a broad-chested hunter with one eye and a face disfigured as though half of it had been torn away in red eclipse by the stroke of a great paw. He had come into the sub-cave the while the woman stolen from an Attic vase had been feeding Clair on a piece of fish and a handful of green, rush-like things; he was evidently a late arrival from the hunt, and the woman his squaw. Clair had shuddered at sight of his face,

and then saw that the hideous grimace on it was an interested smile. Her pyjamas again, of course. He had reached
out and down an inquiring hand – and then withdrawn the
hand, shamefacedly, as the woman said something to him,
sharply. . . . Squaw!

Clair looked over her shoulder at them in the cave-silence
now. They might have been Iseult and Tristan together in
that unshielded embrace.

She closed her eyes – and instantly opened them again.
Somewhere close to the cave-mouths a savage snarling had
broken out. Clair raised herself on her elbow. She could just
see through the nearest entrance, greatly pillared by nature,
like an archaic temple. In the pearl starshine stalked two dim
shapes, long-bodied, sinister. They seemed smooth-skinned
in that light, like great hounds. Were they coming into
the cave?

They growled again, and she realized the brutes were
hesitating, seeking to summon up courage for just such a
raid. But while she thought so a figure beside one of the far
fires arose, stirred the fire near him to a blaze and with blaz-
ing torch came sleepily down the length of the main cave,
stirring each fire. Lights yellow and red and lilac fountained
with much crackle and twinkle. The beasts in the starlight
vanished. Clair sank down again, watching the man with
the torch.

He stopped beside her fire, stirring it as he had done
the others, but more cautiously. Then he laid down the
torch and crossed towards where Clair lay. She closed her
eyes, fast.

With that blinding of herself the silence of the night and
cave fell upon her senses acutely, like a sharp pain. It was actual physical relationship, not of hearing alone, this silence.
The crackling fires had ceased their crackling, burning now
in a steady loom. Outside, the wind had died away, perhaps
awaiting the moonrise – or even the dawn, for how could
one know the hour? And bending over her was a naked
savage.

She bit her lips, hearing the fervid beating of her own
heart. He also would hear it, and at that thought she tried,
foolishly, to ease its noise. She almost suffocated. Should she
shout for Sinclair?

She opened her eyes. She knew him then. It was the grey-eyed hunter. And it was someone else; *the face of the boy who had died outside Mametz bent over her in dim scrutiny.*

So, for a moment, then he turned and went, and Clair laid her head in her arms and slipped into unconsciousness.

CHAPTER VII: A SLIP IN THE TIME-SPIRALS

*Subchapter i*

IT was next afternoon.

Clair Stranlay lay sleeping in the sunlight of the bluff that fronted the caves across the river. She was high up there, and had found a place where the sere grass was less coarse than usual, and soft to lie on. She had not intended to sleep, but to lie taking mental stock of the forenoon's impressions, brooding over the symptoms of a mysterious insanity hourly displayed by Sinclair, watching the unending play of life in the cave-mouths opposite. So indeed she had done for a little after climbing the bluff, seeing the remote golden figures of hunters or women stroll out against the limestone pillars of their habitations, seeing the moving, hasting, recumbent dots that were children sprayed out in all directions from the cave-mouths to the river. Then sleep had come upon her, unawares, yet gently, so that even sleeping she was conscious that she slept and slept comfortably. Almost it was as though she were deeply asleep and dreaming that she slept.

So the new-comers over the grass, from the opposite way up the bluff that she had taken, did not greatly startle her. She opened clear, undrowsy eyes and watched Sir John Mullaghan and the American sit down beside her, one on either side, so that all three had view of the cave-mouths opposite.

"You've been a long time," she said. "If there *is* time in this place."

The two men glanced at each other, swiftly, queerly, then looked away again. They said nothing. Sir John passed his hand over his grey hair in characteristic gesture. He had begun to fray badly, Sir John; he seemed to have frayed overnight. He still had trousers and coat, but the trousers were now shorts, the coat lacked sleeves. Sinclair —

Clair glanced at herself, and made hasty redraping of her rags. "Goodness, our tailors will do a thriving trade when we *do* get back!"

"If we ever get back," said Sinclair.

Clair had half-expected some such remark. Yet it startled her. "So there's something behind their friendliness? Do they – do they intend to do something to us?"

"Eh?" The American looked blank for a moment. Grinned without mirth. "Oh, the cooking-pot or something like that? I imagine they've never dreamt of cannibalism. No, it's not that. We're prisoners – but only as result of the most fantastic accident. Frankly, Miss Stranlay, I don't think there's any chance of us getting back to civilization again."

"But – we're not going to stay here always? We can start out exploring again, and we're bound to reach some place in touch with civilization. Some time."

"I doubt it."

"Why?"

The American looked round the lilac, sun-hazed hills. Below them went on the drowsy play of activity of the naked figures at the cavern entrances. Curlews were crying over that stretch of marsh across which Clair and the grey-eyed hunter had run the night before to escape from the giant hyenas. . . . His gaze came back to Clair's face.

"Because I don't think there's such a thing as civilization in existence. I don't believe there's a restaurant or a dress-maker's shop or a doctor's surgery anywhere in the world."

Clair nodded, chewing a stalk of grass. "I know. I felt like that last night. . . . But it's only an illusion we play with, of course."

Sir John struck in quietly. "Sinclair means it seriously, Miss Stranlay."

Clair sat up, looking at them both. Sunstroke? But Sinclair was merely scowling, as he always did when brooding on a problem, and Sir John's face was sane enough.

"Seriously? But – we came out of – civilization five or six days ago." She indicated the frayed rags that clad her. "This sleeping-suit was made in the Rue de la Paix."

Sinclair drew up his knees in front of him and clasped them. "I don't mean anything illusory, symbolic or allegorical

when I say there's no such thing as civilization. I just mean
it, Miss Stranlay. There's no such thing; there won't be any
such thing for thousands of years."

"Perhaps you'd better detail all the evidence, as you did
for me, Sinclair."

"Yes." The American turned his square, firmly-modelled
head. Clair, troubled though she was, had a little shock of
enlightenment. Of course – that was it! The hunters had
heads like that! "Let's go back to the beginning of all these
happenings. Miss Stranlay —"

"Oh, let's. But why?"

"A minute. Remember what happened on board the
*Magellan's Cloud*? First, there was that submarine earthquake.
Then the airship's wireless failed to get any message from
outside, though the set was quite undamaged. Then it grew
inexplicably cold for that time of the year, and we saw islands
appearing in mid Atlantic – and quite evidently islands not
newly risen from the sea. And then – the moon appearing at
the full, though no moon was due for another five days."

Clair wriggled herself flat again in the sunlight. She felt a
strange uneasiness. "Yes, I remember all that. And it was a
different moon."

"It *still* is a different moon," said Sir John. "I went out
of the cave early this morning and saw it. Intense volcanic
activity must still be going on up there."

"More than likely. You've got all these facts, Miss
Stranlay? Then, the *Magellan's Cloud* was wrecked against a
mountain in a land that couldn't exist. . . . We spent a deal
of argument in the last few days trying to guess what the
land was. I suppose it was necessary to argue to keep sane.
I was never very convinced by my own arguments. Now
we've had time to think, it's plain that the airship didn't
diverge sufficiently from its course – or go at such an altered
speed – as to reach back either to Africa or forward to Canada
or Patagonia."

"Yes. But we're somewhere."

"Obviously. But it isn't any place you ever heard of, is it?
It is, in the geography of the twentieth century, an impossible
place, because the airship couldn't have reached it."

Clair had begun to see. "Then – it's a new country,
somewhere in the middle of the Atlantic? . . . But that must

be nonsense. The sun's got at us all. . . . It's too big not to have been discovered before. It must be as big as ancient Atlantis."

There was an unnecessary silence. Sinclair brooded, Rodin's Thinker in rags. Sir John had turned his face into the blow of the sunlight wind. Sinclair spoke.

"Exactly. That is where I'm convinced we are – in that continent which once filled the eastern trough of the Atlantic."

*Subchapter ii*

Clair covered her ears. "'Once filled it?' Stop, please. . . . I feel as muzzy as a fly in honey. *Once.* . . . That was thousands of years ago, Atlantis. How can we be in Atlantis *now*?"

"Because the now *is* thousands of years ago."

Clair laughed and patted her ears. "There's something wrong with my hearing. You'll have to examine my ears."

"It sounds very confusing, Miss Stranlay, but I think Dr. Sinclair's cumulative evidence is unimpeachable."

"Evidence of what?"

Sinclair seemed to have lost something of his old-time, ready exasperation. He did not rave at her stupidity, Clair reflected, as he would certainly have done three days before. His voice was very quiet.

"Let me go on with the evidence first. We three survived the *Magellan's* wreck, we found a plateau practically without animals, and entirely without human beings in its northern-most part. And there was a long mountain-chain that must be a vent of the central fires of the earth, with thirteen unknown volcanoes on it."

"Were there thirteen? I never counted."

"Yes. Towards the end of the plateau we sheltered in a cave and were almost killed there by a sabre-toothed tiger. And in the cave I found the bones and skull – fresh bones and fresh skull, not fossils – of a Neanderthal man. We came down from the plateau and were chased by a mammoth. We saw an Irish elk, and late last night, hyaenodons. All these animals – and the Neanderthal man – had long been extinct before the twentieth century. And, last of all, we were made prisoners by these people" – he waved his hand towards the caves – "whom at first I thought were merely an unknown tribe of savages."

"And aren't they?"

"I don't think so. I know what their language is now, and why I answered in it so readily. It's Basque – an elementary and elemental form of Basque. My mother was Basque. I haven't spoken the language since childhood, but last evening found myself speaking and thinking in it half-unconsciously. . . . It's the loneliest language in twentieth century Europe, as I suppose you know. No affinities to any other, just as the Basques have no apparent racial affinity to any existing group. It's been speculated that they're the pure descendants of the Cro-Magnards – you've heard of them?"

It sounded to Clair foolishly remote from their trouble of finding a way back to a knowable coast and civilization. She wrinkled her sunburnt brows. "I think so. Yes – I went picnicking to the Cro-Magnon caves once and drank bad Moselle there. They were the Stone Age people who painted all those French and Spanish caves, weren't they? Painters!" Apparent enlightenment came on her. "And you think our hunters are a stray tribe of Basques?"

"No, I don't. I think they're proto-Cro-Magnards – ancestors of the French Cro-Magnards and remote ancestors of the twentieth century Basques."

"*Ancestors?*"

Sir John patted her shoulder. "I think you'd have done better to tell her your theory right out, Sinclair – rather than lead up to it with evidence."

Still, miraculously, Sinclair kept his temper. "All right. Plainly, then, Miss Stranlay, and fantastic as it may sound, I believe we're not in the twentieth century at all – that through some inexplicable accident connected with that submarine earthquake the *Magellan's Cloud* fell out of the twentieth century into an Atlantic atmosphere that had never known an airship before. That was why she could get no reply to her wireless calls. This is not the twentieth century."

"What is it, then?" Clair heard her voice in the strangest, attenuated whisper.

"I don't know. But from all the evidences, I should think

we're somewhere in the autumn of a year between thirty and twenty thousand years before the birth of Christ."

*Subchapter iii*

"It will always remain unreal – and oh, nonsensically impossible to believe!"

More than two hours had gone by. Clair's face was more pallid than either of the men had ever seen it, and indeed it had required something of her disbelief and horror to make them realize the thing themselves, albeit they had met that desperation of hers with irrefragable fact after fact. Now Sinclair pointed down to the mouths of the caves where the golden children played.

"Are these people unreal?"

Clair looked down. "No, they are real enough." She spoke in a low voice, so that they hardly caught her words. She thought for a moment and then smiled from one to the other of them. "Thank you, It's – a devil of a thing. I don't think I'll think about it much . . . if I can. Or at least not deliberately try to go mad. . . . All this stuff about the time-spirals and retro-cognitive memory – maths have always given me a headache. The world used always, I thought, to roll along a straight line called Time, instead of looping the loop with a thousand ghosts of itself before and after it. And none of them ghost, and none the reality."

Sir John said: "I'm not a mathematician either, Miss Stranlay. But I take it they're all realities in the loop-spirals. And for a second – at the moment of the submarine-earthquake – two of the loops touched, and the *Magellan's Cloud* was scraped off one on to the other."

"Like a fly off a pat of butter?"

"Something like that." He smiled at her from behind his grizzled beard. That was better. The Cockney was coming to her help. Clair said, very softly:

"Please. It's a September afternoon in London now. There are dead leaves in the parks, and a lot of people at the Zoo drinking tea under the trees. The motor-buses going round Trafalgar Square and the pigeons are twittering on the roofs of St. Martin's in the Field. And there's been an accident in

Hammersmith Broadway, and an ambulance has come up, and the policeman is shooing back the crowd. And Big Ben says it's twenty past three, and Jean Borrow in my flat is writing a Lido novel, and there's an unemployment procession, and there's Bond Street and shops and early door queues in Leicester Square for an Edgar Wallace play. . . . Just now. And it's not now. It won't happen for twenty-five thousand years. Year after year. I've been speaking just a minute. And it's a long time until sunset. And till the sunset of to-morrow. And until the winter comes here on those caves. And until the spring of next year. Year after year, till we're all three dead. And years after that, till this country's dead and no one really believes it existed. And years after that, with spring and summer and birds over the hills and belling deer, and people in love and sleeping together and having babies and watching them grow up, and the babies becoming old men and women, and dying, and *their* descendants seeing another spring. And an Ice Age coming – slowly, through thousands of years. And passing away through thousands more. And at the end of that time – London will still be in the future. . . . It's not now, it never can be for us, nor for anyone now alive. . . . Up through thousands and thousands of years we'll never see —"

Her voice had risen; it cracked on the last word. Sinclair was on his feet. He took her by the shoulders and shook her. Laughing and crying, she stared up in his eyes. Sir John half stood up also, made to interfere, refrained. Clair struggled. Her hysteria died away. Sinclair's fingers relaxed. Clair found herself staring at him resentfully, flushed, rubbing her shoulders.

"You beast!"

He was panting. He sat down. "Anything you like. I tried to be an effective counter-irritant. Feel better?"

Clair shuddered. "Don't look at me, you two, for a bit."

They didn't. After a little they heard her say: "Sorry I went like that, especially after my promise."

"I felt like going that way myself last night."

"Did you?"

The American nodded. "And we're to make a compact, all three. If one of us ever feels that way again, we're to get to the other two at once. Promise?"

"Yes."

Sinclair nodded to Clair's spoken reply and Sir John's nod, and they said nothing for a little. Clair's mind felt as though it were slowly recovering from a surgical operation. *Atlantis!* She said: "And what are we going to do?"

"What *is* there we can do?"

This was Sinclair. Clair turned her eyes to the armaments manufacturer. He smiled at her. He looked ill, she reflected. He said, gently:

"At least, we have all our lives to live – now, as in that time that is not yet, that time that is thousands of years ago. And they are our lives. . . . There's the sun and the wind on the heath, brother. I wish I could remember more of Borrow." Below their eyes, in the still sunshine, the life of the cave-mouths went on. "And those people among whom we've come – if we can live their life, they're livable companions, aren't they?"

"Oh . . ." Clair sat up again. "I knew there was something you two had left unexplained. Most important of all. You can't explain it." She turned to the American accusingly. "If these are the ancestors of the Cro-Magnards who are to become the ancestors of the Basques —"

"And perhaps our own ancestors. Your own remote ancestor may be one of these children playing by the river there, Miss Stranlay."

"Oh, my good God!" She was checked for a moment, and again the curtain of horror waved before her eyes. And, queerly, something came to her aid. It was memory of the grey-eyed hunter. "But that doesn't matter. Won't bear thinking about. If these people are as far back in time as you imagine – they're remoter from civilization than any savage of the twentieth century."

"Far remoter," said Sinclair. "Their weapons and implements are palaeolithic flints. They seem to have no knowledge of even the elements of agriculture. They wear no clothes at all, they haven't even arrived at the idea of storing water in calabashes – as I found to my discomfort last night."

"They've no tribal organization," said Sir John. "That is plain enough already. None of the ultimate divisions of power and responsibility have been yet evolved."

"But – *your* theories, Sir John, and yours, Dr. Sinclair.
. . . Where is the raving Old Man with his harem of wives?
And where's all the cruelty and fear and horror? They're not
savages. They're clean and kindly children. Listen!"

Some jest of the caves. The shout of laughter came up
to them on the bluff-head. Both the men were silent. Clair
thought: 'Oh, shame to wreck your nice theories!' and said:
"So it must be the twentieth century and Patagonia or some
such place after all."

The American shook his head. "It's not the twentieth
century; our data is stable enough. It's just that all the history
books and all the anthropological theories of the twentieth
century tell the most foolish lies. It's just that Sir John
Mullaghan and I and thousands more have been victims of
the shoddiest scientific lie ever imposed on human credu-
lity. . . . These proto-Cro-Magnards, these earliest true men
on earth – absolutely without culture and apparently absolutely without superstitious fears, cruelties, or class-divisions.
It means that Rousseau was right (or will be right? How is
one to think of it?) and the twentieth century evolutionists
all wrong."

Clair said, steadily: "These – like our ancestors; perhaps
some of them our own ancestors. . . ." For a moment it
seemed to her that her two companions were ghouls squatting beside her in the sunlight. "And I knew it – women
always knew it! But you two and the thousands of others
who led the world swore that men were natural murderers;
you killed five million in France to prove your theories. All
through history you've been doing it. . . . The boy who died
on the wire outside Mametz – he was one of these hunters, I
saw his own face last night. And you and the world told him
he was a murderous beast by nature and ancestry!"

She was aware of the armaments manufacturer looking at
her, doubt and a grey horror in his face. "Perhaps this is only
a stray tribe of primitives unlike all others."

"No." Sinclair spoke. Abruptly, as with an effort. "They
are no stray tribe. You are right, Miss Stranlay. You are
woman, for that matter, of fifty tortured centuries accusing
us. . . . And we've no defence. We never tried to find out the
real facts of human nature. . . . By God, but some did! Some
were trying. I've just remembered. There was a new school of

thought in the world out of which we came. The Diffusionist. And we thought them fantastic dreamers!"

"What did they dream?"

"Why, that primitive man was no monster, that it was the early civilizations and their offshoots that bedevilled him. If a Diffusionist were here at the moment he would say that these are men as Nature intended them to be. So they will continue for thousands of years till by an accident in the Nile Valley agriculture and its attendant religious rites will be evolved. And from that accident in 4000 B.C. will rise, transforming the world – the castes and gods, the warrior and slave, the cruelties and cannibalisms, Sir John Mullaghan's armaments, the war that murdered your lover, Miss Stranlay, and my League of Militant Pacifists."

They stared at Clair uncomfortably in the bright sunshine. A party of hunters came over the eastward hills – golden figures against a golden background. They were singing, these dawn-men – godless and fearless and hateless and glorious, Sinclair thought, they who should have slouched through the sunlight obsessed and obscene animals ! . . . Sir John was greyly conscious of Clair's silent figure.

"But I still don't understand. If this is the world of twenty-five thousand B.C., as we've calculated, what is its population? Are there other men? Is there a Europe? And that Neanderthal skull – it didn't belong to a species of man like one of these hunters, surely?"

The American made an abrupt, half-despairing gesture.

"How can we know – *now* – since all our other beliefs about these times go phut? Something like this, I imagine: Atlantis here is a great waste of land, the youngest and most unstable of the continents. It must stretch at points almost across to the Antilles and America. And wandering through it are possibly a few scarce family-groups like our hunters. Possibly – but our hunters may be the only true men as yet in existence. They must have been wandering this land for thousands of years. In the east there, towards Europe and in Europe itself there are Neanderthal men – unhuman, a primitive experiment by Nature in the making of man. They also must be few enough in number, though their species probably spreads far into Asia and Africa. And somewhere in Central and South-Eastern Asia at this moment may be other

family groups of true men, not so very different from these
golden cavemen of ours, slowly wandering westwards. . . .
There is an Ice Age coming, a few thousand years hence,
and at the end of it the Neanderthalers will die out and
these hunters, or rather their descendants, reach Europe and
spread over it and intermarry with those remote kinsmen of
theirs from Asia. . . . Something like that."

He jumped to his feet. "Oh, by God, if one could only tell
them – those hunters of ours!"

"Tell them what?" asked Sir John.

"History – the world that is to be. Remember that kindly
chap who took you and me prisoners – we thought we were
prisoners and we weren't at all! He's never heard the words
for war or prison. Or that hunter who brought Miss Stranlay
to the caves. . . . If they knew what their children there in
the sunlight are going to inherit – thousands of years away!
All the bloody butcheries of the battlefields, the tortures
and mutilatings of the cities still unbuilt, the blood-sacrifices
of the Aztec altars, those maimed devils who die in the
coalmines of Europe. . . ." He looked down at Clair. "You're
a novelist, Miss Stranlay. You were born in the slums – thirty
thousand years in the future. Do you remember it? Think
that it still has to happen – for these."

Clair said, in a pale, quiet voice: "Will you two leave me
alone? Oh, I won't go mad again."

"Don't stay too late. We'll watch for you from the cave."

"All right, Sir John."

She heard the scuff-scuff of their receding footsteps. She
was alone. A lapwing came wheeling over the hill-brow and
passed towards the marshes. Drowsiness had settled on the
caves. Clair Stranlay laid her head on her arms and began to
weep – to weep and weep as she had done never before in
her life.

*Subchapter IV*

For a little, weeping, her thoughts were a static confusion.
Then they combered into a wild clamour – an affrighted
clamour, though the fear was of a different order from that
which had horrified her into hysteria in the presence of
Sinclair and Sir John.

"But what am I to do? Oh, my good God, what *am* I to do? If we're here for ever – but I can't, I can't! I may live to be a hundred – days and days and months and years – among horseflesh and fires. No books. Never read a lovely piece of prose again. Never have the fun of correcting my own proofs. Or lying on a soft, clean bed. Or smoking cigarettes. Never talk to the people who like my kind of jokes, or twist an argument; or be clever and bright. Or wear pretty clothes and have men want me. . . . And be safe – safe and secure. . . . I can't do it, I can't!' The grass rustled under her as she lay and wept, terrified. She closed her eyes, tightly, to make sure that this country and the American's talk were all part of a dream. Ever so tightly. In a moment, when she opened them, she'd know. It couldn't be, it couldn't be. . . . She opened her eyes on the afternoon of the pale Atlantean hills.

As she looked across them with misted eyes, far and remote, and heard by her for the first time since their coming to the caves, there rose and belled and quivered in the air the sound that had startled the mammoth miles away by the side of the great oak. It rose and fell, rose again, died on a long, strange note, that mysterious lowing. Wonderful thing. Breath-taking thing to hear.

If only she had a notebook and pencil!

Both of them thousands of years away.

'Let's think calmly, then. If this were only a novel – one of the kind you've wanted to write for a holiday. Think that this isn't yourself; only your heroine. It's she who's lying on a hill above a lost Atlantis cave, watching the children of the dawn-men playing by a lost river. . . . And you're comfortable in your Kensington study, planning out the synopsis. What's she going to do next? How's she going to live? She *must* live – you'd never be mean enough to kill her. But *how?*'

It was late in the afternoon now – those afternoons that seemed to contract so steadily with the wearing of the week. She saw the smoke far up the opposite hillside – from some high vent that aerated the caves – thicken from pale blue to violet black. They were building up the fires. Soon the main body of the hunters, that had left at dawn, would return. The individual hunters must long ago have returned. Sinclair and Sir John waiting for her. Hungry. Hungry herself.

She stood up. The wind had turned cooler. She shivered.

Her ragged jacket flapped, and the pyjama-trousers blew against her legs. She looked down at herself – and, looking, started at the thought that came to her. Opposite, the loitering figures by the cave-mouths. All her life among them . . . 'Do it. Sometime you'll be forced to do it. Goodness, why wait till then?'

A fox prowling up the side of the hill heard her laugh, and at the sound stopped and bared his teeth, brush cocked. He crept behind a tussock of grass and wormed his way through the heart of it and looked at the strange hunter with the uncouth skin. . . . He bristled a little at sight of what the hunter did, and waited till she was gone, and for nearly an hour later circled slowly round a strange, grassy fluffment that was yet, he knew, no grass, and intriguing, though very unlikely eatable.

*Subchapter v*

Sinclair was the first to see her coming, splashing through the shallow natural ford of the river. Reaching the near side she paused to shake the water from herself. The sunlight caught her then, dazzlingly. Deliberately, walking with head down-bent (in thought, somehow he knew, not in dejection) she came up the incline towards the mouths of the caves.

Sinclair said: "By God, well done!"

"Eh?" Sir John Mullaghan had not seen her. Now he did. He hesitated, then nodded. "Splendid. Sensible girl."

"I'll go in," said Sinclair.

"That would be a mistake. Much better to stay here and look at her and talk to her as we would have done yesterday. . . . Hello, Miss Stranlay. That is the sensible thing to do. I wish I weren't so old, otherwise I'd follow suit."

Clair thought, 'You dear,' gratefully. She looked at both of them, and found it now very easy. Sir John's eyes were naturally kind, the American's at the moment deliberately so. She said; "It feels good. Especially coming through the river. And I always hated bathing-dresses. . . . Only I hope winter doesn't come too soon."

"Both Sir John and I will be forced to it in time, anyhow," said Sinclair. And added, easily: "Shall we walk over to your fire with you?"

Clair realized, suddenly, something of the ordeal of that. Or need it be? She felt her nether lip begin to tremble; stayed it.

"Oh, no thanks."

She smiled at them and went into the cave; and, so seeing her for the first time, the women of the cave rose like a flight of birds and settled around her.

Unreasonably, abruptly, Clair felt not afraid at all. Standing smiling and nude, pearl and rose, under the touch of their friendly golden hands, she thought: ' . . . as though I were freed from a horrible skin disease – free for the first time in my life. Oh, winter, don't come too soon! I want to live!'

*Subchapter i*

B UT that night the rain set in, blowing squallily into the mouths of the caves, so that the flames of the fires danced and spat and flickered, and long serpent-shapes of smoke wound and whorled everywhere. Amid them blew sharp, piercing shafts of wind, and Clair began to realize something of the life of those people in the winter months. She lay wakeful beside her fire, and Sinclair, who could not sleep either, came over to her while the beating gusts shook the limestone hills and moaned far away in the subterranean depths of the ancient river-bed.

"Shocking night."

Clair stirred the fire gently with a bough, and nodded to him. He stood, naked of shoulders and legs, looking into the fire himself after that first sharp appraisal of her. He said: "Missing your clothes?"

Clair wound the odorous bearskin more closely round herself. "I suppose I am – in spite of my immunity from cold. Silly perhaps of me to part with them."

"Let me feel your pulse."

He did. It seemed quite normal. She startled him with a question. "Do you think we'll pull through the winter months – especially Sir John?"

"What?"

"Oh, you know. *You* will, I think. You have physique for it, and most of the other advantages. I may – through the accident that winter-bathing was my hobby – though goodness knows I feel like a white snail without its shell among all these golden people."

"You looked lovely enough for the Parthenon frieze."

He said this impersonally. Clair nodded. "I know I'm not unsightly. But mentally – coddled and cowardly. Best-selling never trained me for a winter in Atlantis."

He was silent. He bent down to place a burning twig more evenly. The wind whoomed, blowing his hair and beard, as Clair saw looking up at him from the shelter of her bearskin. In shadow and in flickering light the Cro-Magnards slept, disregarding rain and squall – all, except three very young babies who wailed softly in the far corner of the cave. These apart, even the very youngest slept soundly though the wind occasionally lifted a skin covering and drifted it yards, leaving exposed those nude bodies that had indeed the colours of a fresh gold coin. As though made of gold leaf. Outside, against the cave-mouths, the wavering curtains of rain. . . . Atlantis! Lost in Atlantis and pre-history! Clair, forgetting the silent Sinclair, leant on an elbow, gazing round at the sleeping hunters with golden, easy bodies. And for some strange fantastic reason she thought of lines in Tennyson:

> 'Ah, such a sleep they sleep,
> The men I loved!'

These cavemen, the men of the dawn! And suddenly it was to her as though they lay dead, they and their women and children, and over them indeed came stalking those ghoulish shapes with which the world remote in the future was to identify them – great beasts, manure-flanked, slime-dripping, with fetid jaws and rheumy eyes, tearing at the throats of these dead men of the dawn, mangling and destroying and befouling the human likeness from the lovely limbs and faces. . . . She started, hitting her head against the sandy floor. Sinclair had turned *his* head, sharply, looking at her.

"You're sleepy now. Good night."

"Oh – I was dreaming awake. Good night – it's ridiculous to say Dr. Sinclair. What is your name?"

"Keith."

"Good night, Keith."

"Good night, Clair."

Alone again, she lay on the verge of sleep, and thought: 'Those babies. Poor things. Awful for them.'

Two of them had been born that afternoon. Both had been dead before sunset. Their bodies had been carried along the river bank to the edge of the marsh and abandoned there, Sinclair had said.

"Awful. How it's raining! Drumming like a London roof under rain, almost. London roofs – but you mustn't think of them. Nor all your London days. Over, all days, very soon, I suppose.'

She grew wakeful again at that thought. Sinclair had gone without answering her question. Over: all the bright, burnished hours, the days of summers and autumns, the good things to eat, the ease and pleasantness. . . . To come to an end and a blinding in darkness at last, somewhere, in some dark cave, without medical attention or understanding. And someone, unless Sinclair or Sir John was still alive, would carry her body outside the range of the caves; and leave it for a beast to devour.

She looked, and so for long until the fires died continued to look, into a night that was a pit of terror.


*Subchapter ii*

But that next dawn —

She awoke luxuriously, in the embrace of a strange, secret exultation. Why? Something awaiting her? She put aside the fur and got up and shivered in the dawn chill, and saw then that it was but barely the dawn.

No one stirred. Far at the furthest fire the watcher of the fires was smoothing a stick with a flint. He heard her, lightly though she walked, and looked round, and flung back his hair from his face, and smiled. A boy. She smiled herself and warmed herself by the fire of another household, scraping away ash and refuse and replenishing the cone-shaped structure with boughs from a pile stacked near. Then she went to the nearest mouth of the cavern, and at her appearance the sun that had been hesitating behind the hills came over them, and she stood and shivered with pleasure in its first beams. The guard hunter came to her side; said something unintelligible; motioned towards the river. A lion and a lioness, grey beasts rather than tawny in that light, were standing watching them, not twenty yards away. The hunter gestured with the half-smoothed bough in his hand. Promptly the lion disappeared through the soft, wet grass. The lioness growled and stalked after him despondently.

The hunter laughed.

The caves began to stir. The naked women awoke and fed their babies. The men, naked equally, arose and drifted about and were scolded, and grinned, and crowded the cave-mouths as though in casual gossip. Clair saw Sir John Mullaghan rising, with some appearance of chilled joints, from a heap of boughs. A Cro-Magnard helped him up. A frizzling smell began to pervade the cavern. Breakfast. It was deerflesh, cooked in the same monotonous way as always. Frying-pans, pots and pantries were as unknown as gods, chancels and torture-chambers. Afterwards the Cro-Magnards would wander down to the river in twos and threes, and drink.

Clair ate her charred venison with a hunger that surprised her. She had learned a few words of the proto-Basque in the past twenty-four hours, and with their aid gathered from the woman, Zumarr, that Belia, the hunter with the mutilated face, admired his guest's new appearance. So, apparently, and with much astounded calling one to the other, did as many of the Cro-Magnards as had not seen her before in natural garb. They dropped pieces of venison and came running to look at her. Zumarr shooed them away, vigorously. The others who had come to look at her the night before laughed.

And Clair thought a surprising thought: 'These people without religion are the most spiritual the world will ever see! They are quite unaware of their bodies. They aren't personal possessions to them, as mine is to me. They must feel through them, impersonally, just as they feel pleasure in the painting of sky and earth by sun and mist. And they don't dream of refusing other people the right of looking at sky and earth . . .'

The men went away in the early morning, after drinking at the river and indulging in some horse-play when three of them were thrown into the water, and the others – apparently in a mood of self-retaliation – flung themselves in on top. Watching them, Clair said to Sir John: "But I thought swimming was a very artificial acquirement of human beings?"

"Perhaps this family group has wandered from the shore of some inland sea in Atlantis. They're certainly very cleanly, most of them, though it's plain it's not because of any code. They are because they enjoy it."

"Where's Keith Sinclair?"

Clair saw him approaching then. It was apparently for him that the watcher of the fires had been smoothing the bough through the night. He carried that bough now, straightened, and with a carefully-knapped sliver of flint wedged and bound in it. Clair reached out her hand and took the thing and examined it, and some of the women came and looked at the three of them, smilingly. One, a girl, giggled. And Clair thought:

'I hope I'm not examining it too intently. I should be just as casual as he was.'

The American nodded as she handed it back. There was a flush on his dour face, a sparkle in his eyes. "I expect I'll be the worse kind of amateur. At the stalking as well as the running – in spite of my atavistic legs."

"Atavistic?"

"Hadn't you noted them? I'm fairly Cro-Magnard altogether in physiognomy. And the twentieth century seems to have guessed correctly from study of the fossil remains of these people found in the French caves that their long shin-bones were developed by racing game on foot. . . . By the by, this is a feast day."

"Feast?" Sir John, a grotesque figure in his rags, had sat down. He smiled at them, greyly. "I'm sorry, Miss Stranlay. I'm still a trifle upset internally. . . . Did you say a feast, Sinclair?"

"Yes."

"But from what you were telling me of the Diffusionist theory of history last night I understood that ritual feasts came only with civilization?"

"There seem to be two exceptions. Perhaps they're memories of the old pre-human mating seasons. In spring and autumn they occur, as far as I can gather from the old flint-knapper, Aitz-kore; and the autumn one comes after the first night of rain."

"What's it for?" Clair asked.

"Why – You won't be shocked?"

Clair laughed. Even Sir John, with closed eyes, smiled. The American hefted his flint spear.

"It's the time, I understand, when the men and women choose their lovers for the winter – or those already mated exchange."

"Will there be —?" Clair's question hesitated in her eyes. Sinclair's reply hesitated on his lips.

"I don't think so. But I don't know. Sir John and I will take you out for a walk when it comes off, if you like."

"No. If we're here for the remainder of our lives that would be too suburban. . . ." She suddenly gripped his arm. "There's my hunter."

No other. Clair had not seen him all the day before. He went and sat down by a fire and ate some scraps of venison surviving the breakfast. A baby came and fell over his feet. He righted it, absorbedly, and put it aside. The baby procured a bone, and sucked it. Clair shuddered.

"Been out on a lone trek, I should think," said the American. "They often do that, the young and unmarried, according to Aitz-kore. Wander off sometimes and don't come back. Hello, they're waiting for me!"

"Good hunting!"

"Thanks." He called over his shoulder. "Don't stray far from the caves, either of you."

Scouts had already gone. Others straggled westwards by the marsh, going casually, for there was no game near at hand. The American pacifist joined a golden-skinned group and companioned them out of sight, his white starkness very conspicuous. Standing in the sunlight of the cave-mouths, Clair looked after him and stretched her own smooth-skinned body luxuriously, and sighed deeply. Sir John looked up inquiringly.

"?"

"Nothing, Sir John, except – did you ever sleep on Box Hill on a Sunday afternoon?"

He shook his head, his face gentle still, if a little twisted. She did not notice. She was twenty millennia away.

"Heat and stickiness and someone playing a melodeon, and poor, life-starved louts prowling among the bushes. Goodness, the stickiness and the taste in one's mouth! Horrible clothes. When we might have been like this. . . . Box Hill!"

Sir John also had fallen into a dream. Box Hill! His

company; his constituency; that journey to America. . . . Here
in the sunshine of Atlantis one began to doubt them. Had
they ever been? . . . He found he had been thinking aloud.
He found Clair's hand on his shoulder. Her lovely face was
lighted but dreamy still.

"Perhaps they were, but – *need they ever be*? Perhaps men
dreamt the wrong dream. We are such stuff of dreams. . . .
Perhaps it was only a nightmare astray on Sinclair's time-
spirals out of which we came. . . . It feels so here this
morning. As though all the world could begin again —"

Begin again? Sir John put his head in his hands. Begin
again! Who indeed knew what was possible in this fantastic
adventure – if only the pain would go and he could see and
understand more clearly. . . . Begin again? Poets had dreamt
it, and they had changed the world with other dreams. . . .
Shelley, of course! Long since he had read Shelley:

> 'The world's great age begins anew,
>     The golden years return.
> The earth doth like a snake renew
>     Her winter skin outworn:
> Heaven smiles, and faiths and empires gleam
> Like wrecks of a dissolving dream.'

*Subchapter iii*

It was mid-afternoon.

The caves had emptied their entire population on to the
plateau east of the river bank. They had trooped out in little
groups, men and women separately for once. A couple of
jackals, roused from a bed of reeds, had distracted somewhat
the attention of the processions, the entire tribe engaging in
an idiot chase of the beasts, pelting them with stones, shouting and hallooing, until long after the snarling brutes were
out of sight. Clair, laughing and panting, a Greek among
Polynesians, rejoined Sir John and Sinclair, grey-haired the
one, black the other, and now with her red-tipped mop
coming between them.

"Feel as though I were going to the world's first picnic!"

Beyond the nullahs was a flattish stretch of grass, short-cropped perhaps in the hour-passing of some enormous herd. Right of it lay the river. Over the westward hills beyond the marsh hung the sun, high up. The grey-gold land drowsed. And the Cro-Magnards' laughter went up a little wind that turned back from the east towards the deserted caves. The women and children grouped themselves, sitting or standing or lying, round the eastwards verge of the sward. The men held over to the other side and also lay or sat. A silence fell. The three survivors of the *Magellan's Cloud* looked at each other in some doubt; finally reached a spot that seemed neutral, neither for men nor women. They lay down, resting on their elbows. The silence went on.

Suddenly a blackbird began to pipe in a thicket near at hand, breaking the tension for the three aliens at least.

"'And we have Box Hill here and now'," misquoted Sir John Mullaghan, gently.

The sound had stirred the Cro-Magnards also. A man rose slowly from the midst of the male embankment, and slowly walked across towards the gathering of women. The sunshine glided over grey-black hair.

"It's the old flint-knapper, Aitz-kore," whispered the American, interestedly.

So it was. Still the silence went on as he passed over the grass. The rustle of his passage if not his footfalls could be heard. He arrived at the end of the women's line, and, slowly, passed up the ranks of the women, scanning each face. They looked him in the eye. One or two of the younger ones giggled. But for the most they kept the initial silence. Sir John whispered:

"His wife is there in the middle."

Aitz-kore neared her. Clair found herself holding her breath. The flint-knapper passed the woman without a change of countenance. Something seemed to contract in Clair's throat.

Aitz-kore reached the end of the line, paused, shrugged, turned back, walked slowly over the track he had already made in the grass, his face like his name, a pointed hatchet, old and sharp. He halted in front of the woman who had been his wife. She had sat with head down-bent, but she raised it now. Clair was too far off to see her face, but she

knew she was weeping. The flint-knapper held out his hand.
The woman took it and rose up. A yell of delight rose from
hunters and women alike.

"He's selected her again from all the women of the tribe,"
Sinclair explained.

The two of them walked down to the southwards end of
the plateau, turned leftwards, in the opposite direction from
the caves, and were out of sight before Clair glanced for them
again. She had been intent on the second venture.

Again a man had crossed the open space, walked the
line, and made selection of a woman – a young woman, and
comely even among the comely. But he had less luck than
Aitz-kore. The woman shook her head. Thereat the hunter,
after a moment's hesitation, walked back to the place from
which he had come.

It was now the woman's turn. She rose. She was enceinte,
but comely enough in carriage still. Leisurely she crossed to
the seated rows of men, hesitated not an instant, but held
out her hand. Instantly a young man – a mere boy– sprang
to his feet and took her hand. Again the strange cheer went
up from the gathering. Clair's eyes sparkled.

"Kidnapping."

"Young enough," Sinclair agreed, absently. "Wonder if
he's the father of her baby – or that man she has just
refused?"

Clair wondered that also, looking after woman and boy as
they broke into an easy, long-legged trot, southwards, across
the sward, and then turning east and racing for the hills.
Another woman rose up and crossed towards the men's side,
stopping mid-way to fling back a cloud of russet hair from a
flushed, high-cheekboned face.

"She has a lovely figure," said Clair.

"They all have," said Sinclair.

And it was true. Neither the steatopygy of the savage nor
the pendulous paunch and breasts of corset-wearing civilizations were here. They mated as they chose, those golden
women; they bore children, many and quickly, unless they
tired of mating; they died in great numbers in childbirth, they
and their children. And they lived free from the moment
they were born till the moment when that early death might
overtake them. The eager, starved, mind-crippled creatures

of the diseased lust of men were twenty thousand generations unborn. The veil, the priest, the wedding ring, the pornographic novel, and all the unclean drama of two beasts enchained by sex and law and custom were things beyond comprehension of the childlike minds in those golden heads or the vivid desires of those golden bodies. ... Golden children in the dawn of time, they paired in the afternoon sunshine and in pairs melted away into the east. Clair, warm and comfortable, her breasts pressed in the grass, found herself nodding drowsily. Every now and then, however, she would start to half-wakefulness as another shout went up, another nuptial couple wheeled out of the gathering. Suddenly, in a long quietness, she started fully awake.

"Keep cool, Miss Stranlay."

"By God. ... Ærte."

Clair raised her head. An intenser silence than ever before had fallen on the gathering. Few of the Cro-Magnards were sitting now. All stood to look. And the reason was the grey-eyed hunter, Ærte.

He walked from the far end of the men's line. His head was a little down-bent, as though in deep thought. Under his left arm was his spear. Disregarding the waiting line of women he came, straight towards where the three survivors of the airship's wreck lay. Clair thought, breathlessly: 'Cooler, now. Must get back to the caves soon. Sir John – wonder if he's feeling better? ...' Defence. Not thinking. Taking no heed. But in some fashion she felt as though she had just finished running an exhausting race. Sinclair, his eyes on the hunter, said:

"Just shake your head, Clair. There's no compulsion among these people."

But Clair's head he saw as down-bent as the hunter's own. She saw the nearing feet in the grass, but nothing more. And then he was close; had halted. She raised her head.

They looked at each other for a long time. She heard the American say something; something quite incomprehensible because of that drumming noise in her ears. She was looking up, even in the still sunshine, not into the face of Ærte alone. Her heart was wrung with a sudden, wild pain of recognition, and then that passed, leaving a tingling as of blood, long congealed, that flowed again. ... A gentle voice came nearer and nearer out of the aurulent silence. Sir John's.

"He'll go away. It's just that he doesn't realize that you are different."

"I'm glad."

They saw her swing to her feet. For a moment the long, sweet lines of her figure also glimmered pale gold. She stood beside the hunter.

"Miss Stranlay!"

There was urgency and appeal in the simultaneous cry. Clair looked back at them, shook her head. They had grown the mistiest of images.

And then she put her hand in the hand of the hunter, Ærte, felt that hand close on hers, felt herself drawn forward, heard a groan from Sir John Mullaghan.

She closed her eyes, and when next she opened them found before her the eastern hills and two shadows treading a deserted land.

*Subchapter iv*

Rain came on again that night. Winter was not far off from Atlantis. Distant in the north the volcanoes smoked and sometimes, in the lifting clouds of rain, could be glimpsed as the beating of damp beacons remote in the mirk. Clair, lying sleepless with her lover for the dark days, saw them, pregnant, dark blossoms high up in the sky. Remote there was the plateau crossed by herself and Sinclair and Sir John only three days before. Fantastic journey. Fantastic climax to it, this. . . . The hunter stirred, dreamlessly, dark and golden and close, and she peered at him, then at the passing curtains of rain.

A lover for the dark days! A lover dead and dust twenty-five thousand years before she had been born! What dream was this that had led her feet from a Kensington flat to that running across the hills from the mating place of the dawn men?

They had run beyond the sight and sound of that mating place, and then, at the over-quickening of Clair's breathing, the hunter had slowed down and looked at her inquiringly. They were in a treeless stretch of long grass, the river deserting them and holding southwards. Across the grass, a mile or more away, two great hairy beasts shoggled through the afternoon, one after the other. Wooly rhinoceroi. Clair, panting, had brought her eyes back to Ærte.

They had smiled together. Clair had thought: 'And where from here?'

He had answered that by taking her hand again and breaking again into the trot that was probably his customary pace. The trees drew nearer. Clair saw that they were beeches, with great open spaces between. The rhinoceroi had disappeared. Clair, breathing desperately, lay down. Ærte halted, laughed, gestured, his black hair falling over his face. Then he laid the spear down beside her and vanished among the beeches.

When she had recovered her breath she heard the sound of him returning, and saw what he carried. It was a great water-melon. She sat up, looking at him lightedly. His grave eyes laughed down at her. Abruptly he dropped the fruit. She found warm, aurulent arms round her. The grass was warm. A cricket was chirping. Clair shook her head, and saw that gestured denial, unreal and unconvincing, in the eyes so close to hers.

"Not yet."

And then she had thought, with a cool clarity, as he put his hand on her shoulder: 'But that's a lie.'

So it had been. Lying with her hands clasped behind her small head on which the hair was already too long, she had thought: 'I'll hear that cricket all my life long.' And then she knew with utter certitude that at last was here fulfilment of a phrase that twenty thousand years away was to sing like a bugle-call through a dank ritual mumble. "*I thee with my body worship.*" For one moment the knowledge had been merely terrifying, as though she stood in the imminent threat of mutilation. She had struggled a little, but the singing of the cricket was already lost. Some other song came and shaped to a clamour in her heart, till she knew it one with herself, and never would she be wholly herself again. . . . She had reached up and kissed the Cro-Magnard's lips, and then, perhaps a full minute later, with that wilder music dying in her ears, heard suddenly the chirping of the cricket, and realized that it had never ceased . . .

Where would the night find them? Back in the caves?

Ærte had shaken his head when they stood on their feet again and she gestured that question. He picked up his spear. On the young, bearded face close to hers she saw, with a quiver of wonder, a mist of perspiration. He looked down at her, grave again, though with shining eyes. Haunting face . . .

He said: "Over the hills."

They had perhaps half a score of words between them. As they went across the sunset land he taught her three. One was his own name. And for the other two Clair looked in his eyes, wondering again, suddenly so pitiful that she almost wept, and then suddenly laughing so that she found herself caught and held again, and it was still longer before the hills came in sight.

But at length they drew nearer, great redstone masses unusual enough in the Atlantean scene. Gorse in thickets climbed their flanks. Birds rose whirring at their approach. Plover. It grew cold. Suddenly their shadows began to race hillwards.

"Do hope you've some place in mind where we can shelter."

Strange jargon in that sunset land! The English speech, so fine and splendid and flexible an implement, fashioned from the bood and travail of generations of Aryans yet unborn. Thousands of years yet before from Oxus bank dim tribesmen would drift across the Urals, and the first English word issue from barbarous lips. . . . She became aware that they were threading in single file a long cleft in the hills. Golden flanked as the hills, Ærte led the way.

Beyond the winding cleft, she realized they had swung north-eastwards. Across the savannah waste, remote, towered the plateau where she had journeyed from the wreck of *Magellan's Cloud*. A week ago!

There lay the lake in the dying light. Perhaps if they listened they would hear that lowing again. She had caught the hunter's arm then, and stayed him, listening. But from the dimming plateau-world and its foreground had come no sound other than a faint rustle, as though it were a painted screen rustling in the wind.

They climbed. The lake receded, blurred, vanished. And at length, on a bush-strewn ledge, Ærte had drawn aside a

bush and shown their shelter for the night. She understood
then the reason for his disappearance the day before. Some
twelve to fourteen feet deep, the shelter, though not more
than four feet high. Round the walls were things that
looked to Clair like paintings, but the light went then and
she could make nothing of them. The hunter motioned
her inside. He was standing against the sunset. It was very
still. She heard the beating of his heart and thought that
were the light clearer she might verily see that beating. . . .
Almost a shadow, some Titan threatener of the ancient gods,
against the coming threat of darkness. His black hair blew
softly in the wind. And Clair, sitting, rubbing her shapely,
surface-chilled self, remembered more Tennyson:

> 'Man, her last dream who seemed so fair,
>     Such splendid promise in his eyes —'

Man. Ærte. One and the same, here in the night that was
the morning of the world. And if she closed her eyes for a
moment she would see him hanging on the barbed-wire entanglements of a Mametz trench, hear again that moan that
shuddered still, undying, unceasing, in a night twenty-five
thousand years away: "Clair! *Oh, Clair!* . . ."

She had called him in then, startledly, her face quivering,
and he had come, and ceased to have any symbolical significance whatever, and had been merely the strange, dark
hunter, and again, of course, the lover. And, lying on the
verge of yet another abyssal descent to that place where
all colours and sounds merged in a harmony that God had
used as model when He painted the first rainbow, Clair had
thought, very practically: 'In a minute I shan't be able to
think at all, but just now, Oh, my good God, I *am* hungry!'

The thought and the fact of her hunger had returned,
however, as they sat again in that twilight, her arm round the
bare shoulder of the hunter. She told him in a slow murmur
of words of which he had no understanding, and he had
understood and brought from the back of the cavelet cooked
fish, several of them, wrapped in great leaves. She sat and
ate with great appetite, wiping her fingers in the grass, and
reflecting on the amount of germs she must be eating. . . .

Her world had been haunted by the wriggly shapes of germs, even as the world of the Middle Ages by devils.

Then she had found herself drowsy. So had been the hunter, untroubled by either germs or devils. They had lain together and from the cave recesses he had brought forward an unfamiliar skin; she was to discover in the morning it was a lion skin. It was warm 'if smelly'. The hunter lay athwart the entrance. He piled the skin round her, laid his head on her breast, kissed her there and was asleep in a moment.

But at that, somehow, sleep had gone from her. The cold had closed it, despite the hunter and her rug. She thought of Sinclair and Sir John, several miles away. Wondering about her? They would go back to the great cave sometime . . .

She abandoned that train of thought, hearing the soft coming of the rain. The volcano lights forty miles in the north seemed to spit and hiss through the intensity of the downpour. They drove not into the shelter, bright, splashing spear-heads as she saw them in the ghostly light. The hunter slept as lightly and soundly as a child.

A child. For that was what he was. So she had said of him and the others, and so they were. Lover! It was she who had abducted a boy. She was twenty thousand years older than this head that lay so close to her, and the hair that tickled and the shoulder grown chill and the hands that touched her. Behind her marched the bloody ghosts of all history; behind the ancestry of this golden boy beside her in the dark was nothing but long millennia of vivid, harmless lives, reaching back to the time when men were not yet men . . .

A child. Instantly the word had a different meaning for her. Her lips grew dry. Beyond Ærte was the rain-curtain. She reached out her hand to it. Damp and cool the fingers she brought to her lips. And already her startlement had passed.

A child.

She laid her head by that other in the darkness. She lay in quivering wonder, unafraid, on the brink of sleep. A child. Spring-time fields at night under the fall of the rain . . .

Wonderful thing if *that* should happen in some to-morrow of this dream!

CHAPTER IX:   SIR JOHN A PROPHET:   HIS PROPHECY

*Subchapter i*

IT did not rain the next day, nor the next. Instead, they burned with the vivid radiance of a Mediterranean summer; they burned their sights and sounds into the soul of Clair Stranlay. Each evening found her and the hunter back in the painted cavelet – an aurochs stood in challenging regard of a chrome-red lion in that cave, and Ærte was the artist – but nights and evenings were only so many jade beads on the golden garments of the suntime hours. Clair in those hours discovered the wonder of her own body as she discovered the wonder of the earth itself – as though it were a thing apart from her, yet no more apart than grass and trees and that aurochs' calling and the cry of a wounded deer. This body of hers! A stranger that was yet herself, one with whom she went out into mornings that changed from dull grey to amethystine clarity and a hold-your-breath silence, from that to a nameless stir and scurry and beat that brought the sun orange and tremendous above the Atlantean hills, pringling with warmth on chilled back and face, though one's feet, running in the grass, were chilled still. These, and the smell of the smoke from the fire kindled in the bright weather and drifting blue wavelets across the face of the hunter. Noon, and lying together in sunlight in a sunlight dream, with each pore of her skin hungrily drinking in that sun, and the smell, the chloric smell, of the crushed grass under her head. Crickets chorusing; it was a land of crickets. Sunset and the hasting homewards of bird and sun and cloud and themselves. These the background for hours such as neither she nor any of her century had ever lived.

But the second nightfall a troubled, brooding look came into the grave eyes of Ærte. He turned at the mouth of their shelter and pointed towards the plateau that with each falling of dusk kindled its volcano-torches to watchful brightness. He gestured ineffectively. He and Clair looked at each other dumbly in the dusk. Something —

And next morning they went out from the painted cavelet of sixty hours' residence, and Clair never saw it again. For that morning they went west before the sun, slowly, in no great hurry, yet with intention. Once they stopped to bathe in a lagoon from which they were evicted by the splashings and blowings of a great beast such as Clair had never seen before – a thing with a body like an unfortunate beer-vat, four stumpy legs, a hide that seemed to suffer from mildew and a head that was a bewildering confusion of teeth, tusks, horns and bosses. It splashed and paused and pawed, watching the bathers, and Clair felt the hunter tug at her hair. She turned, treading water, and followed him. Nor any too soon, for the multi-horned animal at that moment charged them from the bank with the speed of an express train and something of its whining uproar. Clair it missed by inches, but they were good as so many miles, for the beast's speed carried it into deep water where it floundered and squawked piercingly, evidently unable to swim. Its musk odour lay like a scum upon the water. Eyeing it, the hunter hefted his spear thoughtfully, and then shook a regretful head as it gained a sandbank and stood blowing and dripping there. Bogged, he would evidently have considered it a titbit.

"I'd sooner eat a goods-wagon," Clair told him.

She told him many a thing as unintelligible. She found it a saving necessity to keep herself in remembrance that a week before she had been Clair Stranlay, not a naked wanderer (albeit with a comely enough nudity, as the pools still told a disinterested survey) in a love-cycle with a savage through a land lost in the deeps of time. A savage! At that her laughter went up to the soaring circus of carrion birds gathered in haste to watch the shoreward meanderings of the ill-tempered monster. The hunter's contralto laugh joined in, shortly, his grey eyes upon Clair, and lighting as they were wont to do.

And suddenly, in the aurulent loveliness of the day, Clair felt sick with a strange, queer dread.

*Subchapter ii*

Sinclair saw their home-coming in the late afternoon of that third day. Sitting a little beyond and above the cave-mouths, peeling a long wand and binding either end of that wand with deer-gut, he saw them come. He paused at work and shaded his eyes with his hand. He swore, with the ancient outward mechanism of emotion that the days were indeed wearing to meaninglessness.

Clair Stranlay!

(Ten days before: *Magellan's Cloud*; passengers' gallery; a languid loveliness in an expensive frock, with painted lips and ironic, inquiring gaze . . .)

'Safe, anyhow.'

Safe they seemed. They came over the hills, the hunter pony-laden, Clair carrying his spear. She was a white slip-painting on an Athenian vase; in the blaze of the sun setting she saw the American and waved the Old Stone Age spear. He waved in reply and then returned to work on the peeled wand. He was almost alone at the cave-mouths, for of the mating couples who had taken to the hills, Clair and Ærte were the last to return.

They splashed through the river, stopping midway for Clair to lave the hunter from head to foot, for he was very warm, having killed the pony on the run only a few minutes before. Sinclair descended from his ledge.

"Hello, Keith!"

"Hello, Clair."

She found his stare impossible to meet. A slow wave of colour ebbed into her cheeks and passed across her breast. She thought: 'I *will* look at him,' and look at him she did, resolutely, then. His gaze passed over her shoulder. She leant on the spear, pleasantly tired and looked round for Ærte.

He also stood looking at Sinclair. And then a queer thing happened. A shadow came on his face; he seemed to flicker before Clair's eyes, to vanish. . . . Moved, of course. Slipped into the caves . . .

"Good God!"

Clair said, standing wiping herself with her hands, there being nothing else with which to wipe herself: "Why?"

"Your hunter. Where is he?" The American looked round about him in some puzzlement. "Sight of him with you makes me realize more than anything else the damnable impossibility of it all. Where did you go?"

She told him something of the two days. A boy came wandering out of the caves, saw her, gave a hail of welcome that brought out Zumarr and others. She stood in the midst of a laughing, friendly throng, unalien to them, as Sinclair realized, as she had never been to her own century. Clair Stranlay, the best-selling novelist, had shrugged aside the dream of civilization and come home to the welcome and understandability of an Atlantean cave!

Darkness was very near. Now the radiance from the cave fires stole out across sedge and savannah in pursuit of the hasting daylight. Returned, the hunters were singing in unison, and Sinclair heard their singing with voices from his childhood:

> "I followed my brother into the sun,
>     In the sunrise-time.
> And we crept beyond the place of the bear
>     Sleeping and sad and a foolish bear
> In the sunrise-time,
>     To the ridge where the wild horse run!
> Running and pawing and making their play
>     In the sunrise-time.
> And we lay and awaited, still as a deer
>     In a thicket at bay:
> Till the stallion came near with the mares
>     Of his choice
> In the sunrise-time.
>     And my brother slew with a blow of his spear
> The stallion red like the sun himself
>     In the sunrise-time.
> But I, I followed the mare that was grey
>     Swiftly out of the place of the ridge
>     Swiftly past the lair of the bear,
> The sleeping and sad and foolish bear,
>     In the sunrise-time,
> And we ran with the sun
>     Swift and swift and the mare was mine

*And I slew the mare with a blow of my spear*
*And I drank its blood and I warmed my hands*
*In the blood of the mare*
*In the sunrise-time."*

"What are they singing?" he heard an English voice.
He found Clair alone with him again. The others had
drifted back to the caves to join in that song. A chill wind
came down the Atlantean river.

"Singing? I suppose it is a song. About killing a horse."

"Filthy business. I helped Ærte to kill one."

"You helped at the same business before you met him.
Remember that little deer up on the plateau?"

Clair remembered. "And I thought we were in West
Africa. Instead —"

The instead was beyond speech. Sinclair looked across the
river. He said, abruptly:

"You and the hunter – I hope you've taken care there
won't be —?"

She stared at him, shook her head. "How could I – here?
Besides —"

She heard then a child wailing in the caves, one of the
innumerable children who could and did die so easily. She
shivered. But another thought had been with her throughout
the past two days, and she put it in words now, to herself
more than to Sinclair.

"I want one! We're here for life – however long our lives
may last. If we come through the winter we may live as
long as the average. . . . And we can alter things – we have a
doctor among us! – change things so that babies won't die so
readily. . . . Oh, I'll hate the bother of it. But I'll have one –
next spring."

"I wouldn't."

"I know."

She could not resist that. The Battersea imp was a
ghostly presence enough these days, but undead still. Sinclair
laughed shortly, straightening up where he sat, clasping his
hands behind his head.

"Listen, Miss Stranlay, we're here by such kind of
accident as probably never happened before. Twenty-five
thousand years or more before the birth of Christ. It means

hardly anything saying those words; but they have meaning. We're here, members of a tribal group that, for all we know, are the only human beings yet on earth. Certainly it's ancestral to the Cro-Magnards and half the modern population of Europe. And there is no Europe yet, there is no modern population." He spoke very slowly and casually.

"And if you have a baby and it lives and also has children – can you see the road they'll travel in the next twenty-five thousand years? This is the Golden Age of the human race. I don't know how long it will be before the Fourth Glacial time. Perhaps three thousand years. But it's coming, and by then the descendants of these people – the descendants of your baby – will have drifted across to the fringes of Europe. Through thousands and thousands of years they'll drift with all the chances of famine and starvation and mauling and killing by beasts that are Nature's chances, and may be shared by this baby of yours and its children, and endured because of the things between that will be like the happiness in the lives of these present hunters – like those two days you've spent with the hunter Ærte. But this life does not last for ever.

"In the Nile Valley, four thousand years before the birth of Christ, an accident is to transform the human race and human nature. Do you know that there will be descendants of yours whom they'll stretch out on sacrificial altars – babies of yours – and rip their hearts out of their chests? Do you know that babies of yours will be tortured in dungeons, massacred in captured cities, devoured at cannibal banquets? In Tyre they'll burn alive those children of yours inside the iron belly of Baal, Rome will crucify them in scores along the Appian Way. They'll chop off their hands in hundreds when Vercingetorix surrenders to Caesar. Can't you hear the chop-chop of that axe, and hear mounting down through the years the cry of agony from those children of yours that may so easily be? I can. I can close my eyes and hear the dripping of their blood."

So could Clair. "I never thought of that. Oh . . . horrible and terrible!" She covered her face. "Why did you tell me? Perhaps – *perhaps there were babies of mine who died on the barbed-wire there in France, who are starving in the London streets now, drowned in some awful Welsh mine. . . .*" She took her hands from her face. "But it's a lie. I don't believe this can ever end. Oh, Keith – help me —"

He did not move. He said to her, as she stood weeping: "Fantastic stuff we are, Miss Stranlay! Not you and I only. All the human adventure. . . . Here, on an autumn night in Atlantis. On the edge of an adventure that probably no other thing in the cosmos will ever attempt. . . ." He paused; he stood up with clenched hands. "By God, if we should ever get back!"

"Back?"

He laughed. "I still can't forget, still can't realize that this is reality for us. Of course there's no going back."

He stood beside her, silent. Clair's thoughts were a grey blur. There came a drift of laughter from the caves. It was as though they stood, an old man and woman, outside a children's playground. And then Clair knew some more immediate matter worrying her. She touched Sinclair's arm.

"I'd forgotten. Where is Sir John?"

*Subchapter iii*

Sir John Mullaghan lay wrapped in a long, dark skin that might have been a dyed sheepskin but for the fact that there were no sheep in the world where he lay dying. Clair, kneeling beside him, knew that he was dying, even as he knew it himself. His face, grimed and hirsute, as though it were the face of the one-time armaments manufacturer dead and dried and smoked in some head-hunter's hut, looked up at her and then suddenly shrivelled and then grew bloated in one of the spasms of pain that were unceasing.

The odour of that corner of the cave was horrible. But Clair knelt unhorrified. The din of the golden communal life was stilled about them – strange thing this prehistoric foreshadowing of long sickroom silences round many a bed of pain through many a thousand years! In the roof-spaces of the cave the great aurochs stood belling eternally, the mammoth walked the open plains with flailing trunk, the uiratherium strayed from his geological epoch still bunched in frozen charge. . . . Clair saw that the night had come down.

"I'm glad you're back safely, Miss Stranlay. Nice honeymoon?"

She smiled down at him, unsteadily. "Lovely."

"That's good." His grey head moved dimly, the words came staccato, as by an effort. "Unfriendly – if I'd gone – without waiting for your return."

"You're not going. It's just difference of food, Keith says. We'll hunt up berries and green stuff for you to eat. You'll be well as ever in a day or so."

"Sinclair didn't say that, I fear. I'm poisoned – very unpleasantly and thoroughly, and can't eat anything. All in all, a very shocking exhibit, Miss Stranlay." She saw the ghost of a smile. "Nature didn't design me for a caveman, I'm afraid. . . . You've come back in time. There is the rain again."

So it was. Thunderously. Suddenly, beyond the cave-rims, the cup of darkness cracked. Lightning played and shimmered in the interstices, filling the cave with echoes. Then the darkness closed again. Clair saw Sinclair standing beside them, kneeling beside them.

"Drink this, Mullaghan."

"What is it?"

"Herb broth. I found a hollow stone and have had it cooking the last two hours."

The grey head moved upwards painfully. Clair looked away. Then:

"Sorry, Sinclair, I'm afraid I can't."

"All right. Don't worry. I'll bring some water."

For a full minute after the American had gone he lay so silent that Clair thought he had fallen asleep. But he moved, again in pain. He chuckled, unexpectedly, surprisingly.

"The head of the League of Militant Pacifists acting as sick-nurse to an armaments manufacturer!"

"I'll help him now I'm back."

He spoke, but did not seem to answer her. "And Clair Stranlay, the pornographic novelist. But there are fine things in her, I think, though her books are the nonsense of the half-educated. Fine things in her, Merton, though she was born in a Battersea slum. Courage and honesty and a happy pessimism. . . . Her books? They are just such desperate, half-articulate, half-unconscious protestings as Sinclair's threats of sabotage and assassination. . . . The savages of civilization . . .

"'Savages!' My God, Merton, the fantastic nonsense we

have been taught! I lived in the midst of a Palaeolithic tribe twenty-five thousand years ago. Heroes and kindly women, kindly children all of them. And you have spent your life blackening the memory of them in your lectures and classes – and I have spent mine in murdering their descendants.

"I didn't *know* . . ."

He quivered. Clair put one hand on his forehead, the other under his neck.

"Sir John! Don't worry. None of us knew. Do sleep and don't worry."

He said, in a whisper: "We murdered her lover – a boy – on the barbed-wire outside Mametz. She told me. That was why she went away with the hunter that afternoon. Lost somewhere in the Atlantis hills . . ."

The night wore on. Sound of human voice in the great communal cave ceased but for those occasional whispers of clear-headed delirium. Once Ærte came and touched Clair questioningly, but she shook her head, and did not watch him go. Sinclair came and went continuously, with water which he boiled above the far, bright fire by the near entrance. Once he said to Clair:

"You can't do anything. You had better go and lie down."

"Not until he sleeps."

"Mr. Speaker, in moving support of this Bill for disarmament by example, I am aware that I am contradicting previous utterances of my own and taking a line of action in direct opposition to that pursued by the great party to which I belong, and to my own private interests. But I plead for my former attitude an ignorance of the essential nature of man as crass as any member of this House may ever have confessed to. I lived the scientific delusions of my age – strengthened as these delusions were by the act of a stray madman which brought a very bitter tragedy into my own life. . . . But the wreck of the airship *Magellan's Cloud* on the ancient continent of Atlantis and my experiences there in company with two other survivors, amongst primitive men who were our own ancestors – literally, sir, opened my eyes.

"I found no 'howling primordial beast'; I saw nothing to indicate that man is by nature a cruel and bloodthirsty animal. It became plain to me that the vicious combativeness of civilized man is no survival from an earlier epoch; it is a thing resultant on the torturing dreads of civilization itself. The famous Chinese poet and philosopher, Lao-Tze, writing of a Golden Age which has been considered mythical, yet describes in vivid detail the character and conduct of those Old Stone Age primitives among whom I lived during an eventful fortnight:

"'They loved one another without knowing that to do so was benevolence; they were honest and leal-hearted without knowing that it was loyalty; they employed the services of one another without thinking that they were receiving or conferring any gift. Therefore their actions left no trace and there was no record of their affairs . . .'"

The sound of the rain! Clair heard it rise gustily and drown in momentary volume of sound the speech that Sir John Mullaghan, remote in space and time was delivering to the English House of Commons. The helpless pity of the first hour of watching was past. In an unimpassioned clarity her mind went on with that speech, as though she also were addressing an unborn multitude in that future from which she had come, and which she would never see again. . . . *No Record?* Except that somehow Zumarr and Ærte and Belia, each and all of them sleeping here in this wild night, were to live through the ages, to pass undying through them, to rise again in the Christs and Father Damiens, the Brunos and the Shelleys, the comradeship and compassion of the slave-pit and the trench. No record! They were to live though all else died; they were ghosts of a sanity that haunted mankind.

This adventure in pre-history! As if any woman whatever who had loved a man and been by him loved, known him in the intimate hours when the tabus passed and he lived as man indeed – as if she did not know the true nature of the kindly child immortal, though cult and environment twisted his mind and instincts, though press and pulpit shouted that he was by nature a battling animal, a sin- and cruelty-laden monster! What slum-dweller did not know his neighbour a peaceable man unless one of civilization's innumerable diseases drove him to momentary madness . . .?

She started drowsily, sleep pressing on her eyelids. Sir John talking or herself thinking? She heard him then, his voice clear and sharp:

"Gentlemen, we must transform our factories to other

purposes. There are still bridges to be built and tunnels to be excavated. Flying machines. . . . We have barely glimpsed the universe in which man adventures, yet you and I have sat in this room and planned murder and destruction and called it business and patriotism . . ."

He murmured a phrase: "The Militant Pacifists . . ." Then: "Sinclair? We will have him on our board."

Sinclair came tiredly through the red-ochred mirk at that moment, and again held water to dim lips. All the cave was as some gigantic Akkadian sarcophagus; it seemed to Clair, as once before, that it was a place of the long-dead in which she knelt, and overhead washed the Atlantic. . . . Sir John said, very distinctly:

"Miss Stranlay – I thought she was here?"

"So she is. Here she is."

He peered up at them, his eyes very bright. "I've been dreaming – that next war. You two – promise me you'll get back, get back and tell them!"

"We'll get back," Sinclair said, steadily.

"You *must* get back. They're planning it again. . . . Tell them, Sinclair. Fight them even with your bombs if they won't listen. . . . They *shall* listen. For there was hope even in that age out of which we came – more hope than ever before since civilization began. Else we could never have dreamt this dream, we three who are its children. The slaver and the soldier passes and Man will walk the earth again . . ."

He began to speak in a low, singing voice, so low that Clair had to bend nearer to hear him:

> "*The world's great age begins anew,*
> *The golden years return,*
> *The earth doth like a snake renew*
> *Her winter skin outworn:*
> *Heaven smiles, and faiths and empires gleam*
> *Like wrecks of a dissolving dream . . .*"

Clair felt the American's hand on her shoulder in the ensuing silence. He gave a sigh of relief.

"He's sleeping now. We can take it easy. If you're as dead-beat as I am – Hell, what was that?"

CHAPTER X: EXODUS

*Subchapter i*

IT was as though a great beast stirred in dreams under the floor of the cave. Clair was instantly on her feet beside the American. She saw it was close to dawn; the river glimmered beyond the fires. The watcher of the fires himself squatted not far away, nodding, undisturbed, though the faintest rustle of a nearing beast would have roused him to instant activity.

Clair whispered: "What was it?"

"Remember back beside the lake? Some kind of earthquake shock. . . . Here it is again."

The cave rocked. They held to each other for a moment. The shock passed. Clair peered past the drowsy fire-watcher. "These people must be used to it. None of them have wakened."

Not a hunter or a woman had stirred. They lay and slept in healthy disregard of the earth's freakish moods.

The fires burned low, yet glowed enough to show the painted uiratherium still bunched with head eternally lowered. Funny to think that that beast ('at this moment!') in the twentieth century might still survive in this cave long sunk two miles or more below the level of the ocean! . . . The thought made Clair whisper another question:

"Wasn't this continent sunk in an earthquake?"

She saw a pallid flicker of a smile on Sinclair's face. "*Will* be. . . . Let's see if anything's happening outside."

The fire-tender nodded to them. They paused at the cave-entrance and looked out. Nothing. The rain had cleared away. The sky was pallid with the waning lights of the stars awaiting the morning. The crispness of the air caught at their throats. But there was also in that air an unusual quality.

"Sulphur," said Sinclair. "Stay here. I'm going out to look."

He vanished, tall and white, into that waiting unease of the morning. Clair thought: 'Dictatorial still. But a dear.' Yawned. 'Oh, my good God, what wouldn't I give for a cup of tea!'

Startling thought! Years, surely, since she had visioned such wistful amenities! . . . She yawned again. 'Thank goodness Sir John's asleep at last. . . . Eaough!'

She became aware of a pillared whiteness, like Lot's wife, against the remoter greyness of the morning. It was Sinclair, beckoning.

The grass was wet and cold. The morning wind blew chill on their unclad bodies as they passed together outside the furthest flow of the cave-fires' radiance and climbed over the smooth back of the bluff. And, as they did so, the smell of sulphur increased with every step they took. Nearing the top of the bluff, Clair, loking upwards, suffered a curious optical illusion. It seemed to her that the grass on the knoll, that the whole summit, was lighted to an unwonted glow, as though a great fire were kindled on the other side. But, the summit attained, she saw she had suffered from no delusion. She gasped and stared.

In that hour they should have seen but a little way across the jumble of foothills and nullahs towards the mountain land from which they had descended a short week before. Instead, all that landscape which should have lain in morning darkness was lighted uneasily, a welter of unstable candle-points of flame, and backgrounding it, mile on mile, from one end of the horizon to the other, was a dark-red glow that glimmered and faded and grew to purple being and then died again, yet never quite, like a fire that lives in a half-charred stick. Momentarily, as they watched, the red and ochre faded from the glow, yet that was through no waning of its strength, as they saw, but with the coming of the morning. And with that coming the mystery grew plainer. The whole of the dim mountain-land of their first adventures had vanished into some fissure of the earth from which now arose the corona of its destruction. Twenty miles away to the north the vivid line of flame stalked the horizon, and in the nearer distance they saw a pale advancing gleam.

"Floods – it's the sea!" said Clair.

Sinclair peered forward from beneath his hands. "Hell, and it is! We'll have to run for it."

But he did not. He said, a second later: "It's advancing no longer. Only through the light growing it seems to be. The floods have stopped."

So it seemed, now. Daylight was almost upon the land, and the havoc of fire and water grew clearer. The sea had come far in – in places it was not more than two or three miles distant. More than that. They stood now on what was a great promontory, for this was higher land than to east and west. And, advancing out of the water-threatened, cobalt valleys were long trains of moving objects that ran and squealed and jostled. Clair saw them coming, up out of the morning, dipping and rising, here and there covering the hills in dun hordes.

"Trek of the animals," said Sinclair. "Look – the mammoths!"

A great herd of them led the exodus. They came at racing speed, great tusks uplifted, trunks uplifted, untrumpeting, with flying coats of dun red hair. They thundered past not half a mile away. Then Clair saw her first aurochs, also running in herds, the gigantic beasts whose lowing she had listened to many a time since that first night by the lake. Horned and maddened, with belching breaths of spume they ran, swinging round the corner of the bluff so that Sinclair, seeing the danger there might be to the cave-dwellers below, turned and ran down the hill, calling to Clair to stay where she was. Safest place. . . . Clair sank down in the wet grass, staring appalled. It was as though the hills were the contours of a wet corpse, hideously, titanically be-magotted.

"Oh, horrible!"

The hills drummed with flying hoofs. Great deer, an Irish elk, a pack of lions like loping St. Bernards, here and there a trundling bear. Then herd on herd of ponies, with manes in quivering serration. The day brightened, and with its brightening the glow in the north abruptly flickered and vanished. The pulsing flight of beasts thinned, but the birds still passed overhead in great flocks, tern and snipe and partridge either momentarily startled or out on definite migration through the weaving of some mysterious instinct. Up till then no animal had attempted the scaling of the bluff, but now two leopards did so. Sly and suave, they came in loping bounds, not greatly frightened, evidently, though in flight. One had been swimming, and the water glistened on its sleek black coat. They slithered leftwards at sight of the kneeling woman. Then one crouched and snarled —

The charge of the brute rolled her on the ground. It had charged, not leapt, being over-hungry, and had hit her with its shoulder, instead of pinning her to the earth. Its body sprawled across her, furry and musk and smelling vilely of the cat-house. She thought vividly: 'My throat!' and screamed, and saw the other leopard looking away, with pricked ears. She caught the wurring muzzle of the brute above her. Screamed again. Thereat, unaccountably, it vomited blood all over her. She was dragged to her feet by Ærte. She wiped her face; she laughed hysterically.

All over in a minute. Three of the hunters, Ærte included, had seen the leopards and raced them up the opposite side of the hill. She saw Sinclair ascending more slowly, now that she was safe. Ærte laughed. She could not look at the smoking, furred thing on the ground. The other leopard had fled.

When Sinclair came up she was still trembling, as in the throes of a fever.

"Goodness – I – always did hate cats. Never bathe. . . . Silly to shake, but I can't stop it. I think I'll go down to Sir John."

Sinclair looked at her apathetically; sat down. She was safe; the caves were safe. He felt he wanted to sleep for a month.

"Sir John is dead," he said tiredly.


*Subchapter ii*

The sun lay brave on the hillside. The day marched bannered across the Atlantean sky. Little clouds tinged with purple went sailing by, free and very fleecy and lovely. More of the bird-flocks came from the north, holding into dim southern regions of the Pleistocene earth. Far below, in the open spaces between the caves and the river, the

Cro-Magnards cut up the meat which had come, alive and maddened, past their doors in such abundance.

And on the hill-brow Clair and Sinclair watched the passing of the day. Clair lay with her breasts to the earth, thinking, and yet trying not to think. She raised her face once, looking at the American.

"But it can't be! He can't have died. We don't belong here; it couldn't have happened this way in time! Else he was dead long before he was born. This would have happened to him before we knew him. Before the *Magellan* was wrecked he was dead." She giggled a little and dropped her head on the grass again.

"We've been talking to a corpse all this last fortnight."

Sinclair said nothing, bleakly. Clair, exhausted, dozed. Later, she felt a hand on her shoulder, and aroused to Sinclair speaking at last:

"I won't leave you long. Shout if anything comes near."

"Where are you going?"

But he had gone. She sat, clasping her knees, sun-warmed, earth-kissed, vividly aware of the beauty and pleasure of her body. And below, in the Cro-Magnard caves, was that other body, finished with this and the sun and the rain and the hearing of laughter for ever. Impossibly dead in an impossible country in an impossible epoch. She remembered, numbedly, half-forgotten things about him – his courteous care of her, and her flouting of it, in that march across the plateau; his pathetic adaptations to Cro-Magnard ways. . . . 'Oh, my good God, I am *so* tired!'

She looked back over the bluff. Sinclair and two hunters, burdened, were coming up. A few feet from Clair they halted. One of the hunters was Ærte.

They lowered something to the ground.

Next instant she found Ærte beside her. He put his arms round her. He laughed, gravely, and pointed down to the river in the sunlight. His brows knitted puzzledly as she shook her head and indicated the body wrapped in the pelt from the cave. He glanced at it indifferently, smiled again, and tried to pull her to her feet. She shook him off; his touch was suddenly as shuddersomely repulsive as that of an unclean animal.

"Keith – *send him away.*"

She did not look round again as the American spoke to the two hunters, but she heard the sound of a lingering, puzzled retreat through the low, brittle grass. Then the noise of Sinclair digging with a hand-axe. At that she rose and went and helped him. They worked in silence.

"Stand away, Miss Stranlay."

She stood aside and looked down over the flood-sodden lands. Already the darkness waited for them. She heard Sinclair dragging the body to the shallow pit. Then a sound of scraping and the fall of earth. Sinclair said:

"Throw some earth, Miss Stranlay."

She turned round, seeing the grave almost completed. She picked up a handful of clayey dust and dropped it through her fingers. Sinclair replaced the turfs and walked over them, stamping them gently.

Then he held out his hand to Clair and she went to him.

*Subchapter iii*

It seemed to her that something had numbed her body and brain alike, through and through, in the next twenty-four hours. The second nightfall Sinclair came and sat down beside the fire of Zumarr, who glanced at him questioningly and from him towards another fire at which the hunter Ærte had again taken up quarters, as in times before the Mating for the Dark Days.

"Clair."

She roused a little. "Oh, it's you, Keith."

He stretched himself out beside her. His square, dark head was oddly similar to Zumarr's. She thought apathetically: "They might be brother and sister." He put a twig on the fire, absently, scowlingly, as was his habit, and watched it consume. Abruptly he said:

"This can't go on, you know."

She said, dully: "What?"

He seemed to be considering his answer. Then:

"These people aren't to blame, Clair, but you. I mean your hunter and the others when they thought Mullaghan's death and dead body of no account. Neither, really, were they. Death *is* of no account in fundamental human values –

the things these people live by. Your hunter saw a man lying dead – one to whom he had never talked, a puzzling stranger, a man who had presumably lived to the full, and was now dead, as was the order of things. And if your hunter thought about it at all, it was simply that he himself would also die some time, but meantime there was living to be done – eating, and sleeping with you, and painting his pictures, and hunting, and every moment in which to live his body before he also was dead. That was all. It was perfectly natural."

"I know. And it has made me sick and frozen."

"It has no cause to make you any such things. If he'd seen Sir John lying ill or wounded he'd have carried him miles to safety. You know he would. They are absolutely unselfish and absolutely natural. Nothing horrible in death to them; there *is* nothing horrible in death. It is merely that you and I are laden down with the knowledge of that past that is not yet – with all the obscene funeral rites in our memory and that ritual of sorrow that isn't natural at all, but was an artificial thing foisted on human nature in a matter of mistaken science. It is these people who are clean and you who are diseased."

"I know," Clair said again. And suddenly she found words. "Oh, Sinclair, I'll go mad, I know I will, in this horrible place, among these horrible people! Natural and clean? Of course they are. Splendid and shining and lovely, all of them. Ærte – he's been my lover and is closer to my life than the blood in my body. . . . And they're not kin to me at all. I'm separated from them by a bending wall of glass. I'm not human if they are. I'm the diseased animal, and it's not the winter or the memory of Sir John that'll kill me. It's realization of a fact. I can't go on with it, I *can't*!"

"You filthy little weakling."

He said it in a low, even voice. Clair suddenly found herself in the cave. Something seemed to cataract and then clot about her heart. She stared at the American. He looked at her evenly.

"You little gutter-slut of the London slums! I thought you had guts in you. You haven't. You've a pious, rotten romanticism that's no relation to reality. Think I don't know – that I haven't watched your antics ever since I was fool enough to drag you out of the *Magellan*? And I *was* a fool; I fooled myself about you. Here, especially. I thought this place and these people had done to you what they did to me and poor Mullaghan – discovered the human in you. But there wasn't a human to discover. You're only a sack of second-rate opinions and third-rate fears. Human! A thing like you!—"

Clair shook herself and leant forward to the fire and also put a twig on it. Then she laughed and gave a long sigh, and, looking at Sinclair, shook her head.

"Thanks. But it's really not necessary. . . . Or not now."

He flushed, suddenly, darkly. "I thought it might work."

"It has, in a way." She raised her head and looked across the cave towards Ærte's fire. "Goodness. . . . Sorry I've been all you said."

"You haven't of course. . . . But I need help as well, Clair. All this stuff I talked – about the naturalness of regarding death casually – I know as well as you do that it's impossible for us, just as it's impossible for us ever to live the lives of these hunters. I know that wall of glass as well. . . . But Mullaghan's gone, and if you went and I were left on my own – I also don't want to go mad . . ."

Clair said, soberly: "I'm both sick and sorry. Oh, I'm damnably selfish." She held out her hand. "I don't think we've ever been friends. Can't we be?"

He held her hand a moment. She thought: 'Funny how like his eyes are to someone's —' He said: "This is the last night in these caves."

She was startled. "Why?"

"You haven't heard, of course. They've left you alone, thinking you're sick. But the exodus was decided on this afternoon. There's no game anywhere in the flooded country round about, nor anywhere to the south as far as the hunters have penetrated. That earthquake and the sinking of the mountain-land has left this section a deserted peninsula. The cave is going to be abandoned to-morrow."

"And where are they going?"

"Southwards, somewhere, in pursuit of the game. And it's not the threat of famine, of course. You haven't noticed, not being outside the cave. But there was frost this morning; the new lagoons, half salt at that, were covered with ice. It'll be a winter of such terrors as these people have never endured – at least as far north as this."

Clair looked at the painted animals overhead. "And they're to leave. . . ." It seemed that she herself had occupied these caverns for months. Then: "We knew that this happened in pre-history, of course – or will happen. . . . Goodness, tenses do get mixed in the time-spirals. . . . Is this the coming of the Ice Age?"

"I don't think so. It's just that Atlantis is the most unstable of the continents. That, of course, we know from the future out of which we've come. It's doomed."

"And these people?"

"They're the ancestors of the Cro-Magnards from Cro-Magnon in France, remember. So some of them at least are to push eastwards, and some years or generations hence strike Europe. Or at least, that preceded the future in which we lived."

"Isn't it bound to happen, then?"

"Not necessarily. Perhaps the future we came from was one of many possible futures —"

She leant forward in excitement. "I thought that – once – but I'd forgotten."

"There was nothing fixed and real about that twentieth century of ours, Clair. Civilization as we knew it – it has still to happen. Perhaps it need never happen. Perhaps we can prevent it, sabotage it in advance —"

It had grown dark again. The Cro-Magnards were turning to sleep. The evening was frostily clear and set with frosty stars. Clasping her knees and looking out as she listened to Sinclair, Clair thought of Sir John Mullaghan. "*Think but one thought of me up in the stars* —" said a vagrant line. . . . She turned her attention to the American.

"There is no need for the processes of history, as we knew them, ever to take place. You and I can alter the very beginnings. Listen! We're going south, and it will get warmer. Somewhere beyond the southwards mountains we saw from the plateau these people will find new hunting-grounds. Then you and I can get to work. We can teach them the beginnings of civilization without any of civilization's attendant horrors."

"What, for example? I'm horribly ignorant."

He shook his head. "It's just that you don't realize what you know. Pitchers – they've never thought of using gourds

to store water at night. That for a beginning. Then in hunting:
I'm engaged in making a bow. But these are the lesser things.
Somewhere beyond those southwards mountains we'll find
a river and wild millet or barley or corn. We can start the first
agriculture – ploughing and seeding will be simple enough.
That for next spring. And in the summer get them to build
a corral and drive wild cattle into it; they can tame them in
a few years. Next autumn take a party prospecting in the
mountains – I know something about metals. . . . Flax or
hemp growing, perhaps. Even with crude metal implements
and rough fibre bandagings I could save half the women who
die in childbirth. And iodine and suchlike are easy enough
extracts. . . . We can leap twenty thousand years and take
these people with us if we plan it carefully. Preserve this
sane equality that's theirs, take care that no idea of gods or
kings or devils ever arises in their minds. We can transform
humanity."

Clair began to kindle to his words. If they could! "But –
aren't the cruelties and the tabus bound to rise with civilization? Better to leave our hunters alone for the Golden Age
that is still theirs than try and fail."

"We won't fail. Much better to leave them if there was
any chance of failure. If there was no choice for the future
but history as we know it, a thing inevitable awaiting these
people, it would be better for them and better for the world if
we poisoned them all or drove them to death by starvation.
But there's no reason why we should fail. The foul things of
civilization were an accident. . . . Time and history will go on
long after we're dead here in Atlantis, Clair, but there need
never be a pyramid built or a city massacred or a war or a
miners' strike. We can re-make the world."

"Goodness, we will! . . . Keith, there's Gloezel!"

"Eh?"

"Don't you remember reading about it a few years back?
That place in France where heaps of Neolithic relics were
dug up, and were said to be fakes because they were mixed
with modern-looking bottles and jars and the scratchings of a
primitive alphabet? . . . Perhaps this experiment we're going
to try was known to us already in that twentieth century
from which we came! Perhaps Gloezel saw the end of this
plan of yours, and men of those days forgot your teachings,

and the civilizations and the savageries rose in spite of the dream we brought these hunters."

Sinclair laughed and stood up. "Perhaps there have been other voyagers into time than you and I. Perhaps time and history cannot be altered. Yet if they can —"

Somewhere in the depths of the caves a sick child was crying. He stood and listened to it and then looked down in Clair's fire-bright face.

"There need never be a lost baby crying again in the world that we can make."

And with that he left her, and Clair lay down, and saw him stride into the far shadows, and a hunter rouse and look after him. For a moment she hesitated, and a shudder as of nausea passed through her. Then she raised her head and called.

"Ærte!"

So it was that Sinclair, coming back to lie down by his own fire after tending that crying child, saw the hunter and Clair, the lovers for the dark days, asleep in each other's arms.


*Subchapter iv*

And next day the Cro-Magnards of that nameless valley in Atlantis left the fires in the painted caves still burning, and gathered their children and their implements and the skins of the beasts they had killed in generations of hunting, and forded the river, and turned to the south. The rain cleared, and a cold sun shone, and far in the north the new lakes shivered in a brisk wind. They passed through a deserted country, with not even birds in it. They passed out of the Atlantean valley as dream-people pass from a dream dreamt by a drowsy fire. Coming from the east or west hundreds of years before, their ancestors, a people with a no-history of millennia, descendants of the dawn-men who lived in Java and Peking and the Sussex downs, had descended upon the valley, a place of good hunting, and settled there. And the years had passed in the flow and ebb of death and love and birth, times of plenty and times of famine, with neither memory of the past nor fears nor hopes for the future. The sun and the wind, the splendour of simple things, had been theirs; theirs that Golden Age that was to live for ever, a wistful thing in the minds of men. Now they were out on an adventure that followed no road Clair Stranlay could foreplot.

They carried their sick and their aged with them, and they went gaily enough, with laughter and singing, the young men stringing out far in advance across the southern savannahs. They went in no great order, but a friendly southwards drift. Alone perhaps of them all Clair and Sinclair stopped and looked back.

"There will be fishes swimming in that cave years hence," said Clair.

"Poor Mullaghan!"

And that was strange enough to think of also. Thousands of years away, perhaps preserved uncorrupted and incorruptible by the pressures of water and rock, the body of Sir John Mullaghan would lie in that grave they had dug for it with the flint spears of Cro-Magnard hunters. The knoll glimmered.

"And now —" said Sinclair.

So they too turned about and went, their white bodies strange phenomena still in the wake of the golden men of the dawn. The savannahs rose green and brown and cobalt in the distance. Far and remote beyond these, many days' journeyings away, were the mountains where Sinclair planned to change the course of history.

Behind, the winter followed on their tracks.

# BOOK II

## WHENCE?   WHITHER?

*If I have been extinguished, yet there rise*
*A thousand beacons from the spark I bore.*

– SHELLEY

CHAPTER I:   CLAIR LOST

*Subchapter i*

CLAIR Stranlay was lost.

She looked back, shading her eyes with her hand against the pale afternoon sunlight, to the track she had taken across the withering grass to this eminence in the southern foothills. But all the country was desolate and deserted, except by a far loch where curlews called and called. Nothing moved or took to itself animate being in that still land, with the forests marching on its fringes and the sun – silver, not gold at all – brooding upon the quietness. Up that track she had come. But before that?

She sat down to consider the matter. There was the forest. But which forest? The country was ribbed with just such masses of trees, and the rise and fall of nullahs confused all knowledge as to whether one mass was a separate entity or the winding continuation of another. . . . Goodness, such a fool not to watch the course of the sun!

"I'm shockingly hungry," said Clair, aloud.

The silent countryside took no notice. Clair pushed her hair from her eyes and stood up again. It would be nonsensical to rest now. Somewhere, from higher up, she would be bound to see the hunters or the encampment.

She climbed through grass that was sedgy because of a trickle of water from the hillside. A ridge, like the scales on the back of a stegosaurus, ran along its summit. Here the grass gave place to lichened rock – granite rock, she noted, and red granite at that. The sight brought back a memory – oh, holiday bathing at Peterhead in Scotland, of course. Twenty-five thousand years before.

The red slivers cut her feet, hardened though these had grown. But at last, though with some difficulty, she attained a platform-ledge that dominated all the hill and indeed all the country. Panting, she looked again into the north.

Made miniature in distance, the land was otherwise unchanged. No sign of the Cro-Magnards or their encampment
anywhere.

If she made a fire —

Realization of a startling fact chilled her a little. She had
nothing with which to make a fire. She glanced down at
the short-bladed flint spear in her hand. Flint. But no iron
pyrite. The hunters used tinder and a drum-stick – things she
was incapable of operating. No chance of raising a fire. Must
watch for one instead.

For how long? She looked at the sun. Perhaps three
hours more of daylight. She turned round, slowly, in a circle,
looking about her. So, very suddenly, she became aware at
last of the mountains of the south.

From her stance, and for the first time in the southwards
trek she saw them uprise plainly. Not only so, but gigantic.
They filled all the southern horizon with their tumbled
shapes. Distant, Andean, some trick of refraction allowed her
to see the sun filtering into immense canyons, splashing in
remote upland tarns, crowning each point with quicksilver.
The significance of that last gleam dawned on her.

'Snow.'

They were perhaps twenty miles away. From right to
left of the horizon they stretched unbroken, tenebrous and
question-evoking. Were they passable?

She thought: 'Keith's plan to take the hunters south of
them – he may never be able to carry it out. Necessary to
try out our experiment on a southwards river, protected by
mountains in the north. . . . Wonder what he's doing now?
Missed me? Sure to.'

She had an afterthought, and smiled at it, absently. 'And
Ærte as well, I suppose.'

How far away, both of them? Miles and miles, surely.
Goodness, what a fool —

But thinking that wouldn't help.

It was nine days since the beginning of their trek from the
ancient cave. Acting on the apparently casual suggestion of
Sinclair, the Cro-Magnards had held as directly southwards
as the nature of the country allowed. It was to them a matter
of indifference what direction was taken, so long as game
grew more plentiful. And certainly neither to left nor right

was there that plentitude. But one colony of lions the general exodus of the animals had left behind, and on the fifth night of the trek these beasts, made bold by hunger, had raided the camp, a score or more of them. Clair and Sinclair had been awakened by the screams and shouts, and stirred to see a fire geyser under the impact of a lion landing from a misdirected spring. Clair had caught up a torch and thrust it into the face of one brute. Near her Zumarr had been killed and nearly disembowelled by the stroke of a huge paw. The fighting in the semi-darkness about the fires had gone on for many minutes. Then the lions had retreated, dragging several bodies with them. Devouring these, they had squatted all night in a semi-circle beyond the fires, evidently determined not to abandon the neighbourhood of this store of food which had descended on their famished land from the north. Sinclair had gone about, binding up such wounds as grass and sinew seemed capable of salving. Ærte had come to Clair and crouched by her, looking towards the noise of the lions' grisly banqueting and gripping a spear in either hand. Then, towards the dawn, the Cro-Magnards had begun to move out towards the lions, discovering them replete and somnolent, all but two or three cubs which had had little share of the human meat. Out there, beyond the camp, a running fight began, three men and more to one beast, until the morning came. Half a dozen or so of the lions escaped. The rest, dead, were skinned, and the Cro-Magnards cooked and ate meat from their haunches. Both Clair and Sinclair had refused it.

Throughout the next day and the next, holding south again, no game at all had been encountered. Food was growing very scarce, and the half-dozen lions, made cautious, but still hungry, followed up the trek, roaring despondently at night-time but venturing on no more raids. But, on the morning of this day on which Clair sat lost on the summit of her hill, a boy, slipping out of the camp in the early hours on some boyish foraging of his own, had wandered for several miles and then returned in a glow and much excitement. The lions had vanished from about the camp, and he knew the reason. A herd of mammoth, many bulls and cows and three young ones, was gathered feeding near a stream and a hill.

The news had emptied the camp, at racing speed, of the golden men. Clair had caught up a flint spear and ran by

Sinclair's side, the spear a thrilling complement. "Though goodness only knows what for. Unless to tickle the mammoths. . . . What, for that matter, are any of us going to do with spears against a mammoth?"

"Ærte was telling me," Sinclair had said. "We'll drive one of the animals into the river and attack it there."

So they had done. One bull, perhaps the leader of the herd, had charged the yelling attack of the Cro-Magnards, a magnificent spectacle of wrath with uplifted trunk and threatening tusks. Him they had allowed to pass without casualty, and, once past, he had stood a moment meditating discretion or valour, and then taken to the open land and safety. The others, all but the selected two, had followed him. Driving those twain into the river was the task. Under the urge of a hail of stones one of them at length galumphed forward into the muddy embrace of the waters and sank to the knees and was held there, like a fly in glue. And, as by so many hornets, hewing and stabbing, he had been instantly assailed. Not so the second. It had broken away to the right, trampling several hunters underfoot and impaling one on a great broken tusk. Sinclair had taken abrupt command, his dour face flushed; perhaps the first commander in the world, for even in hunting parties the Cro-Magnards had no leaders. They were an orchestra without a conductor, yet a fairly efficient one at that, acting with a serene co-operativeness that suggested to Clair telepathy. But, under the direction of Sinclair's shout, such of them as had already attended the panicked antics of the second mammoth broke into two parties. One raced for the hills, the other held in the track of the beast. Clair had joined the first group, and ran with them, feeling in a very glow of health, and had slipped and fallen; and had laughed and scrambled to her feet and reclaimed her spear. Then she had found herself alone and lost.

As simply as that. For a time she had heard receding shoutings and once a wild trumpeting of agony that made her cover her ears. She had made in the direction of both sounds, as she believed. Neither could be more than half a mile distant. And no sign of hunters or hunted had met her eyes. She had found herself in a series of low valleys, one fitting into the other with the suave necessity of shallow boxes in a Chinese puzzle. And when finally she had emerged from the labyrinth into open country again, it was a country of which she had no knowledge. No river was in sight, other than one glistening far across the savannah. It had seemed too distant to be the one where the first mammoth had been killed, and she had disregarded it and searched in other directions. And when she would have sought for it again it had disappeared.

She had wandered the deserted Atlantean country since then, once stopping to drink at a pool, once finding a nest with three eggs in it, curious speckled eggs which she had broken and eaten raw, very thankful that they were fresh. She had even thought of the curate's egg while doing so, and laughed, feeling refreshed. Then she had hunted on again.

And this seemed the day's end of the hunt.

Bound to follow her. But could they? With a certain uncertainty gripping her she turned now from survey of the gigantic bastion in the south, and looked at the country out of which she had climbed. They had no dogs, they had no special scent themselves; scent was nothing to primitive man, was probably a later acquirement of specialized savages. She would have to wait until darkness and then look for the light of a fire somewhere down there. And food —

Beyond her hill, eastwards, was another, and between the two of them a gleam of water. She realized the thirst parching her throat, and began to descend from the scaled back of the granite stegosaurus. The sun flung her a long shadow eastwards as she walked, but it was only as she neared the foot of the hill and the water was near that she saw a mist was rising or descending from nowhither. Between her and the distant, nameless Andes the undulating, sparsely-forested land was sheathed in an uneasy garment of damp wool. By the time she had knelt and drunk and stood up again, the mist was all about her. She stood in uncertainty of it, walked a few steps, halted, determined to climb her hill again. But the hill had disappeared. Or rather the hill-summit had.

Now she walked along a rolling shoulder of earth that was either of the original eminence, or of that second hill she had seen in the east. A tickling sensation disturbed her chest; then her nose. Abruptly she began to sneeze, desperately. She sought for a handkerchief she did not possess. The fit passed in a moment but not the constricted feeling in her throat. She thought, dismayed: 'Goodness, if I'm in for a cold!'

She came to another tarn. It reflected her face and body as her feet touched the edge. She leant on her spear and looked down at herself.

'Pretty thing still,' she said, and rubbed her chill arms and flanks, still regarding herself. A woman had come into the water and looked up at her gravely, from under a heavy, short-cut mane of brown hair with the red slightly bleached from it. But the red tints were still in eyes and brows, and her face had a brownness set on it evenly, as though out of a jar. So indeed her whole body was tinted, yet in some fashion that left it none the less white. Rubbed to warmth, she picked up the spear again, and, leaving that reflection of herself to dream of her for ever, perhaps, in that lost pool, went on into a mist that presently cleared, like a curtain drawn aside, to disclose the splendours of the sunset on the Atlantean Alps. They changed and took separate form and advanced and retreated as she looked, like a company of warriors in gold and grey and the panoply of war.

With purple from the murex the sunset had garbed them, and with the red of rust, and a blue – an ultramarine blue that must have found its colours in those high, glacial snows. ... Clair had never seen such a sunset, and the stalking approach of darkness at her lower level was almost upon her before she noticed it. With that darkness came a bitter coldness and a wind that seemed somehow dissociated from the cold, but cold itself . . .

And suddenly Clair knew that she was being tracked.

The beast had snuffled in a peculiar way. She wheeled round and saw nothing. Then – a hump of rock she had not noticed when she passed that way. It was not a hump of rock. The beast was crouching. There was not light enough for its eyes to gleam, she saw merely the dim shape, hunched, and the twitching of its ears. She thought: 'Is it going to spring?'

She turned round and went on. The padding came on as well. This time she wheeled so rapidly that she saw the beast, not crouching this time, but on its feet, its ears still twitching.

*And it was not a beast!*

*Subchapter ii*

To Clair it seemed that she stood and faced the thing through minute after minute of horror-struck silence. The spear was gripped and useless in her hand, for the blood had deserted her hand. It grew momentarily darker, in wave on wave of lapping shadow from the sunset fire in the mountains of the south. And still Clair Stranlay stood and stared wide-eyed at that hideous apparition out of pre-history.

It was a male, with the bigness of a gorilla and something of its form. It was hung with dun-red hair; crouched forward, its shoulders were an immense stretch of arching muscle and bone. Its gnarled hands almost touched the ground. It smelt. It stared at her filmily, and a panting breath of excitement came from its open jaws.

A Neanderthaler!

The thought flashed through her mind and was instantly disputed and dismissed. For the thing had an immense bulge of forehead and no downwards-pressing neck constriction such as she had read the lost race of Neanderthal possessed. Nor had it a single implement or weapon about it. It crouched, a strange, strayed, hungry, pitiful beast, looking at her. What it was she did not know, was never to know, that member of some lost, discarded genus of sub-men that time was utterly to annihilate. Lost as herself she suddenly realized it was, and with that realization blood came back to her hand. She raised the spear and shouted, "Shoo!"

The thing, half in sitting posture though it was, sprang back a full yard, and then, as Clair, desperately afraid, made at it, turned and shambled off in a rapid baboon-like scrabble. And as it went it uttered a strange moaning cry, growing louder and louder as the body behind the voice receded and finally vanished into the evening. Clair, sobbing hysterically, no sooner saw it out of sight than she turned in her original direction and ran and ran, slipping and falling over rocks and once becoming desperately entangled in a soft and hairy bush which seemed to grasp at her with clammy hands. When finally she stopped, panting, there was no echo of that moaning ululation to be heard in the deserted hills, nor any sign of her stalker.

The running had warmed her, but now, stopping, she

felt the wind drive against her bare skin icily. Some shelter she must have before the night came. And there was little chance in these hills, for they were of granite, not the familiar limestone so frequently honeycombed with caverns. Yet, in the thickening nightfall, she had not gone more than a dozen steps when fortune favoured her and up the brow of the hill she saw an indentation. Attained with panting effort, she discovered it a fault in the strata that left a roofed, triangular recess some nine or ten feet deep, inadequate enough, but better than nothing.

Grass. Grass to warm it and herself.

She laid down her spear and ran to the foot of the hill where grass, sere and dry as hay, rustled and whispered eerily in that voiceless country. She tore up great armfuls of it and carried it up to the ledge. Meantime the force of the wind had increased, and as she made the last journey sleet began to pelt her body, as though she stood in an ice-cold spray from a bathroom tap. But the ledge was a heaped fuzz of hay. She ran inside, seized the flint spear, lay down on the hay and wound herself into the swathes, rolling over and over till the faintly burred heads had entangled her in a great coverlet from head to foot. She left her right arm bare and gathered more of the hay and piled it above her in blanket-like layers. The exertion had warmed her again, faintly, but her whole body was still an icy numbness. When she finished and raised her head it was to see the blackness complete but for a strange phenomenon. A white curtain wavered and shook in front of the ledge of refuge. And the rock sang as it waved and shook.

Hail.

Winter.

She found she had forgotten hunger as she had forgotten to be afraid. Yet the numbness of her body had not spread to her mind. She found herself thinking and remembering in a passionate dispassion.

She thought of Ærte and that first night she had lain with him in the cave far to the north, watching the volcanoes burn in the land that the seas were soon to devour. And instantly the memory passed from her. Neither Ærte – his face seemed to take shape in the darkness and then fade at once – nor that pitiful shade of Mametz seemed of importance. She thought of Sinclair, and he passed from her mind, a dour, enigmatic ghost. Sir John Mullaghan – less than a ghost. So with all she had ever known, all the tenants of the ancient world of comfort and security. Only in the sound of the bitter hailstorm that thudded upon the hills, remained one piercing memory; the face of the beast-man, lost and desperate as herself, astray in time and the world.

Had he found refuge or was he out in this? What a jest of God! Millions and millions of years ago He had brought a warm fetid scum to anchor on some intertidal beach. And it had fermented through long nights and noons; and it was life. And life climbed and branched and flowered from it. And the dragons passed and the mammals rose and the great apes walked the hills of Siwalik. Westwards they wandered, through millennium on millennium, gathering their little skills with stock and stone. And one by one God murdered and discarded them. For they bored Him. Heidelberg man with the mighty skull, the ape-hunter of Piltdown, the chattering beasts of Broken Hill and the Java jungles – they passed and were not, bloody foam and spume on a sea that whimpered cruelty and change. Till this Atlantean night of hail all these experimentings of Nature's thousand millennia – they ended here in a nameless hill-land with the ape-beast and herself, last representatives of their kindred experiments . . .

She quivered to a misty drowsiness, even while a faint voice protested through her frozen serenity: "But you are not the last!" Last she was. Poor humanity, that had dreamed so much and so splendidly – to end its dream with her! . . .

Thereon, warmed by the heat her body had engendered in the hay, utterly exhausted with her day's marchings and searchings, Clair laid her head on her hand, and slept, while the hail ceased and the hand of winter drew back, hesitating a cosmic moment, from the night and hills of Atlantis.

*Subchapter iii*

It began to freeze as the night wore on. The cold grew more intense. But it did not penetrate the grass coverings wherein Clair Stranlay lay enwrapped. Not cold but cramped position made her awake, and, shifting her aching hip, she saw that the hail had ceased and the moonlight had come. It flooded all the uplands and came in little waves into the recess. She lay and looked out, suddenly vividly awake. What had she been imagining before she fell asleep?

Suddenly she remembered and laughed a little at the memory. The night bent eagerly in to listen to her. She thought: 'You were hysterical, I suppose. The last woman in the world. . . . Still, supposing Keith Sinclair is all wrong, and it's into the future we've strayed, not the past? Then this damn hunger of mine must be the accumulated hunger of centuries. . . . *Paté de foie gras* sandwiches – remember them? They were very good. And spring lamb. And black coffee. And green chartreuse. And – you'd better not go on.'

She pressed her hand against her small, flat stomach. Her back ached. Those kidney-pill people would give anything to have her as an illustration. "The Cavewoman's Bowels. . . ." Every picture tells a story.

Bright moonlight.

She wriggled a little, cautiously if light-headedly, towards the fore part of the cave. Now she could see the moonlit lands. The silence of the day that had encompassed her wanderings was as nothing to this. Over a crisp white shroud that draped the countryside, nothing moved or cried. Had she indeed dreamed? Was this not perhaps verily the end? Far below, to the right, a stretch of water gleamed icily, burnished and unrippled. Silence and the sweetness of death in the silence, and beyond the water the black armies of the trees.

> 'Forest and water, far and wide,
> In limpid starlight glorified,
> Lie like the mystery of death.'

And God? Was there indeed no God, were He and His variants no more than mistaken science – results of that seasonal ritual that grew in the Nile Valley when men ascribed the time of flood and ripening to the mysterious, animate sun? No more? And the Christ and the Buddha and their dream of a Father Who knew if a sparrow fell? Were these

no more than thin plaints of this lost adventure of mankind, crying for warmth and safety and comfort?
*'Lo, I shall be with you alway, even unto the end of the world.'*
*'Until the day break and the shadows flee away —'*

*'Father, in Thy gracious keeping,*
*Leave we now thy servant, sleeping.'*

Phrases innumerable, lovely and gracious and shining, came to her out of the silence. Things from the Anglican burial service, from the poets, from forgotten hymns . . .
*'Our birth is but a sleep and a forgetting . . .'*
*'For God so loved the world that He gave His only begotten Son —'*

*'So runs my dream, but what am I?*
*An infant crying in the night,*
*An infant crying for the light,*
*And with no language but a cry —'*

Was *that* God only the Anglicized version of the Nile-lands sun? A dream, Himself a hope and a terror as yet unborn, undreamt of here in the wastes of Atlantis or elsewhere in this world that awaited the coming of the last Ice Age? Before Adam – this was a night before the birth of God!

Omnipotence and Omniprescience still unborn. Far up there in the stars God still lay unborn and unawakened. . . . Or dead, dead indeed if this were the last night of the world, swinging now a frozen star about an extinct sun.

'Then what am I? Why was I born to think these things? Oh, somewhere, surely, in some age to come, there's explanation. Of me and Sinclair and Sir John and the beast-man lost in these hills. Somewhere . . .'

She covered her eyes from the bright moonlight. No sound, no answer came to her. None had ever come or ever would come.

And then Clair felt no longer afraid. She dropped her hands. She addressed the frozen world in a whisper.

"You lovely thing, you can kill me and finish me. Very

easily. But not that question. It's beyond your killing. It'll live long after you're dead yourself."

*Subchapter iv*

In the morning she encountered and speared a half-frozen hare by the verge of the loch. Shuddering, she cut the throat and drank its blood. By nightfall she was far from the ledge where she had sheltered, holding across the savannah towards the southwards mountains. That had seemed the only hope left. Towards those mountains Sinclair was guiding the Cro-Magnards and somewhere on the verge of them she would overtake or intercept the trek.

The sun had risen, powerful and hot, and the thin frost-rime went fast from grass and forest. Clair ran as much and as often as she could, but many times had to sit and rub her numbed feet, agonizingly, back to circulation. No wind came across the hill-jumbled plain, and the southern peaks seemed to come but little closer with the passing of the day. Yet the hills where she had encountered the ape-man receded almost into flatness. She made up her mind to perch in a tree during the night; so all day she kept near the winding forest-belts, lest darkness overtake her remote from the shelter she had determined on.

For shelter, cold apart, would be necessary. The land now swarmed with game. Once she came on a nest of hyaenodon, rolling and playing and snarling happily in the sun. They desisted at sight of her, and crouched with lolling tongues, looking at her quizzically. Two, hardly more than puppies, got up and cantered after her, falling over the grass-tussocks and their own legs, foolishly. A great gaunt female the size of a young heifer whined them back. Further on she saw a herd of aurochs among the trees, and remembered the Latin tale of these animals having no knees and being unable to kneel or lie, or sleep otherwise than unchancily poised against the bole of a tree. The Romans had been misinformed. Many of the great beasts squatted, cud-chewing and somnolent, with bulls on guard here and there. Clair passed too far off for them to take offence at her. The wonder of this passing through a land filled with wild beasts, and passing unharmed, wore off in the trudging hours. She thought, with a return of her usual gay irony: 'I'm the essential Cockney still, I suppose, and can't get rid of the notion that it's really Regent's Park or the Bronx – and if any of the beasts break loose I can scream for a keeper.'

But in late afternoon the direct sunlight vanished, extinguished in a driving storm of snow, soft, powdery stuff which felt almost warm at first, but speedily lost that quality. The landscape became a wavering scurry, as though the very savannahs were seeking shelter. Clair turned into the safety of the trees, treading a great nave of pines with underfoot a thick carpet of needles which pricked her feet. Scotch firs grew here as well, and under one of them she crept and sheltered, watching the afternoon pass greyly and the storm continue unabated.

She could still see the land she had crossed, and, presently, in a late clearing of the snow-squall, a figure nearing the forest. A human figure.

She knew it a dream or a mirage and looked away, and rubbed her eyes, and looked back again. Then she started to her feet and found herself running towards him, calling and sobbing. He saw her, dropped his load, and came running towards her and caught her in his arms.

"Ærte!" she cried.

It was Keith Sinclair.

## CHAPTER II: A LIGHT IN THE SOUTH

*Subchapter i*

HE said, breathlessly, "Clair! Are you all right?"
And she could not answer because her head was pressed against his chest, and she was breathless with running and surprise, and felt she never wanted to speak again; only to hold to him and hold to him and never let him go. So for a time they stood in each other's arms, and then somehow they were apart, Clair looking up at him, still unbelievingly.

"You *are* Sinclair? I'm not the last left alive? Oh, Keith! . . ."

He turned away and picked up the bundle. It was a great bearskin. Beside it he had dropped a hunting spear and something else – a huge, stringed bow that reached almost to his shoulder. He turned round to find Clair drying her eyes ineffectually. He saw her slim and brown-white and grimy, with snow in her hair and a ripple of gooseflesh across her shoulders. Bless her for those winter dips of hers. . . . He said: "My God, it's a long way to Kensington!"

"I thought I was lost for ever. I thought —" She darted forward and seized his spear and bow. "You dear to find me! I've got a tree to shelter under. Come along!"

The snow had begun again and they ran for the shelter of the forest. Under the Scotch fir no snow came, and only a waft of faint ice currents from the wind. Sinclair dropped his bundle and bent and untied it, not looking at her as he asked the question:

"Have you had any food?"

"I killed a hare this morning and drank its blood."

"And no fire? How did you pass the night?"

"Sheltering in a ledge up on the hills back there. I saw all the world lying dead last night, Keith."

He said, with a grimace of dour humour: "Why didn't you wave to me? That's what I felt like!"

He was gathering pine-needles and broken branches. He placed a little circle of rotten wood fragments round the heap and then fumbled in the bearskin. Some tarnished thing shone in his hand. Clair drew a long breath.

"Sir John's lighter. Does it still light?"

"He never used it after we came among the Cro-Magnards, you know. And the wadding is still a little damp with petrol – I hope." He flicked the lighter open. A tiny, white-yellow flame kindled the wick. Shielding it, he knelt to the heap of twigs. The wind had ebbed round and came from the north now. The flame ran swiftly along a twig. Clair, standing, stared at it fascinatedly. A fire again! Sinclair put up a hand, iron-cold even upon her chill-accustomed skin, and pulled her down.

"Sit here and don't let it out. I'm going to erect a break-wind."

He bent and disappeared out of the sheltering circle of the fir-fronds, returning in a moment with an armful of boughs. He went back, foraging, and she heard him snapping off others. Presently he was beside her again, and began to construct the break-wind, interweaving from the ground up to the fir-fronds a wall of boughs. Abruptly the wind ceased to blow upon Clair's back. The fire changed from a sulky negligence to a gossipy crackling. Sinclair lay beside her.

"That's that. God, I am glad to see you."

She saw then that he was utterly exhausted. His face was pinched and dented with cold and other things, his eyes bloodshot. Also, his feet were so torn that the blood had splashed in long streaks up past his ankles. She gave a cry at sight of them.

"They're all right." He was lying with closed eyes. "Stopped aching, and the dirt in them's clean enough." He tried to rouse himself. "There's pemmican in that parcel. Twine the bearskin round you. Keep up fire . . ." His voice trailed off into unintelligibility. She thought he had fainted and leant over him in some consternation.

He was asleep. Probably he had not slept all the previous night.

She undid the bundle and found inside it smoked meat, as he had said; strange spongy stuff she had never seen before. Mammoth meat? In the bundle was a package of stone-tipped arrows. Nothing else. She cut off some of the meat with the blade of the spear which had companied her, and mounted the spongy slices on arrow-heads, and crawled out from below the tree to collect more fuel. There, beyond the shelter of the break-wind, she realized the salvation of Sinclair's coming. The snow had ceased again, but the wind was almost a solid thing, and awful in its numbing coldness. Darkness was driving across it, an opposing force, and she stumbled chilledly in shadows, presently sobbing through her teeth as she faced about to return to the fir. There she found the meat smoking and Sinclair still fast asleep. She flung the skin over him and tucked it about him, and he stirred a little and muttered something; and she bent to hear what it was.

"Road to the south. She'll have taken the road to the mountains."

So he had guessed and followed on that chance? But a hazardous enough guess, and when had he made it? Not until he had reached one of those hills in which she herself had sheltered last night. That was obvious. . . . Keith Sinclair! And she had thought – she had *known* as she ran towards him – that he was Ærte.

Where were the hunters?

Useless questions. She thought: 'Oh, it *is* good to eat,' and ate the meat slowly, carefully, wondering if she should awaken Sinclair to share with her. But he was obviously more tired than hungry. The saltless stuff in her mouth went over without effort nowadays. But a drink – it might be impossible to find any water. She looked beyond the break-wind and saw only a smouldering landscape on the verge of night. But the break-wind had collected a drift of snow, and she gathered a handful and ate it, though she knew she invited stomach-ache. But her mouth and throat felt instantly cold and moist, and she finished the sliver of meat in her hand, and looked for the rest, and gave a little gasp. Oh, my good God, had she eaten all that?

So it seemed. She piled more boughs on the fire. Now the wind was crying overhead. The Scotch fir drummed like a harp played on by a blind harper. She found handfuls of camp leaves and cones and packed them about the fire, their resinous smell homely in her nostrils. Then she crept to Sinclair's side and lay down beside him. Under the bearskin his body had generated a grateful warmth, and now an additional warmth came out from the fire. She stretched herself beside him and he moved in sleep, as if making way for her. She patted his shoulder, soothingly, and saw his shadowed face in sleep, not so worn now, but blued still under the eyes. He moaned a little as he moved his torn feet. She lay in compassionate alertness, not touching him. The firelight flickered and flapped in a stray eddy of the wind. Clair tucked the bearskin around herself and then leant over and tucked the other side round Sinclair.

So raised, she looked out from below the whistling fronds of the tree, into the darkness of the forest and tundra, a darkness based on a ghostly greyness that was the snow. She felt a drowsy content upon her. She thought, withdrawing a chilled arm into shelter: 'Goodness, how little we need for comfort!' Two naked savages in a forest on a snowing night. A fire, food, a break-wind and a bearskin. And men had toiled and planned and invented elaborate explorer's equipment and central heating and safety lavatories when they might have had this for nothing – and conquered the stars and split the atom in the generations devoted to worrying over houses sound-proof and wind-proof, and, as they had had at length to construct them, fool-proof. . . . Her hair blew a little; she felt it rise and undulate pleasantly on her head. She was about to lie down when something in the night, far away, caught her attention.

At first she thought it was a star and then realized the impossibility of that. The night was too dense with storm-clouds. And, though it had the twinkling immobility of a star, it was too low down there in the horizon of the south. But it gleamed brightly, like a torch in an unsteady hand, winking, as it seemed, across the leagues of tundra in the drive of the same blizzard as whoomed against the break-wind. What could it be?

Another volcano? But there had been no sign of a volcano during all her southwards tramp of the afternoon. The Atlantean Alps were great, glacier-studded masses, not like that line of fires that had marched to the right of the original trek of Sir John and Sinclair and herself from the wreck of *Magellan's Cloud*. No volcano. It must be a fire.

But kindled by whom?

Staring across the night, a maze of drowsy speculations unfolded in her brain. Other Cro-Magnards? But were there any, other than those she knew? Perhaps – who knew! – another party of explorers from the outer rims of Time, sucked into this epoch by just such accident as wrecked the *Magellan's Cloud*. No impossibility. People perhaps out of an age even remoter than the twentieth century, stray Utopians perhaps from A.D. ten thousand, with the most fantastic notions of the twentieth century, and never having heard of the Cro-Magnards at all . . .

Still – perhaps simply a consignment from the same age and era as had caught the *Magellan*!

She lowered her head, and then, he being at last fast asleep, snuggled close to Sinclair. The remote, mysterious fire had vanished from her range of vision. She closed her eyes. Other twentieth century explorers! . . .Who would they be if she had the selection of them? The Archbishop of Canterbury, of course – to see what he thought of a people who knew not God; Mr. H. G. Wells, to find out what he thought of primitives who were neither stalking ghouls of the night nor those vexedly flea-bitten savages who scratched throughout the early pages of the *Outline*; President Hoover and Mr. Ramsay MacDonald – to learn a little about the original nature of man, and be shocked to death to find their ancestors so unwarlike that they needed no elaborate conventions to restrain themselves from throat-cutting and the disembowelment of babies; Mr. Henry Ford, with his tight, narrow face, to die of a broken heart in an auto-less world; Charlie Chaplin to poke the aurochs with his stick . . .

A small and sleepy chuckle stole out to the fire, and the two under the bearskin lay very still indeed the while the night went on and the wind rose to a super-blizzard, rose to the roar of a Russian *shoom*, and then fell and died. But all through these hours, and into the pale coming of the next dawn, enigmatic, the fire in the southwards mountains winked across the wastes.

*Subchapter ii*

The American was the first to awake, what of his un-quenched hunger from the previous day. All his trunk was very warm; but his feet ached as though they had been frozen and were now in the process of thawing. The fire was out and the wind had died away and it was the beginning of daylight. He put aside the bearskin from his face and discovered then the reason for some of his warmth. Clair lay with her arms around his neck, fast asleep, her grimy face laid in the hollow of his shoulder.

He remembered at once, and then, not moving, lay and looked at her. For a moment the temptation made him dizzy. All the repressed and thwarted desires of his ancestors for six thousand years were behind him, urging him to it in that Atlantean forest that was to be a rotted myth before those ancestors were born. But there were other and older ancestors. . . . He scowled.

"You scabrous lout," he commented to himself.

He withdrew his shoulder as gently as possible and stood up and shivered in the waiting coldness of the morning. A moorhen twittered. Water was not so far off. He stepped gingerly towards the fire and collected charred boughs, and scrunched around in search for Sir John's petrol-lighter, and found it laid neatly at the base of the fir, in company with his bow. His spear was nowhere to be seen, because at the moment Clair lay on it. He started a fire and then crept out from below the fir and held down through an avenue of pines to that twittering that told of the moorhen's splashings. The sun came up over the eastward tundra at that moment and followed him. He found the water, a stream that meandered southwards towards the mountains, and sat down on its snow-covered bank. He was half-frozen already with his walking through that snow, but the cleansing of his feet at once was imperative. He set to work with handfuls of ice-cold water. Several times he felt he was about to faint in the spasms of agony that travelled up his body. Clair's voice spoke behind him.

"Keith! Why didn't you ask me to help?"

He looked over his shoulder and saw her shivering behind him and carrying the bearskin. "Go back to the fire."

"Don't bully. We'll go when you're all right again. Sit on this and I'll bathe them."

He rose and then sat down, as she had told him. And then she saw a curious thing. His black hair was almost ashen grey. She stared at it appalled, half-kneeling in front of him and looking up. Sinclair said: "What is it?"

"Your hair."

"My what?"

Of course he didn't know. She hesitated, beginning to lave his feet. He scowled at her, inquiringly. He put up his hand to his head. "Seems all right."

"It's turned grey," said Clair, gently.

"What!"

He was astounded for a moment. He laughed. He muttered something unkind about the influence of Hollywood and was palpably ashamed of himself. But Clair kept her head down-bent. Had he been through as bad a time as that? Hers had been nothing to it. Of course he had thought her lost for ever, killed most probably. . . . His feet made her shudder, and he shuddered himself as she tended them and drew out long slivers of stone from the right one.

"That was from the time I had a slip and glissade on those infernal red hills."

"If only we had something to bind up the cuts with —"

"I'll make some sandals from part of this bearskin. They'll do, thanks. Let's get back to the fire."

At the fire Clair knelt and toasted herself and more of the mammoth meat. Sinclair made his moccasins. "How did you find me?" Clair asked.

"God knows, How did you get lost?"

She told him of the circumstances the while the day brightened; then heard of his own Odyssey. Her absence had not been discovered by him until the afternoon of the day on which she had been lost. He had hunted from group to group, asking about her, and finding her nowhere. Presently the whole camp was aroused and, excepting those Cro-Magnards engaged in the boucanning of the mammoth meat, every hunter and woman had set out in the search for her. From one of the hunters the American heard of Clair's joining the party which had made a dash through the hills to intercept the second mammoth. Thereat, in company with Ærte and three or four more, he had set out to retraverse that route. In the hills they had scattered and presently Sinclair, in a muddy patch on the other side of these hills, had come on the imprint of a naked and recent footstep which he knew was Clair's —

"How did you know?"

From the arching of the instep. There had been no more than that single footprint, but it had pointed southwards, towards a range of hills. He had set out to reach that range.

The range had been gained as the darkness was falling, and with no further sign of Clair, nor sound of her or answer to his shouts. He had hunted the range all the night, and with the coming of morning had gained the top of it and considered the situation, deciding correctly that if Clair lost were still Clair alive she must have determined to make the southwards mountains in the hope of intercepting the trek of the Cro-Magnards. So he himself had set out in the direction of the nameless Alps and – then he had heard her hail him.

She said: "We've always been cut apart and strangers in some way, Keith. Why did you do it? – all this tremendous search for me?"

He had made the moccasins by then and was fitting them to his feet with gut as string. He looked across the savannah to the mountains.

"Any of the hunters would have done it. Ærte is probably searching for you still."

"Yes, I know. But we are different. So why?"

He said in a very still, strained voice: "It's because I love you, I suppose. And there isn't any supposing about it. It's just that."

She stared into the fire. "And I love you also. I think I always loved you. From that day I saw you on the gallery of the *Magellan*. Remember it– twenty-five thousand years ago. Oh, Keith!"

He dropped the moccasins and came towards her, grey-headed, his eyes alight. She shook her head. She spoke in a whisper. "But there's still Ærte – my lover for the dark days."

"Eh?"

"There's still him. We've still got to find the hunters again, and there's still Ærte. He's as remote and impossible as a boy in a fairy-tale. But I'm his and he's mine for the dark days at least. . . . I thought you were Ærte last night. I could have sworn you were."

He sat down again. He said: "It's damned nonsense."

"I know."

"Ærte will make no claim on you if you come to me."

"No, he won't. But that's the point, Keith. Oh, my dear, don't you see? It's for you and your sake and the sake of your dream that I must keep by Ærte. Unless you've given that up? Are we to look for the hunters again?"

He nodded south towards the mountains. His face had the savage sulkiness of repressed wrath she remembered from the days of crossing the upland plateau. "We'll go on and wait their coming there. Even if they don't go further than this stretch of country we'll be able to see them and return to them."

"But you want them to go further. You're going to lead them south of the mountains and find a river and plant corn and teach them to build houses and cast metals? Remember? You and I are going to change the course of history there, somewhere beyond these Alps. Do you think we can do it without keeping faith in every detail with the hunters? They'd laugh and say nothing and only pity Ærte a little, but they'd never take counsel from you again."

Sinclair sat down and completed the binding of his footwear. Clair laughed, a little shakily.

"It's me or the future of history, Keith! . . . And don't leave it to me now, else I'll forget that other lover of mine who died on the wire in France, and I'll forget all the black oppressions done in this wild world under the sun, and think only of you, and the dearness and adorableness of your dear, sulky head and the queer sweetness of your body and the heart-breaking miracle of that grey hair of yours and its soft lie on your head, and the loveliness of that clean, crude, splendid mind of yours. I'll remember only these things – and you'll never forget the others, though all our lives together you'd pretend you had forgotten them."

He said: "I think you've cured me. Bless you. We'll go south and await the coming of Ærte and the hunters."

*Subchapter iii*

"Oh, that light last night. I forgot to mention it."

"Eh?"

They were on the road to the southern mountains, though no road had ever crossed that wild belt of land. It was past noon. Here and there the snow still lay in patches, or shivered and wilted into slush pools under the heat of the sun. And over all the landscape was a steaming haze that rose a little, but patched the ground in great areas to indistinctness. Sinclair strode nude as when he was born, but for the bearskin moccasins. Clair, barefooted, was elsewhere wrapped in the remnants of the mutilated skin.

They had crossed a good eight or nine miles of country since leaving the encampment of the night before. Now the mountains before them changed shape continually, but visibly grew greater. They towered as tower the walls of the Colorado Canyon from river-bed level. Crowned with snow, the great massif stretched from horizon to horizon, with in front, leftwards, an extended arm, a crazy jumble of broken peaklets and poised glacierettes. It was somewhere in that extended arm, Clair thought, that she had seen the light.

Sinclair scowled down at her questioningly. "Light? What kind of light?"

She put her arm through his. "Funny how that scowl of yours used almost to intimidate me! . . . Fun to be alive, isn't it, Keith?"

The scowl went from his face. He pinched her shoulder, absently. Then:

"The light?"

"Oh, yes. It was like a camp-fire."

"Couldn't be. At least, I don't think so. The hunters have no story of other groups living so comparatively near."

Some half-memory vexed her mind. She could not secure it. "But there might be."

"I don't know." They passed into a winding trackway made by beasts, between two stretches of marsh, and climbed up from that low patch to firmer ground, a re-beginning of the savannah-land and dotted with deer and aurochs herds.

"There might be, but on the whole I doubt it. Our hunters are perhaps as yet the only human beings in Atlantis – perhaps in all the world."

She found that a breath-taking notion. "But there were other peoples in pre-history besides the Cro-Magnards."

"Later, yes. But at this epoch? Mayn't the others have been helped into full humanity by imitation of our proto-Cro-Magnards? . . . We can't say. But all these things are accidental, dependent on a multitude of chances that might arise in one district and nowhere else. Perhaps in the world at the moment there are only tribes of sub-men at various levels, and our hunters constitute the only group that has as yet emerged into full humanity."

"Then —"

He smiled down into her grave face, and bit his lips because he desired her, and there were other things than desire, but none so warm and immediate as she was. Clair looked back at the land behind them.

"Any accident might change the nature of things for ever. If our Cro-Magnards were suddenly wiped out —"

"There might never be such a thing as history. At least – we can never know."

"Oh, the awful loneliness of men! They couldn't help making gods when they found some shelter and security in an agricultural society. . . . Pious, rotten romanticism, Keith – remember what you once told me I was addicted to? – but that night I was lost on the hills back there I began to think that perhaps there was some God after all. Not just a god. Something, Someone . . ."

She looked up at him. Thousands and thousands were yet to look up into the faces of their fellows for confirmation of that wild hope. . . . He said: "An honest god's the noblest work of man. I don't believe there's anything to shield us from the darkness, Clair. And not even for the sake of poetry do I think we should carry the idea to our hunters in that world we're to make beyond these mountains. . . . If we ever get beyond them."

"Tremendous things, aren't they?"

They were. Somewhere at the foot of their slopes, how-ever, the Cro-Magnards would arrive in time, and there was nothing for the two of them but to press on and await that arrival. Clair said, being dragged out of a squelchy boggy place: "The light – we never settled about that."

"No." Sinclair, assisting her to her feet, abruptly pulled her down again and lay prone himself. "But we can now, I think."

Clair, her breath shaken from her, wriggled out of his grasp and looked in the direction in which he pointed.

*Subchapter iv*

The tapering tip of the northwards spur of the mountain-range was already a sierraed toweringness to the left of them. It was not more than three miles away. The forests climbed its base in green attack, even skirmished remotely up into valleys and ledges of the heights. That for background, with directly south the still remoter, more gigantic background of the range proper, a good six miles away. Here and there, in the angle so formed, grew clumps of larch and fir and great stretches of gorse. Amid these fed the herds of aurochs Clair had noted before. One herd was very close – a herd that had ceased to feed and stood on the *qui vive*, bulls with gigantic tails uplifted, cows and calves sniffing the air. And the reason for the alarm – a dozen reasons – became at length obtrusive to Clair's gaze.

They were less than a quarter of a mile away, but had remained unperceived by her because of their dull grey colouring. It seemed to her that it was on all fours they were creeping from bush to bush, nearer their quarry, the aurochs. But indeed it was merely that their arms were so elongated as naturally to reach the ground. Across cavernous, hair-matted torsos were strapped crude skin-wrappings. From each pair of shoulders, on a short, squat neck, a strange, deformed head, chinless, browless, enormously eye-ridged, projected forward so that the Thing could never look directly upwards. Even at that distance they were horrible, dreadful and awful caricatures of familiar and lovely things.

Clair felt sick. "What are they?" she whispered.

"Neanderthalers," said Sinclair, also in a whisper.

CHAPTER III:   ALL OUR YESTERDAYS

*Subchapter i*

NO snow fell that night, but a bitter wind sprang up with the coming of darkness and blew into the great triangular space formed by the forest lines and the bastions of the unknown mountain-ranges. At first the darkness, for there came neither moon nor star-rise, was heavy and complete, without even the usual brooding Atlantean greyness. And then, as if lighted one by one, there became obvious far in the base of the triangle and ranging up northwards towards the open country the glare of great fires. Sinclair and Clair saw them pringling brightly in the night, from their own camping-place in the heart of a thicket of broom-plants and larch. They also had kindled a fire, dangerous though that procedure might be; they had kindled it mid-way the thicket, however, so that there was little chance of those alien firetenders seeing it. But both, after they had eaten, went out to the verge of thicket to watch that bright sentinelling of the mountain-base. Sinclair stood with his arm round Clair, and pulled her back into the thicket after a moment to still her shivering.

"Then they can make fires – they *are* men," she said.

"They are men, but not Man. They are the sub-human species that are almost men, and are to be in occupation of most of Europe when our Cro-Magnards wander there thousands of years hence. If they do so wander."

The fires burned steadily. Clair remembered the creeping beasts of the afternoon and shuddered with disgust. Yet perhaps that was unreasonable enough. Perhaps there was nothing of savagery about them, any more than among the Cro-Magnards. She saw the dim shaking of Sinclair's grey head.

"Their conduct didn't warrant it. Men – the Cro-

Magnards and the stock that produced ourselves – are decent, kindly animals of anthropoid blood, like the chimpanzee and gibbon. But there *is* another strain – the gorilla and perhaps these Neanderthalers – the sullen, individualist beast whose ferocity is perhaps maladjustment of body and a general odd, black resentment against life."

"Like the militarists and the hanging judges and the gloomy deans of the twentieth century?"

"Exactly." But his voice sounded absent. "I wonder. . . . Look, here, go back to the fire. I'm going out to see what they're really like."

"What?" She was startled enough at that. "Then I'll come as well."

"Can't. One of us must go, Clair, and must take the bearskin for covering against this infernal wind. And it must be me. I'm stronger than you and I can run faster."

"But why must? We needn't go near them at all."

"We must because our hunters will be down from the north in the next day or so, and there's no telling what will happen then. If they're peaceable or cowardly beasts there's nothing to fear. If not —"

"But we needn't lead the Cro-Magnards anywhere near them. We can take them through the mountains away over there, somewhere." She pointed to the right in the westwards darkness.

"Can we? I wonder. . . . I must go, Clair."

She said, standing beside the fire and helping him to tie the bearskin: "Do take care of yourself, my dear." And thought: 'As though we were in Kensington and I was telling him to mind the buses on the way to the office!'

He said, absently still: "I'll do that." Then he picked up his spear, and put his hand on her shoulder and gave it a little shake, and went off into the darkness.

Clair built up the fire and lay down in the shelter of the break-wind. She took her own spear beside her for company and Sinclair's bow as well, though she knew nothing of the handling of the thing. It was a very lonely vigil. The fire fluffed and rose and fell occasionally in eddies of the wind. But presently that wind died away almost completely, though the cold seemed to grow intenser still. Clair thought: 'I must not think of Sinclair,' and put him out of her thoughts as well as she might, and curled her legs up beneath her, and remembered some picture of a Tierra del Fuegan savage she had once seen in that attitude.

She thought, startled: 'Goodness, I might have sat as the artist's model!'

Where were Ærte and the hunters?

Something bayed close at hand beyond the bushes. There came a distant scuffling; more near, the swift scurry of running paws. The scurry ceased. Then a pad-pad-padding began in a circle, just beyond the range of the fire-glow. Clair, with a very dry throat, stirred the fire and in its increase of radiance saw that she was surrounded by a pack of wolves – beasts with long, feathery brushes and brightly erected ears. Each might have been of the bigness of an Alsatian. Sometimes they sat and rested, staring at her, at other times resumed that scurrying encirclement of the fire. It was difficult to realize that if they overcame fear of the fire they would eat her, sink those bright teeth into her legs and throat and stomach, very agonizingly, in a flounder of hot and stench-laden bodies. . . . Clair got to her feet once and waved her spear at a great, cadaverous brute. He stopped in his pacing, head brightly alert, and cocked his ears. Then, as though grinning sardonically, he bared his teeth, growled, and advanced a step or so. Clair stirred the fire again, and he retreated.

So the night went on. Clair, sitting dozing once, awoke to find – not the beasts upon her as she had dreamt, and dreaming had awoken with a startled cry – but them gone and the fire burned very low, and herself very cold. She fed the smoulder hurriedly, carefully. A mammoth trumpeted, southwards, in some glen of the mountains, the sound eerie and plaintive. The clouds began to clear and presently, with a faint spraying of powdery light, the star-rise came. The heavens were filled with an eastwards sailing of great masses of dark storm-clouds. Clair sat and warmed herself and got up and walked about and sat down again. Still Sinclair did not return.

There came a breath of dawn through the air of the darkness. The stars grew brighter and then faded. And through the dawn Sinclair came back. She heard him calling in the distance: "Clair! Clair!" and ran and found him.

He had been *lost*.

*Subchapter ii*

"Most infernally lost." He was splashed with mud and rimed with frost. His eyebrows and eyelids curled white with frost. He sat down jerkily by the fire and started up again, glancing over his shoulder. "Idiotic to shout, but there was nothing else to be done. I hadn't a notion of where you were. Lost my way completely coming back – as I might have guessed I'd do. . . . Old habit of thinking of the lie of a country in terms of roads and signposts. . . . Wonder if they heard me shouting?"

"I'll go and see," Clair said.

He pulled her down beside him. "Not that, anyway," he said, grimly. "Let's listen."

They listened to that austere world of the Third Interglacial awakening with the coming of the morning over the Atlantean savannah. Sparrows chirped in the trees. Somewhere in the depths of the wood a corncrake was sounding its note. Spite the nearing of the sun, it was still bitterly cold. But there was no crackling of undergrowth under coming feet.

"What are they like?" Clair whispered.

"God. . . . Awful."

He said no more than that about them. Instead, he shivered. Clair cut meat from their dwindling supply and grilled it. Sinclair was nodding from lack of sleep. She asked: "Did you get near them?"

"I lay above one of their caves: I seemed to lie there for hours. Limestone spur, that, and its upper tip here is honeycombed with caves. There must be several hundreds of them. Ugh." He had been eating. He was suddenly sick. "Sorry, Clair."

She ruffled his grey hair. "Don't think of them or speak about them for a bit. Do you think I could use your bow?"

"Why?"

She looked wistfully through the trees towards the sound of the forest fowls. "I *would* like chicken for a change."

He smiled at her from a face as grey as his hair. "Try. But don't go too far. And if you see – any of them – scream like hell and run back in this direction."

She went through the morning-stirred forest, thinking, at first almost in a panic: 'I had to get away . . . Keith, my dear, you've had the devil of a night. Will it pass or are you really ill? . . . Oh, *damn* this thing.'

She stopped and disentangled the bow from a bush and hurried on again because of the coldness. She came to the edge of a clearing. In the charred forest-litter two birds fed, perkily, with quick-darting heads. Partridges. She thought: 'I'll never hit them,' and stopped, and planted the butt of the bow in the ground, and fitted the clumsy arrow. One of the birds saw her and raised its head, regarding her sideways, out of a bright, questioning eye. Her fingers fumbled frozenly at the bow-string. The damn bird imagines it's having its photograph taken. . . . Now.

The arrow whizzed across the space, an enormous lance of a projectile. One partridge rose with a flirr! The other lay impaled wing from wing, and fluttering wildly. Clair wrung its neck and tried to get out the arrow, and desisted, lest she snap off the insecure flint; and went back towards Sinclair and the camp-fire. The break-wind shelter was deserted. She dropped the bird and ran through the trees towards the open country that led to the Neanderthal caves. Sinclair turned about as he heard her coming.

"Sh. For God's sake."

The great triangle was evidently the hunting-ground of the beast-men. Three separate parties, none of them near enough for the intimate study of individuals, were debouching in various directions from that far mountain-wall – one party apparently heading in the direction of their shelter. A little over two miles away, Clair judged it. Sinclair swore, ruffling his bearded chin.

"Are they on my track – or is it just a chance drift after the game?"

Clair stared with him. He gave a sigh of relief. "A chance party, after all. They're just on the prowl."

"Are they? They're not coming in a straight line, but they seem to be following something. Didn't you lose yourself last night? Perhaps they're following your —"

"By God, they are!"

*Subchapter iii*

All that forenoon they fled westwards and south-westwards, the grey beasts behind them. Sinclair's own running abilities might have out-distanced them with ease, but Clair needed frequent rests. Once or twice, reaching the foot of one or other of the rolling inclines in which the land ebbed and flowed, they would glance up and see their pursuers at the summit, sometimes less than a quarter of a mile distant. On flat country that distance grew greater; the Neanderthalers were at a disadvantage on the plain. Once, when a good mile and a half separated them, Clair, lying panting on the ground, asked:

"Shouldn't we strike north? We'd meet Ærte and the hunters."

Sinclair himself lay and breathed in great gasps, watching that loping, crouched-forward trot of the beast-men. "We might miss them completely. Perhaps they're already much nearer the mountains than we've supposed. Anyhow, they'll descend further to the west than this, I think. . . . Rested?"

"Goodness, no." She looked at him, white-faced, and smiled. "If only I'd had training as a charwoman instead of as a novelist!"

"You don't do badly." He stood up. A long, guttural wail came down the air from the beast-men. "I think they don't like us."

"Mean of them."

Funny how one could push the horror back with a remark like that. . . . But they followed on behind, doggedly enough, the horrors. Clair, running stripped and unshod, carried nothing but the light spear she had brought from the far northern camp of the Cro-Magnards. Sinclair had tied to his back both the bearskin, now enwrapping the slain partridge, and his bow and arrows. His feet were still in their moccasins, and from the bloody tracks left behind by his companion he could see that without such aids Clair herself was hardly capable of keeping the pace for long. Running beside her, he glanced at her face, red-flushed, a very sweet and kind and comely face even in this desperate hour. And again he thought, wonderingly and inadequately: 'Pretty thing!'

Open country they had come to then. But the

Neanderthalers seemed tireless. Sinclair looked back to see them not more than half a mile away. Strange – that tenacity of pursuit. Did they recognize Clair and himself as kindred animals, to be killed as freaks, or did they seem just desirable and tirable meat? God, what an end to the business! Messy end, too. For Clair –? Not to be thought of. But it had to be thought of. He said: "If they overtake us, Clair, I'll kill you. That'll be best. It won't hurt much."

"Oh, don't be a fool!"

He almost sulked, and grinned wryly at the recurrence of his ancient short temper. Clair flung herself to the ground again.

"Can't go further – yet. Sorry I said that, Keith. But you *are* a fool to suggest these melodramatics, you know. Here, in Atlantis. Stuff out of Victorian novels. . . . And I ought to suggest now that you should leave me and save yourself. Not so silly. Oh, goodness, my heart. . . . We'll just fight it out together. They'll kill both of us."

"Will they?" He stood above her, desperate, looking backwards. Clair lay flat, breathing ('like a stranded lung-fish!').

"Of course they will. Oh, because I'm a woman? I'll seem just as repulsive to them as they do to us. . . . How far?"

"Very near now."

He had unslung his bow. Clair scrambled to her knees. The beast-men were quite close, running with lowered heads and trailing fringes of body-hair, their knuckles touching the ground at every forward swing of their bodies, in their hands great shapeless mallets of stone, mounted on rude wooden hafts. Sinclair knelt on one knee. The bow-string sang like a plucked guitar.

A Neanderthaler to the left – not one Sinclair had aimed at – received the arrow in his chest, almost in the region of the heart. The brute screamed horribly, and its companions, swaying and lurching, halted. They were all males. The beast plucked stupidly at the arrow, and then bent its head and bit the thing clean off where the shaft entered its chest. Then it suddenly crumpled, as though some support had been withdrawn. Sinclair loosed his second arrow, glanced after it not at all, but heard its thud in flesh and the succeeding howl; and dragged Clair to her feet.

"Try again."

They ran hand in hand towards the near belt of forest. Clair felt her lungs bursting. A red mist played before her eyes. Twice she tripped, and Sinclair, savagely, jerked her to her feet again. Again and again the earth seemed to rise up towards her. Sinclair's grasp on her hand suddenly eased. She heard his voice far off.

"Done all we can. Sit down, my dear."

She fell rather than sat, and put her hands to throbbing ear-drums. Sinclair gave a shout.

"Impossible. . . . They've turned."

Clair swung round at that, resting on her elbows also, looking. The Neanderthalers were in retreat, carrying the dead body. One of them went with limp-swinging arm, blood-dripping. Every now and then he bent to bite at the arm. Clair stared stupidly.

"They're . . . going."

He lay beside her, almost as exhausted as she was. "Looks like it."

They had neither the will nor the breath to say more at the moment. Meantime the Neanderthalers, without a backward glance, shambled across the savannah, topped a low rise, and disappeared into the jungle wilderness in the direction of the northern spur. It was past noon. Still there was no sunlight and still it blew as harshly as during the night. Sinclair, with a driving headache, sat erect.

"Can't stay here. Die of cold after the heat of that run. I'll leave you the bearskin and go and make a fire over there."

Clair sat up also. She had the pocked, grey face of a woman of fifty. "I'll come. I can manage."

Somehow they helped each other to the forest-fringe – great beeches standing with shrill, whistling boughs. But further in were more larch, and then a wide grove of stone-oaks. Beyond these: more evergreens, then a wide glade and open country once more. It was no forest, as they had imagined from the east, but only a long, straggling plantation of Nature's planting. Through the glade the open country to the west showed up as differing in no great degree from the stretches they had already traversed. They dropped to earth by a little stream meandering amid the tree-roots –

an indifferent little stream crooning in an absorbed content-
ment – and drank ice-cold water which instantly gave Clair
cramp. Sinclair picked her up and carried her under a larch
nearby.

"Stick it. I'll have a fire in a minute."

It seemed to Clair an unending minute. Then she was
conscious of warmth and of Sinclair kneeling, massaging her.
He had the fire kindled and crackling. The greyness had gone
from his face, and, incidentally, from her own.

"Feel better?"

"Leagues. Goodness –" she looked up at him in the gay,
ironic self-appraisal that survived the *Magellan*, clothes, comfort, and seemingly every conceivable contingency – "*and
hungry!*"

"I know. So'm I. Nothing like a run in the Neanderthal
Stakes for an appetite. I'm roasting your partridge."

It smelt savoury enough. Clair sat up and assisted. They
sat side by side, and despite her hunger and her recovery she
still felt weak, and leaned her head comfortably on Sinclair's
shoulder.

"Adam and Eve."

He smiled at her, his face remarkably un-dour. "Or the
Babes in the Wood."

She dozed a little. So did Sinclair. Then their heads
knocked together and they started awake. The smell of
singeing partridge filled the air. Clair shook herself.

"Shockingly selfish again. It's you who've a right to be
sleepy. Rest when we've had lunch."

"I will. I'm almost all in."

They ate nearly all the partridge. It was very good.
Sinclair, lying down and closing his eyes, nevertheless did so
with a mental reservation. He would keep awake and get up
in a short time and make her take his place. . . . He looked
at her from below half-closed eyelids that each seemed to
weigh a ton. God, if the Neanderthalers —!

Infernal to die and never see Clair again, never hear her
deep, enjoyable and enjoying laughter; or see that bright,
naïve puzzling of hers. Infernal to have died and never held
her in your arms and kissed her from tip to toe, as she de-
serves to be kissed. As you want to kiss her and she wants. . . .
Never see the Cro-Magnards again, perhaps. We'll go west,

far off, and find a passage through the south mountains together, and build a house next spring. Together ourselves. Children – we can make them safe enough. Together . . .

Clair's voice raised in excitement, her hand shaking him. "Keith – oh, Keith, our hunters!"

*Subchapter iv*

He had slept for perhaps a couple of hours, in spite of his resolution. He sat up with a start and looked round scowlingly. "The hunters?"

"I'm sure they are. Away over there by that cramped little wood."

He saw them then. "The hunters right enough." His voice was oddly unglad. "Still on the trek, too."

They had debouched from the wood that Clair thought of as cramped. They were specks in distance, but speck-men, not the strange beasts of Neanderthal. They straggled southwards in happy-go-lucky migration, moving slowly, proving they had no lack of food at least at the moment.

Sinclair got to his feet, stiffly.

"No more Neanderthalers, anyhow. And you'll find Ærte again."

"I needn't. We need never find any of them."

He started: "You've thought that?"

"And you?"

He nodded. Clair said, slowly:

"We could hide from them and wait till they pass. We could go south beyond the mountains, and start a Golden Age of our own. We could be happier than was ever possible in the world – before or after. . . . And we'd be ashamed of ourselves all our lives."

He found a wry jibe: "'Stern daughter of the voice of God!'"

She laughed, pitifully, looking out at the nearing Cro-Magnards. Was ever such a fantastic choice before a man and woman? Sinclair wondered. And wondering, he knew there was no choice, neither for himself nor for Clair. For she brought out of that dim twentieth century of three weeks ago the memory of her boy-lover who had screamed away a

night of agony beyond the parapets of Mametz; and he – he
had brought memories kin enough to hers, dying soldiers and
starving miners, the Morlocks of the pits. . . . Clair seemed to
have read his thoughts.

"We're both playing, Keith, and we know it. Let's go out
to them." She turned away, and then turned back, resolutely.
"But you'd like to kiss me first!"

When he had finished with that they went out across the
cold, knee-length grass, laden as they had arrived. The whole
migration of the hunters paused, in straggling, shimmering
lines in the cold, gold light of the afternoon. And then there
came a shout.

They had been recognized.


*Subchapter v*

Lying in the arms of Ærte that night, Clair Stranlay did
not care to move lest she awaken him. But with the passing
of the hours it grew to a veritable agony keeping the position
in which his golden arms held her. Golden and delicately
fringed with gold, as she could see, for they lay near one of
the camp-fires, two of innumerable such recumbent figures;
and the light came out and lay on the face and arm of
Ærte. He slept in happy security. His lover for the dark days
had returned. She had been lost and she was found, and
he had gone to her and taken her with a simplicity that
had wrung from Clair no protest or repulsion. Only pity.
Sinclair had gone back to his place by the fire of Aitz-kore,
the flint-knapper. Life went on – even life in a dream in
winter-threatened Atlantis.

Life went on. . . . Perhaps she was the first woman in
the world to lie in this sleepless unease because of the arms
that held her. No Cro-Magnard woman would, Clair knew.
There were already several who had tired of their choice in
the mating-time, and their hunters did not go near them.
Here there was no hate, no compulsion in love. These people
played no game of sacrifice, because sacrifice was a stupidity
beyond their understanding. They did not live such a lie as
she had lived a few hours ago, with the bright face of Ærte
close to hers, his arms about her. It was the mentality of the

slave, the bond-woman of all the weary years of civilization that had allowed those caresses while Sinclair went away.

All their thousands of grey, suppressed years! And, hating and resenting all that tradition of sacrifice and servitude, she was herself submitting to it. Why?

There was someone else who was sleepless. She saw him pass and repass amid the fires, though she knew he was not the night's watcher of the fires. It seemed colder than ever, spite the bluff under which the camp was built. Beasts roamed beyond the radiance of the fires, but timorously, perhaps at sight of that white, restless figure within the camp.

The why of it all. Keith and his dream. Keith and Ærte and their dreams! To-morrow and to-morrow and to-morrow —

CHAPTER IV:   NOW SLEEPS THE CRIMSON PETAL

*Subchapter i*

A ND the unaccustomed cold grew ever more intense. Day came and brought no lightening of that burden. Instead, it brought generally sharp showers of hail in the morning hours, and at noon the scurry of a snow-blizzard from the north-west. It was weather of a severity the hunters had never known before in all the long days of their residence in the painted caves of the north. Stumbling campwards at evening both hunters and Sinclair's scouts would come on the bodies of their fellows lying frozen and naked in places where exhaustion had overtaken them. Winter had come to Atlantis – a foretaste of that winter that was gradually creeping down on all the northern hemisphere, presently to crystallize into the spreading glaciers and the long silences of the Fourth Ice Age.

Game grew ever scarcer. The herds went west and disappeared, and the hunters might have trailed in pursuit but for the alien presence of Sinclair in their midst. Hence the scouts that day after day went out under his direction, puzzled yet friendly, even though they might never return from such scoutings, any more than those death-frozen comrades of theirs. Game had almost vanished, but packs of the raiding and scavenging carnivorae hung around the camp, and at night the fires had to be built to twice the usual height, both in order to scare the wolves and hyaenodon and to counteract the bitter frosts.

On the second day Sinclair himself vanished in early dawn together with two of the strongest and wiriest Cro-Magnards. It did not snow all that day, but to Clair, wandering the camp clad in the bearskin Sinclair had once brought for her protection, it seemed that the cold had again increased. They could not long remain in this place. Indeed,

Ærte had gestured to her that they were to follow the game westwards on the morrow. He had no understanding of Sinclair's hesitations. . . . Doubtlessly, however, like other hesitants on other occasions, the White Hunter would follow the main drift of opinion and migration.

Thus Ærte, the while Clair marvelled, chilledly and once again, at these people of the dawn. There was no compulsion, just as there was no acceptance of it. They had grown to know and love Sinclair, perhaps because of that energetic righteousness of his that was so in contrast to their own unhesitating and unswerving kindliness. But he was no magic leader from the void, no story-book hero such as Clair had read of her fellow-authors assigning to the leadership of savage tribes in the pages of many a romance. Here was truer romance. He was merely one who promised good hunting grounds and pleasant days beyond the southwards mountains – better than they would elsewhere find if they took his advice. Now it was evident that he was mistaken, as a man might be. West or east they must go. The game seemed to have gone west. They would follow it.

That night Sinclair came back with one of his hunters. The other had been lost in a canyon of the southern mountains, the great black-blue wall that dominated the horizons of their world. The American came to Clair while there was still daylight and flung himself down by the fire deserted but for herself. He was spattered in mud from head to feet, mud that had frozen on him; his arms and legs were scored with long cicatrices. For a little he lay in silence near Clair. She put her hand on his shoulder in that caress that was his own, and he put up his hand to her hand. He said, as if speaking to himself:

"There's no road at all through the southwards mountains. It is an absolutely impassable wall. We've climbed and prospected ever since we reached it an hour after daybreak. And the other parties that have gone into the west report the same. It's a range that may lie mid-way across Atlantis. And it curves northwards after a bit."

"North?" Clair lay on an elbow and reflected; and suddenly understood. "Then if the hunters go west that will take them into a worse winter. It might even mean —"

"Extinction. These people cannot stick things worse than

they are at present. And it'll grow worse every hour. The
sinking of the northern plateau has done it, of course."

"Then what are we going to do?"

"*I* don't know. God, how I ache!"

He lay so quiet that she thought he was asleep. But
presently he spoke again. "And in the east, beyond that
northwards-making spur, we know there are leagues and
leagues of brackish marsh. Didn't notice them? I did. . . . That
would mean, if we turn the drift east, that we'll have to go far
north again to circumvent the marsh, and turn south again.
It would mean that hardly a woman or child could survive.
Perhaps not any of us. . . . Remember my Utopia beyond the
mountains?" He laughed.

Clair sat and stared at him and the fading of the daylight.
There was still food in the camp. There was still the calling of
greetings and the flaring of fires, there was still the sight and
being of unfearing human life all around them. Southwards:
impassable. Westwards: impassable. In the north: extinction.
And then a great light seemed to flash on her.

"But they didn't die, Keith. They went east, somehow,
some of them, and escaped this winter. We know it from
history, as you've often told me. Our hunters weren't killed.
They reached France thousands of years after this."

He was silent for a little, then he said: "That was in the
history we knew, not in the history we hope to build."

She put out her hand and shook him again. "Oh, we're
playing again, Keith. *How if the history we knew is the history
we helped to build?* How if when you, twenty-five thousand
years away, learned as a student that the Cro-Magnards came
into Spain at the end of the Ice Age – how if you were
learning about an event which you yourself had helped to
fashion?"

"Then I've come back again and can refuse its fashioning
this second chance – even if I knew how." He sat up. "And of
course – there is perhaps a way!"

"Which?"

He pondered, looking at her and not seeing her, as she
knew. "The northwards spur to the east is broken off from
the main mountain-wall. I saw that on the night I crept
out from our camp and went to spy on the Neanderthalers.
There's a long, hillocky valley lies between. Perhaps half a

mile broad, though it seems to climb up to a point at the other side ."

"Keith, you've found the way!"

"By God, I have not! Oh, we're the stuff of dreams, but that's not the dream I'm going to help humanity to dream. We'd crawl through that pass sometime at night, so's not to arouse the Neanderthalers, and gain the country in the east. I don't know how many would ever gain it, but some at least. Not me among them, I think. And beyond that pass in the east lies: Your boy lover dying on the wire in France, Clair, and the crucified slaves along the Appian Way and the Pinkertons shooting down the starving strikers of a Scotch philanthropist. . . . Not if I know it! Better to end it here. Better to make this the end of the human adventure, or go west with the hunters tomorrow and lose ourselves and die in the clean snows of Atlantis. . . . Here's your hunter, Clair. Twenty-five thousand years hence he'll also be a hunter – of human heads in New Guinea, with dried human hands strapped on his chest. Or a gangster in Chicago. Or a Steel Helmet in Germany. Like it'?"

Ærte sat down beside them. He looked from one to the other with puzzled eyes. Clair smiled at him, this child who loved her. She said: "I never had a classical education, but wasn't there some tag: 'They make a desert and they call it peace'?"

Sinclair said nothing, standing up and looking into the darkening west. She knew she was pleading for something immeasurably greater than herself. She could find no words but seemed trite and pitiable ones.

"There were other people than the head-hunter and the gangster. . . . There was Karl Liebknecht; there was Anatole France. There was even yourself in that age out of which we came. There was I."

He turned back at that. She saw more than a bitter denial in his face now. She looked at Ærte and someone other than herself spoke through her lips:

"Do you think they ever quite beat us, Keith – the beasts of civilization? Do you think that Ærte ever quite died, away there in those years? Do you think he won't beat them when civilization has passed and finished? Remember Sir John? – The hunter will come again in the world we left! You and I

and thousands of others were fighting up from the fears and
cruelties of civilization to look at the world through his eyes
again. There are later ages than the one we came from, and
Ærte – he'll walk naked across the world again, and fearless,
but with Orion's sword in his belt and the Milky Way for a
plaything. The weeping and the tears – they're a darkness
yet to fall on our hunters. But it will pass. I know. You
know it will. And it is for that, though your own dream of
changing that chance must finish, that you are to lead the
Cro-Magnards east to the pass in the mountain-wall."

She could not see when she stopped speaking. She
thought: 'Oh! I ache also, and I'm cold and hungry, and I've
been ranting. . . . And I'd like to lie down and sleep and sleep
and forget it all —' She heard Sinclair speaking, and looked
up and saw that Titan resentment gone from his face.

"You've won again, Clair. There was you, at least, in that
age that is not yet. . . . We'll go east tomorrow."

*Subchapter ii*

At dawn the next morning the Cro-Magnards moved out
from their camp and took up the line of march into the east.
In front Sinclair and his surviving scout vanished before-
hand. Clair marched mid-way the migration in the company
of a girl, Lizair, who had adopted her after the death of
Zumarr; it was the same girl who had refused her first suitor
in the time of the mating for the dark days. Now the boy
whom she had chosen walked beside them, solicitous for
Lizair's baby, and a very prideful and manly boy. Ærte had
gone off with a band of other hunters to forage northwards
for game with which to feed the migration.

No sun came, but a pale diffusion of saffron light in
the east. The wind had died away again, but beyond the
forest belt to the verge of which the Neanderthalers had
pursued Clair and Sinclair, the Cro-Magnards saw the rolling
savannah country pelted with flying showers of sleet. Here,
also, the snow lay deeper than in the higher country from
which they had descended, and the trek, a grey trek in a
grey country, moved slowly enough in the direction set by
Sinclair the night before. Children wailed ceaselessly in the

piercing chill. Behind, as Clair could see looking back, there followed pack on pack of wolves, black hordes of skulking raiders which grew ever bolder as the day wore on.

Clair tramped half that day like one in a dream. As in a dream she saw the country close in and open out before them; she was hazily conscious of the passing bombardments of sleet; once of a thunderstorm and a great flare of lightning that played over a wood where they halted somewhere towards midday and ate cooked or raw flesh brought with them, for Sinclair had told them to light no fires. It was there that the girl Lizair began to cough and cough in ever-increasing spasms, until she was coughing blood, and in a little while was dead. They left her there, and others, and the wolves halted for a little time, and then came on again.

The boy who had been Lizair's lover insisted, with a dull obstinacy in carrying her baby. Clair could not bear to look at him.

The northwards spur, not more than five miles or so away, was reddened with the colours of the sunset when Sinclair and his scout fell back on the main body of the trek. Clair was told of their coming and managed to urge her half-frozen limbs to carry her to the front of the march. As she did so the march gradually turned aside, to the south, making another small wood. Sinclair had advised a halt.

She found him at last, Aitz-Kore and a group of other Cro-Magnards about him. They were at the further verge of the wood in which the trek had halted, and in the hearing of the long, easy agglutinative roll of the proto-Basque speech she stood for a while puzzled and un-noticed. Then she heard her name mentioned, and saw Sinclair's face lighten. She went forward and touched his arm then.

He held her in his arms then, while the hunters with troubled eyes looked at them. "How are you?"

She was weak enough to want to sob, but she did not. "Getting weaker and wiser, as the rabbit said when the dog was eating it. . . . I'm lasting, but there have been awful things back there, Keith."

"I've heard. It can't be helped. We must just go on."

"Can we?"

He indicated the open country in front of them. It was the triangle of the Neanderthalers, and apparently quite deserted. "The hunter and I have been watching the place ever since we arrived early this forenoon. There's been no one out on it, and no sign of any of the beast-men stirring, even over by the spur."

Clair peered through the intervening distances. She saw, after a little, lighter patches in the face of the cliff, and in that clear, generally untainted air, there was the ghost of a sharp, *blue* odour.

"Aren't those their fires?"

"Yes. But they don't seem to be moving out of the caves. Probably they have plenty of food and will continue to keep inside, as they have done all the daylight. We'll strike south as soon as the darkness comes and wait in the lee of the mountain-wall for the stars – if there are any. Can't move further in pitch blackness. Then we'll cross and push up through the valley."

"If there's fighting – what will happen?"

"God knows. Our hunters have never fought anything but beasts. They can't conceive a human enemy. It would all depend if they were to find the Neanderthalers human or bestial. . . . We won't have any need to put it to the test, I think. . . . Go and help keep everyone on the move or interested, Clair. No fires. . . . Eh?"

She gave a little ghost of a laugh. "'While shepherds watched their flocks by night' – I never thought I'd play the rôle. I wish we could sing."

"What would you sing?"

"Something comforting."

"Do, then; but not too loud. It'll keep the hunters interested."

She had never thought of singing to them before. They had no songs of the European type, with sharp rhymes and mechanical spacings. But they came round about, from the greyness of the trees, in some numbers as she began to sing, her voice a little hoarse, for she shivered still, but as sweet and sensuous as it had ever been. Sinclair, standing still watching the Neanderthaler fires, heard her voice:

*"Abide with me*
(Clair sang),
*Fast falls the eventide,*

*The darkness deepens,*
*Lord, with me abide."*

Clair's God beyond the gods . . .

The wind rose again. The last of the daylight lingered sharply, on pin-points of the strange world in the beginning of history, and Sinclair's eyes, in a sudden passion of knowledge of how little of this world he had ever made deep acquaintance with, went from point to point as these rearguards of the day quenched their lamps and departed. Clair sang on, a new song now, inexpressibly alien in that wild land:

> *"Now sleeps the crimson petal, now the white;*
> *Now waves the cypress in the palace walk;*
> *Now sinks the goldfish in the porphyry font;*
> *The firefly wakens: waken thou with me.*
> *Now droops the milk-white peacock like a ghost,*
> *And like a ghost she glimmers unto me.*
> *Now lies the Earth all Danae to the stars,*
> *And all thy heart lies open unto me."*

He looked up at the sky. It was pall-black. He moved and stamped frozen feet, thinking: 'I'll have frost-bite soon. And Clair – better not think of her. Of nothing but the pass. God, if only there will be starshine!'

> *"Now folds the lily all her sweetness up,*
> *And slips into the bosom of the lake:*
> *So fold thyself, my dearest, thou, and slip*
> *Into my bosom, and be lost in me."*

He waited while he counted a thousand, and then moved through the darkness of the trees, speaking to the hunters and women. They must walk four or five abreast and follow after him. He heard their pleasant sing-song of response, though many of their faces he could not see, and turned about, and called that he was ready, and held out gingerly southwards on the track he had mentally plotted while the daylight lasted. He held his spear extended, and groped the path with it.

He thought: 'Rotten show if the wolves attack,' and put that out of his mind also. One thing at a time . . .

Beyond the wood the wind smote them as with keen-edged knives. Sinclair gasped, and steadied himself, and plodded forward. Behind, he heard the scuffle of the migration, and looking over his shoulder could see the lighter shadows that were the bodies of the frontwards Cro-Magnards. One slipped forward to his side and kept pace with him. Sinclair said: "Who are you?"

"I am Ærte."

"You had better go back to Clair and guard her. I can lead the way."

Ærte, the Atlantean child-man whom he had never been able to detest, whom even in bitterest moments he had never regarded with other than a grey acquiescence, remained at his shoulder. "Clair sent me here."

So that was that . . .

Once the wolves behind did verily attack, and the whole column swayed and eddied while the rearward hunters turned about and fought and stabbed at the leaping bodies in the darkness. They did it with little noise, and the beasts drew off again. But they took with them the bodies of some half-dozen, half-grown children. Nothing could be done for these, and some hunters also did not return. The march through the darkness went on.

Clair carried Lizair's baby by then, for its boy-father had handed it to her when he fell back to fight the wolves; he had not come again from that baying clamour. It coughed, pitifully, now and then. Presently, in her forward stumblings, Clair was aware that the mite within the bearskin had ceased to cough. Not until the column halted in slow eddyings, and she realized it was a deliberate halt, and sought to use the interval to ease the position of the child, did she discover that it was dead. She put her lips to its and her hand over its heart. There was no movement. A nearing voice called: "Clair! Clair!"

"I'm here."

A lighter form than those she had followed came out of the darkness. "What's that you've got?"

"A baby. Oh, Keith, it's dead."

"It's finished with cold and hunger, Clair. Put it down."

"I can't. . . . Those beasts behind."

He shook her. "We're going into something twice as bad as we've had to face in the last hour; and I'll want your help. Put it away."

She did. The American said: "I want you to walk mid-way the column. Talk to the people round about you. Explain just what I'm doing, and why they must make no noise. Ærte's going to do the same at the rear."

"But I can't talk their language!"

"Lord. I'd forgotten that."

"We're turning towards the valley, now?"

"Yes. It's grown a little lighter." His fingers touched hers, awkwardly. "Good luck."

She would have called him back; but he had gone. In another moment, slowly, in a light that gradually increased with the coming of the star-rise through the frost, the trek was again in motion. In their changed direction the wind blew not behind them now, but on their left. And suddenly, pricking out the bastions of the northwards mountain-spur, seen as they rose to the higher ground that led to that spur, there shone bright and splendid the fires of the Neanderthal caves.

A murmur arose from the Cro-Magnards, but died away at the urgings of Sinclair and Ærte. Over there was danger, no food or help. They must still even the crying of the babies.

The fires seemed to Clair to draw nearer in leaps and bounds. They were fires remote in caves, however; there were no signs of watchers. Right ahead, where the column wound into the presumed valley, was unspotted darkness.

Clair became aware of the fires passing on her left. They had entered the valley. They stumbled up over rocky ground. Clair raised her head once and saw the heavens, unclouded, banded with the glory of the Milky Way.

And then presently another line of fires gleamed directly ahead, a strange, wild moaning filled the air, and above it rose shout on shout – shoutings in Sinclair's voice!

The migratory column of the Cro-Magnards was being attacked at a dozen points by the Neanderthalers of the unsuspected valley caves.

That had been hours ago.

Morning in the air again. It seemed to Clair, looking downwards and around, that this was the land of morning. How many of them had she seen come over the strange, pale hills? Would she see this one?

They were through now, the bulk of the frightened, amazed, uncomprehending Cro-Magnards and their women. Or such of them as had survived the attacks. Or such of them as had not been dragged into those caves of night. . . . But Clair would not look in that direction, nor think of those dismembered bodies the beast-men had dragged there. Here they came again —

Like a pelting rush of shadows. But shadows of sickening substance, with the gleam of low-set eyes in the foreheadless heads. They charged again, with their ululating moan rising to a scream, and the musk odour of their bodies nauseating. Sinclair's yell met the scream, and at sound of it the Cro-Magnards still unpast the valley point bunched forward uncertainly to meet the attack. . . . Sinclair himself Clair saw, dimly, stripped of bearskin cloak and every other encumberment, in his hand a great club of the beast-men.

Then the scurry of furred grey bodies was upon the Cro-Magnard line.

The morning seemed to have heard the impact. It was coming more quickly out of the wild, unknown eastern lands. Clair felt its pale fore-radiance in her face as she darted here and there, heeding to the onward guiding of the main hunter-stream. Betwixt two rocks they filed, into the unguessable valley-country beyond. Clair thought, wearily: 'Will they never get through?' and heard herself chanting again, foolishly: "Oh – do please hurry!"

Sinclair, on the westward slopes, heard that cry. Then other interests engaged him. A great brute tore the club from his hands and took him by the throat. Its breath was fetid in his face. He kicked it, intimately, with a moccasined foot. It screamed and slipped away from him. He found a hunter stabbing methodically on either side. Not courage but comprehension they lacked. . . . Breathing space.

The Neanderthalers were swaying backwards and down-wards again, moaning as they retreated. But, as throughout the hours since the migration had stumbled upon the fact that all one valley-wall was inhabited, other grey beasts were coming at a scrambling, swaying run to replace the rout. Tireless, scores on scores of them, reinforcements from the northwards spur. Rational animals. Men almost . . .

Lighter and lighter the darkness. It was gloaming. Sinclair heard Clair, far up the slope:

"Keith! Keith! All the women are through!"

He stumbled up through the ring of hunters towards the ring of her voice. Dawn near. White in the ghostly radiance. "Unhurt?"

He breathed sobbingly. "All right. Everyone through?"

"Except these dozen with you."

"I'll send them up. Hurry on yourself."

"You're coming?"

"I'll come. In a minute." He grinned at her, grey-faced. "*Do* please hurry!"

He watched her disappear. He found himself sobbing again. Now the false dawn illumined the valley.

It rose in a cone, mid-way, and at the cone-tip the cliffs closed in on either side, allowing barely more than the passage of two men abreast. The red sandstone rocks were already a dun rose colour, though no sign of the actual sun came yet. It was snowing fleecily, but even as he turned back towards the westwards slopes that ceased. The rearguard bunched up towards him, and now in the morning light ad-ded to the light of the cave-fires, he saw the valley alive, like a spider's nest, with fresh hordes of the grey-furred beast-men.

They would follow on in hundreds . . .

"Go through! Go through!"

Panting, leaning against a rock, he saw them file past, the last of the hunters. Below, the grey, hirsute whirlpool beginning to boil again. . . . Two or at the least one must stay with him; he could not do it alone. But whom? Not that old man. Nor this boy. Quick, quick. Whom? Whom? Ærte to guard Clair in the world beyond – ah, God, she had still her hunter! He heard himself shout with sudden strength:

"Turn south beyond this valley – south if you can! Keep watch always."

"But you will be there with us, brother." The last hunter, scarred and torn, swayed round and waited. Keith Sinclair cursed him.

"Go on! Go on!"

He heard the pad of retreating feet.

He found himself alone.

*Subchapter iv*

He started up, gripping his spear. He peered in the faces of the two who stood beside him.

Clair said, sitting down with a sigh: "Silly to think you could hold this place alone, Keith. So Ærte and I have come back."

The light grew brighter on the hunter's face. Sinclair stared at the two of them. Clair leant her chin in her hands.

"Nightmare, Keith – but a wonderful one. Last dawn in Atlantis! . . . And the beasts that follow men —"

Thereat the sunrise, in a great hush that seemed to hold quiescent even the gathering attack of the Neanderthalers twenty yards below, sped suddenly up from the eastern end of the canyon and poured liquid through the narrow defile. Sitting, Clair's head nodded on her shoulders. But she started up at Sinclair's last cry of entreaty.

"Clair!"

She stumbled between the two men. Her eyes turned to the horror below. "I'll stand behind with my spear. They're coming."

Twice they had come, and twice broken and shambled downwards in screaming flight. Clair's spear was gone, the head embedded in a beast-man's chest. Sinclair leant against the canyon wall, his right arm hanging by a pinch of skin, blood pouring from a dreadful stomach wound. . . . His face a battered mask, all human likeness had gone from the hunter. But she saw his eyes turned towards her, glazing eyes lovely and human still. He staggered to his feet. She felt suddenly serene and assured.

"Oh, my dears, it isn't long now! They are coming again —"

*Subchapter i*

S HE awoke in a dazzle of sunshine that blinded her for a moment. She sat up and knuckled her eyes. She felt very tired – sun-tired, as though she had slept a long time in this warmth of the earth and sky. There was a continual drumming splash near at hand, like the sound of the sea heard far off. She took her hånds from her eyes and looked round.

She was lying on a patch of sand on a low beach that sloped up to rocky, verdant mountains. The violent green of the near underbrush waved, languid and warm, in the ghost of a breeze. Overhead was a sky deep and blue and touched with a sailing speck-net of clouds. A score of yards away the sea rumbled unhurryingly on the beach.

*The beast-men of the pass!*

"Keith! Ærte!"

A gull whooped past her. Far up the mountainside a sudden roar grew to a grinding clamour, became a glittering snake in the sunlight, hissed; swept from view again. A railway train . . .

She stared upwards in paralysed affright. Delirium. Of course it was delirium. For suddenly she had remembered. *She was dead.*

Morning Pass – the Neanderthalers – their last charge – a great malachite club descending – Ærte and Keith gold and white and red-streaked veinings of foam under a wave of snarling greyness. She must be still alive and in delirium – the last alive of the *Magellan!*

She closed her eyes again, that the horror might pass, and willed to die also; and the wind touched her cheek and her hair came ruffling across her face, tickling her skin so that her hand went up involuntarily to put it aside. She opened her eyes on the green, warm day. And then she saw something lying a few yards off, and, sobbing, was in a moment kneeling by the side of that something.

It was Keith Sinclair.

He lay unmoving, face downwards in an outpost of the mountain grass. Kneeling in a blur of tears beside him, she thought: "I am mad; it is still delirium." For his body was unmarked by signs of struggle in the Pass – that body from which the blood had welled in great gouts. She shook his shoulder.

"Keith. Oh, Keith, make it real!"

For answer he yawned where he lay, stretched his arms, stretched his legs, seemed to stretch every muscle in his body. Then, slowly and casually, he turned round and sat erect. His eyes seemed to have a grey film over them. He blinked, knuckling his eyes as she had knuckled hers. She sat back and watched him.

As she did so there came again, far up the slope, that muffled roar, the green of the mountain vegetation stirred ever so slightly, and again that metal toy monster swept round a curve and vanished with a loud whistle. Sinclair's head jerked upwards. He stared with fallen jaw. Then he looked round him, smiled dazedly at Clair, and, as she had done, covered his eyes.

"By God," he said, "*we're back*!"


*Subchapter ii*

"We'll go exploring in a minute. Azores or Madeira I should think. . . . Oh, I'm real enough and sound enough. So – and so. Convinced?"

She said, her voice muffled in his long hair: "Still a dream for all I know, for you did that often enough in my day-dreams. O, my dear! You're real and whole. . . . And ten minutes ago your arm was hanging by a thread from your shoulder – and that stomach-wound —"

Sinclair held her close. "But it wasn't ten minutes ago. It happened thousands of years ago, else we'd never see that train."

His arms about her still, he started suddenly; laughed.

"What is it?"

"We were killed, of course – and by some chance didn't die. . . . We're back in the year we left – unless some other accident has happened. It may be 2000."

She withdrew her head and looked at the brightening day. "Real. You and the world and myself. . . . And I know it's the year we left."

"So do I," he confessed. And thought aloud: "The railway trains of 2000 won't burn coal —"

"Keith, where are we?"

"Eh?" He looked round the scene again. Then: "We're in Morning Pass still. Look."

He pointed to the mountain-edge near at hand. Dimly, a ghostly scene in the sunlight, a remembrance shaped in Clair's mind. That boulder, that curve of rock that swept into the sea where the grey men mustered for their last attack. . . . But the leftwards wall of the pass had vanished into a smother of grass that was presently sand; beyond that also the murmur of the sea. . . . Ten minutes ago, twenty-five thousand years ago . . . She knew him looking at her in quick understanding.

"We're *back*, Clair. Don't worry about it. Let's get up and do that exploring."

They stood up together, helping each other. And then it was Sinclair who was seized with an obsessing memory. He looked to right and left and broke away from her, searching. She stared after him. "Keith!"

He halted in his search, looking over his shoulder. "Ærte – he must be here! He died with us."

But he turned fully round again, and they looked at each other white-faced. And then it seemed to Clair that his face had altered, that she knew at last the meaning of scores of puzzling resemblances that had torn her heart now this way, now that. She knew that she might cry again if she did not speak very quickly. She said:

"Don't you understand? I do at last. *You* are Ærte."

*Subchapter iii*

The deserted beach curved northwards round the shoulder of the mountain. Out to sea a trail of smoke grew to being across the horizon, became a triune procession of dots that were funnels, and presently sank again, leaving that scroll-writing in the sky. But neither Clair nor Sinclair moved.

"I am Ærte." He sat with his hands clasped round his knees. "Just as he was the boy who died at Mametz and a score of others. Race-type, race-memory, blood of his blood – who can know? . . . And there was a you also in the painted caves. I didn't know then. Now – I saw her a dozen times, in a look, a way of walking. Lizair who died in the last forest – she was you."

Clair Stranlay stood with the sun in her face, dreaming also. "Oh, Keith, not only these two! Zumarr and her hunter – Aitz-kore – Lizair's boy-lover who died among the wolves – the young men who came back at evening singing —"

"They're here in the world still, all of them, that company that went over Sunrise Pass into the morning we never saw."

"But what happened then – that morning? They must have got clear away."

"Somehow. Perhaps the Neanderthalers never pursued them after our end. Somehow they went east and south and found a place safe from the winter. And then they went east again, into the beginnings of history."

She stood with troubled, lighted face, far in dreams, and he looked up at her suddenly with the gaze of the twentieth century; the custom of weeks fell from his eyes. Unconscious of herself and the beauty of herself in the fall of sunshine, her red hair blown on the tanned gold of her neck, and against the mountain greenery almost merging the gold of her body into the sunlight. . . . *Back!*

She looked down and sighed and sat beside him. She smiled into those eyes that were not of the caves of Atlantis. "Oh, we've awakened. . . ." She looked round the bright weather of the green beach. "We've come back. We'll be hungry in a little, and have to go round that hill, and hear people speak and wear clothes again, and lie in the fug of little rooms and never hear the midnight cry upon the mountains. That's finished and put by. . . . If only it was a pack of hyaenodon that waited us round that mountain bend!"

It was he who stood up now, with a laugh, and she also saw him with eyes that had lost the acceptance of many a day and scene. Keith Sinclair of the *Magellan* – never that

Keith Sinclair again. . . . He smiled down at her. He held out his hand.

"Come along. We'll go and meet the hyaenodon."

She put her fingers in his. "I suppose we must. . . . Love me, my dear?"

"Till the hunters come back to the world again – and after."

She did not stir.

"Then there's still a moment we've never known, Keith, though we dreamt it in the Golden Age. It's still the same sun and earth – for a moment, before we go back to the world that's forgotten both."

Not looking at him, she yet saw his face change strangely, felt the pressure on her fingers alter, knew him kneeling beside her. She put her arms round his neck. He held her away a moment.

"Sure, Clair?"

"Till the hunters walk again."

She drew down his head very slowly, and kissed him tremulously, and the moment came out of the growing day, and waited for them with a quiver of purple wings, and was theirs for ever.

*Subchapter iv*

Senhora Leiria regarded her guest with admiration and uplifted her voice in throaty French.

"But they fit with exactitude!"

The guest raised a flushed, smiling face. "Very sweet," she agreed, and thought: 'Oh, my good God, and I'll have to *wear* the things!'

The thought was appalling. So was the Senhora. Had she never seen a nude body before? Why, if she looked across at the caves there —

But the caves were twenty-five thousand years away.

Clair sat down. "I'll manage ever so nicely now I've had a bath and you've shown me the stuff I can choose from. I'll dress and come down in a minute or so."

The stout Senhora lingered, constitutional languor and aroused curiosity in combat. "The dreadful hours you must have spent, Senhora Keith, after the wreck of your husband's boat!"

"Shocking." ('If she doesn't go away I'll —')

The door closed. Clair dropped the garments entrusted to her, stumbled to the casement window, and flung it wide open. Gasped with relief.

"The ghastly, ghastly smell of the place! Just the ordinary room smell? Wonder how Keith's getting on – or what he's getting on? . . . Those must be the roofs of San Miguel over there."

San Miguel of the Azores . . .

She began to laugh. That servant whom Keith had encountered —

Three hours ago. They'd rounded the mountain bend into view of open, cultivated country, a road half a mile away alive with automobiles, and, in the foreground, on a branch of the road and not more than eighty yards from where they stood, a low and gabled house with a garden and the white shirt-sleeves of a gardener.

Clair had sunk hastily to the ground. "Don't shock them too much, Keith."

He had grinned and set out, long-striding. Almost immediately there was catastrophe. Avoiding the main door and turning rightwards through the garden he had collided with a diminutive female in some kind of domestic uniform. Her shrieks preceding him, he had disappeared from Clair's view for a quarter of an hour, and, just as she had begun to wonder about his safety, had emerged from that main door and approached her.

"It's all right, Clair. Put on this coat of the Senhora's. We're in the Azores. Portuguese. I've told them a few lies to avoid unbelievable explanations."

"Keith – that ulster of yours!" She had struggled into the coat, half-hysterical. Surveyed herself: "And I look like something saved by some ghastly missionary. . . . What were the lies?"

"Coming? Senhora Leiria is going to look after you and get you some clothes. . . . We're the Keiths, an English couple, husband and wife. We've a craze for boating. Tried to reach San Miguel from Santarem in our three-ton yacht —"

"Are there three-ton yachts?"

"Eh? No idea. But early this morning we met a squall

and were upset. Stripped and swam. You're Mrs. Keith, remember."

"But we'll have to tell some of the truth later."

"We won't be able to avoid that. But this is the best meanwhile. I realized just in time that our banks'll refuse us a draft, as they'll believe us lost in the *Magellan*. But I keep an alias account – name of Keith, League of Militant Pacifist purposes – and can always order on it by a code message. . . ."

They were under the garden-wall. "Now —"

Now, with a curious shambling motion, upraised upon the heels of unaccustomed shoes, Clair Stranlay crossed the floor of Senhora Leiria's bedroom and began to descend the stairs. At the foot of the first landing was an open door, and beyond —

"Clair! Hell, what a mess!"

He was tugging to ease an unaccustomed collar. He had risen from uneasy sprawling in a be-cushioned chair. He pushed her away from him.

"My God, did you see that crucifix? And servants – diseased animals sweating to tend diseased animals! Why do they? Why the devil do they? Pack a room like this? All this nonsense of furniture. Pottering in that damned garden. . . . Flowers: they grow much better wild; any fool knows it. You can see them opposite the caves – purple-growing blooms. Sometimes the firelight reaches across the river to them —"

"Keith!"

She closed the door behind her. He sat down and buried his face in his hands. He looked up at her with just such film over his eyes as she had seen on them at his awakening.

"Sorry. Went crack for a moment. . . . All this – God, we can never endure it again, Clair! Beyond this house there are the towns and the filth and the stench. London on a wet Sunday afternoon. The shoddy crowds of the Boul' Mich'. Newsboys screaming, trains screaming. . . . it would kill us after – after that."

"What are we going to do, then?"

"Clear out to the South Seas or some such place."

"Escape?"

"Escape."

"My dear, I'd sooner go down to the sea there and walk out into it." She started to cross the room towards him.

Something snapped, intimately. She put her hand to her thigh. "Those damn things. . . . Let's open that window." She laughed down at him. "Keith, are we to be beaten by a collar and a brassière when the Neanderthalers didn't beat us?"

She knelt beside him. "I'm going to do what *you* are going to do. Go back to the world we came from. Tell them we survived the *Magellan* – and then preach Atlantis till our dying day!"

"Tell them what happened? Who'd ever believe it? Can't you hear the bray of the headlines? – remember how they vilified Mitchell Hedges?"

She smiled the old, gay smile with no irony at all in it. "Different from that. Upstairs I suddenly knew what we would do. We can't desert the world – we've no right to. . . . Not while there are still Neanderthalers alive – in generals' uniforms. Not while they still can lie about the everlastingness of rich and poor and innate human ferocity. Not while our hunters are still in the world – somewhere out there, Keith! – chained and gagged and brutalized, begging in streets, cheating in offices, doing dirty little cruelties in prison wards. . . . Remember that world you planned beyond the southern mountains? It's still a possible world and a possible civilization."

"This disease of mine is merely agoraphobia, of course. It'll pass."

"Then —?"

"Of course." He caught her hand and stood up with her. He winced at his straining clothes, as she did. Clair's laughter had survived Atlantis. He shook her, very gently. "We could never do anything else, I suppose – even though we bring a flint spear against a sixteen-inch gun."

*Subchapter v*

They stood together in the sunset. The sea rumbled again at their feet in the beat of the incoming tide. And out for miles, hasting into the west, the fading light leapt from roller to roller of the Atlantic. Remote above them the culvert belched out another train to sweep the mountain track down to San Miguel. Sinclair's hand fell on Clair's.

"Time we went back. The Leirias dine early, they said."

"I know. But just a minute more. ... To-morrow's so near."

"Eh?"

"To-morrow and all the things of which we've talked. You'll get money and we'll go into San Miguel and sail to France, and begin the fight for sanity; and the world will vex and thwart us and we'll grow bitter, and grow old till those four weeks —"

He put his arms round her. "We're going to work and fight together. We're going to marry. Children we'll have like yourself – keen and lovely as you. We'll do all the things you said this forenoon when the future scared me. We'll light a torch and never let it die."

She did not move, still staring out to sea. "Oh, Keith, I know. This is only a moment with me also, and it'll pass and be forgotten. Do you think I won't love the fight as well? – or love loving you and bearing your babies and taming your temper and – and seeing you always have a fresh razor blade? It isn't that. Only —"

It was almost dark. He held her gently, unimpatiently. "Only —?"

"Oh, Keith, say you'll never forget them! – all those days! Remember that first night? Remember the golden hunters on the western hill? Remember the fires? Remember the laughter and the kindliness of them? Remember the road to Sunrise Pass? ... We'll forget and forget and the years'll come tramping over our lives and memories —"

"But not these memories." His arms tightened round her. "They'll live as long as we do. They're things undying. They live though human nature go into an underground pit for a million years."

She stirred in his arms. She touched his cheek in shadowy caress.

"The Leirias are lighting their lamps."

But as they passed together out of the noise of the sea to the lighted night and the waiting world, Clair caught his hand and turned back a moment to the rolling waste of waters whereneath lies buried these twenty thousand years the mythic land of Atlantis:

"Good-bye, my dears!"

THE END

# J. LESLIE MITCHELL

## AN APPRECIATION*

by

John Lindsey

I came across the work of Leslie Mitchell entirely by accident and I was struck immediately by its authenticity and realness.

His first novel, "Stained Radiance", was avowedly destructive. An orgy of destruction ran through the whole book. His characters destroyed one another mercilessly – they destroyed God, society, sex. And Leslie Mitchell let them do it. They seemed to horrify him as, perhaps, all mankind had horrified him by its unimaginative lusts and frightful, unthinking cruelties, and its appalling hypocrisy.

The book wept and raged with pain so that one felt that here was a man who had indeed been down into the pit, who had seen all the baseness of which man is capable, the poverty, degradation, the wounding laughter: man crucifying man. It was the cry of the over-sensitive artist against the wrongs of the world.

Time and again I wanted to put the book down. I felt that I could not go on: that the pain it engendered in me was too intense, too excruciating to be borne. But I did not put it down. I was forced to continue: even, as it seemed, against my will; because here was something real, that compelled my attention.

And somehow, out of all the pain and suffering in the book, there emerged another thing for which I could find no name for the moment. It was too small, too flickering a light for hope . . .

"Stained Radiance" had many faults. It was over-written. It was restless, allowing the reader no respite; set at too high an emotional pitch, so that one thought, "This cannot go on"; but it did go on, and something else happened! A new idea or thought had to be brought in, thrown before the reader for consideration, snatched away only that another might

196

take its place – another thing that the author was forced to say—

But in his second novel, "The Thirteenth Disciple," he has definitely found that something that flickered in "Stained Radiance". His new characters have found something too: they are in the round, instead of, as in the first book, appearing as flat drawings. The pain is still there, but it is not so intense. The rage is still there, only now it is suffused with pity. The wild anger has gone. There is still anger, but this time Mr. Mitchell has not set out to destroy only. He wants to construct, and, in a large measure, he succeeds.

In "Stained Radiance" he is horrified by sex, it has got muddied like everything else. He hates "strange and disgusting changes in her body." In "The Thirteenth Disciple" he is no longer horrified, except in so far as people make sex cheap and pornographic by clothing it with rosebuds and soft-coloured lights.

The form of "The Thirteenth Disciple" is different: a friend writing the biography of a friend, having had access to certain documents, but, inevitably, restricted in his knowledge of that friend's mentality and emotions. I have read the book through carefully twice. I cannot find that in any single instance has the author stepped beyond those things of which he was allowed to know.

Then again, the book is filled with an amazing "sense of place". To confine oneself to those chapters dealing with Leekan Valley, one is struck by the author's ability to recreate not only the actual scenery of the place, but the implied scenery: the undercurrent of feeling and sensitiveness which this bleak country engenders.

The book is sub-titled "Portrait and Saga of Malcom Maudslay in his Adventure through the Dark Corridor." And I suppose that the word Tragedy would be used to describe it. But it is more than Tragedy in the sense that the book has fulfilment, that Maudslay himself is fulfilled. Out of the "agony in stony places" something new is born, and the whole book is illuminated in the light of this fulfilment.

In his third book, "The Calends of Cairo", a story-cycle, he has deserted – only for a holiday, I think – the urgencies of the Western world. Here is the Modern East: the whole book saturated in a strange, wild spirit – a spirit of unrest and yet tranquillity in the midst of that unrest; full of colour and a noble searching after meaning.

On these three books alone it seems to me that Leslie Mitchell has justified his inclusion among the very few people – men or women – writing today whose work we cannot spare. The work is individual: perhaps almost annoyingly so. It demands a certain mental adjustment on the part of the reader. But, granted that adjustment, it is important work, indicating a certain line of thought that is too seldom treated of: *a certain freedom from preconceived notions of what is right and wrong.* And the explorer along that line of thought is, I am sure, a writer who will have an influence, and that a very definite one, on the thought and literature of the twentieth century.

* Reprinted from *The Twentieth Century*